'Human history has become, more and more,
a race between education and catastrophe.'

H. G. Wells

*With very special thanks to Sue Cook,
the George series non-fiction editor*

THE LATEST SCIENTIFIC IDEAS!

As you read the story and see the sort of future George discovers, you will come across lots of fabulous scientific knowledge and ideas – everything from time dilation to machine learning! To expand this, at the end of the story is a collection of essays written by respected experts that will really help bring some of these ideas to life. It's your future: read about it, think about it – and enjoy it! It is likely to be a truly exciting world.

LUCY HAWKING

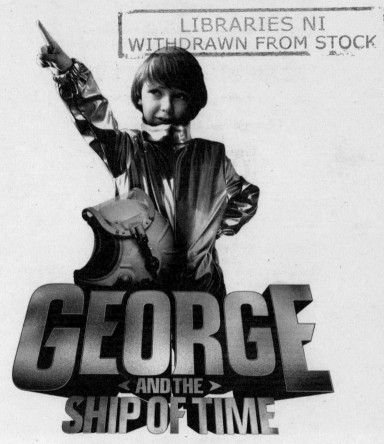

GEORGE AND THE SHIP OF TIME

*The final adventures of
Annie and George*

Illustrated by Garry Parsons

CORGI BOOKS

CORGI BOOKS

UK | USA | Canada | Ireland | Australia
India | New Zealand | South Africa

Corgi Books is part of the Penguin Random House group of companies
whose addresses can be found at global.penguinrandomhouse.com

www.penguin.co.uk
www.puffin.co.uk
www.ladybird.co.uk

First published 2018
001

Typeset in Stempel Garamond by Clair Lansley
Printed in Great Britain by Clays Ltd, St Ives plc

A CIP catalogue record for this book is available from the British Library

ISBN: 978–0–552–57529–4

All correspondence to:
Corgi Books
Penguin Random House Children's
80 Strand, London WC2R 0RL

Prologue

'Message buffered!' The communication system crackled into life. 'Doppler correction implemented.'

Until now, the inside of the spaceship *Artemis* had been eerily silent. But then a human voice broke through. A very angry human voice.

'George! This is your mother!' it squeaked over the tannoy. She sounded absolutely furious.

'Oops!' said Boltzmann Brian, George's outsize robot, his only companion on this enormous spaceship. 'Shall I say hi to your mum? She must be missing us!'

'No!' George floated back to the front of the ship. He had boarded the *Artemis* on Earth, little knowing that it would take him and Boltzmann on quite such a wild ride. It was as though they had jumped onto the back of an untamed stallion that had cosmically galloped away with them. 'Well, actually,' he added, pausing out of range of the receiver so his extremely peeved mother wouldn't be able to hear him, 'I don't suppose you'd like to tell her this was your idea?'

He looked pleadingly at the battered old robot. A high-altitude space jump some time previously had led to Boltzmann's head and body being charred by the heat of re-entry into Earth's atmosphere. This always reminded George that his own human body had no chance of survival outside the ship.

'But it was not my idea,' said Boltzmann, sounding puzzled. 'I do not think our current predicament will be solved by my attempting to fabricate reality to your mother.' Robot Boltzmann had made great progress in mastering human emotions, but still hadn't got the hang of that most basic of human habits – lying.

Anyway, George realized that it was pointless to tell tall stories to his mother back on Earth. No matter how they got there, he and Boltzmann were stuck on a speeding spacecraft, heading in a direction away from Earth . . . and they didn't know how to get home. He picked up the microphone.

'Mum!' he said.

'George!' The tinny voice sounded torn between rage and joy. If it was possible to weep and laugh at the same time, it sounded as though his mother was doing both. 'George!'

'Hello, Mum,' said George.

'George?' continued his mother. 'Where *are* you? And don't just say, "I'm in space!" I know that, thank you very much, George Greenby. George? George!'

'Hello! Hello, Mum!' said George. Suddenly he realized that his mother couldn't actually hear him. Because of the time delay for delivery of messages across space, his mother was talking to him but unable to pick up his replies, which were still travelling towards her across the vastness of space. In fact, his mother could have broadcast her message hours or even days before and no longer be poised to receive his replies. George's heart sank. It was too weird to be talking to his mother and yet not be talking to her at the same time.

'George Greenby!' she carried on. 'What did you think you were doing, speeding off on that wretched spaceship and giving us all the fright of our lives?' The line broke up into static and George just heard a hum and a fizz.

'I didn't realize!' he bleated pointlessly into the receiver, knowing his mother couldn't hear him. 'It wasn't meant to be like this!'

At the time, spontaneously hijacking the spaceship *Artemis* had seemed brilliantly adventurous. But it also felt as though it had a built-in ending. Immediately after launch, he and Boltzmann would gain control of the spaceship, putting it into orbit around the Earth. After a few circuits of their home planet, they would decelerate out of orbit and return home. And, even if his parents were so angry with him that he was grounded for the rest of his life, it would still have been worth it to experience space flight in a real spacecraft.

But this was not the way it happened. The *Artemis*, it turned out, moved to a music all its own. It seemed to come with a pre-plotted course and didn't respond to any attempts to change it. Instead, it had exited the Earth's atmosphere like a cannonball. The grey face of the Moon had flashed past as the Earth receded into the distance, fading rapidly to just a point of light in the dark, one dot among thousands.

Now they were tearing through space, bright lights of stars flashing past the windows. The control panel of the ship had resisted all

Boltzmann's attempts to take over. The two of them were as powerless as the cargo of green lettuces they had found installed in a special growing segment of the ship. Just as the space salad slowly grew, so they would have to wait until the *Artemis* revealed the purpose of this voyage. Were they going to Mars, which George had thought was the original destination for the spaceship? To Europa, one of Jupiter's moons, as he had then been told it had been programmed to visit? That would be a much longer trip. Right now, it didn't seem like they were going anywhere except into the darkness, faster and faster.

'Hello, George's mum!' Boltzmann shouted into the receiver. 'We're having a great time! But don't worry – the ship is fitted with the most amazing inertial dampers so there's no danger of us being crushed in a massive acceleration or deceleration! If that's what's been worrying you . . .'

George hoped Boltzmann's message would get lost in space. It wasn't quite what he thought his mum wanted to hear.

Suddenly she came back loud and clear.

'Eric,' she said, 'is trying to turn your ship round. But he says it may be a very long time before you get back. He thinks the *Artemis* wasn't programmed to go to Europa or Mars at all. You're going—'

'Where?' cried George. 'Where are we going?'

'*Fizz buzzle swizzie tum*,' said his mother as the message broke up. '*Crackle . . . crackle . . . boom . . . hiss.*'

'Mum!' cried George, who wanted nothing more at that moment than to be at home in his bedroom in his ordinary house on his normal, boring street with his little sisters, while his mum was in the kitchen and his dad was out in the garden, chopping up wood to power the family's home-made generator.

This vision of home was suddenly so clear that it was like being there for real. George saw himself walk in from the garden, and sniff the air. His mother was baking some of her famous broccoli muffins, his sisters were building and knocking down towers made out of cherry-wood bricks while the steady *thwack* of his father's axe drifted in from outside. It was home. It was where he belonged.

'*Boom!*' went the amplifier. George's mother was gone and he was back here, in this sterile space environment with its stale air and dehydrated packet food, and only a robot for a friend. The space food tasted OK – it came in lots of different flavours such as 'bacon sandwich' or 'chocolate milkshake'. The ship's recycling facility did a great job of keeping water circulating too, so George was unlikely to run out of food or drink. Even the robot wasn't bad company – but none of it was like being back at home with his family, his best friend, Annie, next door, ready for another adventure. Only this time George had set out on his adventure and left her behind.

His mum was gone, the connection broken. George realized that his last hope – that Eric Bellis, his friend Annie's dad and the superstar scientist and former head of Kosmodrome 2 (the spaceport from where they had launched near his home in Foxbridge), would be able to grasp control of *Artemis*, the runaway spaceship, and bring them back – had disappeared. They were still hurtling through space. But where were they going? He slumped over the useless controls, microphone in his hand. The receiver continued to pick up noises – a crackle, a boom and a strange, high-pitched whistling sound that meant nothing to George.

'Cheer up!' Boltzmann poked him with a long robot finger. 'Look what I found!'

George raised his head, looking bleary.

'Raspberry ripple!' chuckled the robot, brandishing a packet mix in George's face. 'A new flavour! Now tell me you're not excited! Is it dinner time?'

The strangest thing about being in the spaceship was that, as they voyaged on, they had no real idea of the passage of time. George's watch seemed to have stopped. Boltzmann's timekeeping function had strangely malfunctioned, the control panels gave them no clues, and they had no sunrise or sunset to mark out their days.

They slept and woke as they felt like it. George tucked himself into a relatively comfy pod to doze when he needed to, while Boltzmann lounged around, making use of the ship's solar electricity supply whenever he needed to charge up. They passed the time by chatting, with Boltzmann taking copious notes on what it meant to be a humanoid rather than a robotic life form. After a while George noticed that Boltzmann was copying his gestures! It was oddly like having a robot mirror.

Days passed like this – or at least George assumed that they were days. He had no real idea how long it had been before another familiar voice broke through, all the way from Earth.

'George!' the voice cried. 'George!' It was his best friend, Annie. After George and Annie had journeyed to the icy moon of Europa to defeat the most evil man on Earth, Alioth Merak, they had returned to Earth just in time to rescue a bunch of kids who were trapped inside a stationary *Artemis* on the launch pad. Merak's plan had been to isolate the cleverest kids on the planet and send them out on a secret space mission to find life in the solar system on his behalf. But George and Annie had intervened just in time and saved them, although in the process they had accidentally atomized Merak during a quantum teleport. He had disintegrated in transit and would never be reassembled.

Unfortunately Merak had designed and built the spaceship *Artemis* himself, in great secrecy, and only he knew how to operate it. When Merak vanished, there was literally no one on Earth who knew how the ship worked. And, as George had now discovered, even mega-brain Eric – Annie's dad – hadn't been able to divert the *Artemis* from its true destination, whatever and wherever that was.

'Annie!' yelled George, floating over to the comms portal as fast as he could. He was now super-skilled at moving around in microgravity and could do all sorts of interesting flips and somersaults.

'George!' Annie was speaking very fast. 'I don't know if you're even still out there, or if you can hear me, but please get in contact if you can. There's big trouble.'

'I want to!' said George. 'But I don't know how to get home! No one does! And what you do mean, *if I'm even still out here*? Help me, Annie.'

'Everything has changed,' said Annie, her voice suddenly coming over the communication channel as clear as a bell. In some ways she sounded just the same, yet in others she sounded different somehow: more grown up, more self-assured. She also sounded scared. 'Everything's gone wrong,' she said. 'The world – it's turned upside down, George. It's all ruined. We couldn't stop it. George, are you out there? I need you! *Eric* needs you.'

George's blood ran cold. Hearing the voice of his friend, relayed across endless miles of empty space between them, asking for his help when he had no way of giving it or replying in real time, was heart-breaking. Next to him, Boltzmann had frozen too, as though like George the robot was experiencing deep, heartfelt pain at the awful news.

'What *about* Eric?' asked George. But he was aware that Annie couldn't hear him at that moment. He knew that he was just shouting across space, as she was, like putting a message in a bottle and sending it out to sea in the hope that someone would find it and answer.

'No!' cried Boltzmann, very emotionally for a robot. 'Not Eric!'

'Shush!' said George. 'I need to hear what Annie's saying.'

'Eric's disappeared,' Annie's voice continued, much lower, but answering his question almost as though she could hear him. 'He did something, George. And they caught him. Someone betrayed him. He was trying to stop them, but now he's disappeared. We don't know where he is. We're very afraid . . .' She sounded breathless now, as though she might be running.

'Who are *they*?' said George. He knew his questions were irrelevant, but even so he couldn't stop himself from asking.

The only answer from the other end was a scream, which resounded around the large and mostly empty spacecraft, bouncing off the walls time and time again.

'Annie! Annie!' he shouted into the receiver.

But it was dead and unresponsive. George ran to the window, as though somehow he expected to be able to see Annie floating out there in space. But the only view was of the huge unfurling cosmos, full of bright stars and strange celestial objects and huge rocks twirling past in an endless light show.

He felt a chill creep down his back. Annie's message had been a last, desperate call for help and she might not even know that he had heard her.

Boltzmann and George looked at each other

in silence, robot to boy, mechanical eye to human eye.

'You feel it too, don't you, Boltz?' said George. 'Something has gone really wrong on Earth.'

The robot nodded. 'I sense your distress at your dislocation from your home environment,' he replied. 'While not an organic part of your planet in the same way that you are, I too am beginning to feel we have gone far enough. I believe we have accomplished your dream of space flight and it is definitely time to start back.'

'Where is this ship even going?' said George. 'Did Alioth never tell you?'

Boltzmann shook his head. 'My master was a man of many secrets,' he said, floating over to the control panel to begin another sustained attack on the systems governing the flight of the *Artemis*. 'And many games. If he told you the destination of this craft was Europa, then you can be sure that is the one place the *Artemis* will never go.'

'And how long have we been up here? Why aren't there any clocks?' said George. There wasn't much he could do to help while Boltzmann flicked switches and inputted commands. 'Why is there no time up here?'

'There is always time,' said Boltzmann. 'And it

always goes forward. But we just do not know by how much, or how fast we are moving. Although the inertial dampers on his ship have made me suspicious as to the speed at which we are travelling . . .'

'We have to get home, Boltz,' said George decisively. 'It doesn't matter what it takes! They need us.'

Boltzmann made another vain attempt to hack into the system and wrest control away from whatever invisible force was directing the ship. Outside, they saw the brilliant rainbow of lights as stars flashed past. George paused for a moment, lost in wonder at the thought that he might be the only human being who had ever been this far from Earth! But would he ever get home to tell the tale – and, when he did, what would he find?

Boltzmann wiped his forehead after the exertion of trying to change the ship's course. George almost laughed to himself – robots don't sweat, so he had no need to wipe moisture out of his eyes, but he had picked up the gesture from humans and rather enjoyed doing it as a signal that he was working hard.

But then, just as Boltzmann had given up once

again, the ship itself decided to speak to them.

'*Apex of outward journey achieved,*' it announced, causing both George and Boltzmann to jump out of their skins.

'What's happening now?' George cried. But he didn't really need to ask. The huge spaceship, which had been determinedly charging through the darkness of space, almost came to a halt, and then, finally, it started to turn.

'Boltz!' said George. He didn't dare to say it. 'Are we . . . ?'

'I think so!' said the robot, grinning from ear to charred metal ear.

'We are!' said George, space-leaping over to the robot and giving him a massive hug. 'We're turning round! We're going—'

'*Home,*' said a chilling voice, blasting out of the communication portal. George and Boltzmann froze in mid-hug. '*Do not leave your homes,*' the voice continued, sharp and distinct. In the background they heard a wailing sound as though a multitude of sirens were blaring.

'*Citizens of Planet Earth!*' continued the broadcast. '*Do not panic. Remain in your homes. Do not resist. This is not a drill. Repeat. This is not a drill.*' As the voice rapped out its orders,

George and Boltzmann heard another sound like a huge violent explosion, large enough to shatter the surface of the Earth and send a vast gas cloud mushrooming through the Earth's atmosphere and into space.

And then there was silence.

Chapter One

The spaceship landed on its back-side with a huge crunch. It wobbled precariously for several minutes but managed not to topple over. Instead, it was wedged into the rocky ground at an angle like a spacey version of the Leaning Tower of Pisa. Clouds of dust billowed around it. It would

have been quite a sight – if someone had been there to see it. Around the ship, for miles and miles, stretched bleached, sandy ground, as empty as a lunar desert under a blistering milky sky.

Inside the ship, the two astronauts stayed strapped in their seats as the rocking motion juddered to a halt.

'I feel a bit sick,' bleated Boltzmann, who hadn't yet opened his eyes.

'Don't be silly,' said George. 'You're a robot, you don't know how to feel sick.'

'Yes I do,' protested Boltzmann. During his time in space with George, he had started to believe that he was not just an intelligent robot but a sentient one too. 'I have feelings!'

George, who preferred facts to feelings anyway, didn't want to discuss Boltzmann's feelings at that moment. 'Is landing complete?'

'Yes, thank you, Boltzmann!' replied his robot huffily.

'Thank you, Boltzmann,' murmured George. 'Interesting landing technique.'

'We are on the surface of a celestial body. I call that landing.'

'Not being funny,' said George, 'but this is Earth, isn't it?'

'I *think* so,' said the robot, looking around. 'But it's hard to be entirely sure.'

'What if it isn't?' asked George. 'What if you've landed us on the wrong planet?' As soon as he said it, he realized his mistake. On their long journey, Boltzmann had become more and more human in his reactions. Any hint of criticism made him very tetchy.

'Look, I've done my best!' cried the robot. 'After all, it's because of you that we went into space in the first place.'

'Yes, yes, I know,' sighed George. 'And thank you for coming on the journey with me. I couldn't have flown this spacecraft by myself.'

'Oh shucks!' said Boltzmann, more happily. 'I've never been allowed to spend so much time with a human before. It's been most educational. As a robot, I never dreamed . . .' He paused. 'Robots don't dream,' he corrected himself. 'I never thought that I would get the chance to have a human friend. And there is no other human I would have chosen. You are the best of your species, astronaut George.'

Unexpectedly George felt a lump in his throat. 'Aw, Boltz!' he said. 'You've been the best of robots. No, actually' – he cleared his throat – 'the best of friends, robot or human.'

Boltzmann smiled, then reached over with his metal pincer hands and undid George's straps.

'Are we getting out?'

'Yes!' said the robot. 'I don't know about you but I'm ready to stretch my legs!'

'How are we going to do that?' asked George. 'Aren't we a bit high up off the ground? Will my bones break if I jump out?'

'Fortunately,' said Boltzmann, peering out of the window, 'by landing the ship upright – a clever manoeuvre, even if I say so myself – I seem to have crushed the bottom half and we're much lower down than we should be. So your bones should be able to withstand the descent.'

On the day of the launch, they had boarded the huge spacecraft through an umbilical tower, which had raised them up to the entry point. As George peered out of the window, he could see that Boltzmann was correct. It was still quite a way down to the surface of this planet – Earth? – but it was jumpable, just about, although the windows must have got really dirty during landing as he couldn't see much of a view – only a sort of flat whiteness.

'Where have we landed?' George checked the

control panel of the spaceship to try and gain some clues as to where they were.

But the spaceship had come home to die. Once an adventurer that had charged beyond the edges of the solar system itself, now the *Artemis* was no more than scrap metal, blank screens and pointless switches.

'None of my devices are connecting either,' said Boltzmann. 'I don't understand why. I hope this is Earth. I don't feel emotionally prepared to greet a new planet right now.'

'Well!' said George. 'There's a more practical problem. If this isn't Earth, I might not be able to breathe the atmosphere . . .'

'I'll go first,' said Boltzmann in a noble voice, 'and test the conditions. I may be gone some time . . .'

'Thanks,' muttered George, who wasn't in the slightest bit worried about Boltzmann stepping out of the ship. Testing the conditions was in no way as dangerous for a robot as it was for a human being. He peered out of the window again. Where on Earth – literally – were they?

'Are you excited?' asked Boltzmann as he busied himself around the exit hatch.

'Yes!' said George. 'I want to see my mum and

dad. And Annie! And find out what's been going on. What was that weird message she sent us? I hope they've managed to fix everything by now ... and I'm hungry! I'd like some real food ...'

'Personally,' said the robot, 'or robotically, I can't wait to catch up with my robot brethren on Earth and share my insights into the human condition. I think they will be fascinated to hear—'

'Yup!' said George, cutting off Boltzmann's musings, which he had heard quite a few times on the space journey. 'Well, come on then. Let's get out of this spaceship before it switches itself off and we're stuck in here for ever.'

'Ta-dah!' said the robot as the hatch swung open, giving them a panoramic view of the world beyond – except the visibility was so bad they couldn't really see anything at all. Air blew in, carrying sticky sand and sooty particles that stuck to them.

'Bleugh!' said Boltzmann, trying to brush the tiny flakes off his metal carapace. 'I don't remember Earth being this dirty. But good news! You can breathe the air – I've run a test and its composition is just about safe for you.'

'What do you mean *just about* safe?' said George, coughing as he took off his helmet. The air tasted nasty and had a gritty feel to it.

'The carbon-dioxide content seems very high,' said the robot dubiously. 'Higher than I remember. Way less oxygen and far more greenhouse gases. But I think you'll survive for at least a few minutes.'

George spluttered a few times as he stuck his head out of the hatch and looked around. He realized that the windows of the spaceship hadn't been dirty – there was simply nothing to see except a blank, featureless desert stretching for miles in all directions, broken only by knobbly, stunted trees. Flinging one leg out of the side of the spacecraft, he prepared to throw himself down onto the surface.

For as long as he could remember, he had dreamed of the moment he climbed out of a space-ship and took a step on a new planet. This felt like his dream had turned into a nightmare – a near crash-landing somewhere on Earth. At least, he hoped it was Earth. But it was a remote and bleak spot and there was no one to greet them, nor any signs of home.

George shinned down to the ground, his space-suit easily gripping the outside of the spacecraft, which was gluey from the thick air in this strange location where they had landed. Boltzmann followed, plonking his huge metallic feet down on the sandy earth, which was strewn with small rocks. George swayed as he tried to steady himself, the impact of gravity weighing very heavily on him.

'Look!' said Boltzmann, pointing at his feet. 'We're standing in a river bed!'

'We are?' said George, examining the cracked surface for clues. 'But where's the water?'

'Dried up,' said Boltzmann. 'But it was once here.'

'What a sad place,' said George, puffing out his cheeks. 'Why did the *Artemis* come here? What made it choose this spot?'

'It definitely wanted to land here,' said the robot. 'It chose the journey and the destination – we've just been passengers all along. My master must have programmed it this way.'

'Why would he do that?' said George. 'Why would he program the *Artemis* to fly through space only to return to this dump? There's nothing here!'

They stood together and surveyed the scene, the boy in his spacesuit and the huge blackened robot gazing out across the empty land.

'Do you see anything?' George murmured, peering into the distance.

'Nope,' said Boltzmann. 'Just emptiness.'

The space rations had just lasted until they landed. Now, as the sun beat down on this dry desert, George realized he needed to find water soon.

But, as they were both staring at the heat haze in the distance, they failed to notice something approaching from behind. Before they knew it, a group of tiny robots making faint clicking noises streamed right past them, tearing towards their spaceship. As soon as the mini bots reached the ship, they started to dismantle it, pulling it to pieces with remarkable efficiency and speed.

'Hey!' shouted George. 'That's my ship!' But the tiny bots paid no attention. They couldn't have been less interested. Entirely focused on destroying the spacecraft, the bots removed the ship's *Artemis* nameplate and broke it up into pieces.

'Let me try,' said Boltzmann confidently. 'They'll want to talk to me.' He strode over to the tiny robots and started addressing them. They gathered round, answering back – and it seemed as though they were laughing at him! Soon the little bots turned back to the ship, cutting it into segments and carrying each piece away like a column of ants. Boltzmann walked heavily back to George, who was now feeling a horrible combination of travel sickness, gravity sickness, Earth sickness, home sickness and air sickness.

'Well?' croaked George. 'What did they say?'

'I don't know,' admitted the robot. 'At first, I didn't understand anything they said – but they thought I was hilarious! I worked out that they were calling me "V minus one point zero".'

'V minus one point zero?' repeated George hazily. 'You were the most advanced robot on Earth when we took off.' He felt very uneasy and a bit nauseous. 'Did they tell you where we are?'

'Sort of,' said Boltzmann carefully.

'What do you mean?' asked George, who was now leaning on Boltzmann as he was finding it hard to stand. He felt so heavy after all his time floating about in space. It wasn't a good feeling – if he could have gone straight back to space at that moment, he would have.

'They called it by a funny name,' said Boltzmann slowly.

'Funny ha-ha?' said George.

'Not so much,' said Boltzmann. 'They called it "Eden".'

'Eden?' said George. 'Where even *is* that? Did they say?'

'Here's the very not ha-ha bit,' said Boltzmann. 'The coordinates for this place tally with our point of departure – we are close to the launch pad from which we blasted off.'

'What?' said George. His head was spinning. 'I'm standing in a dried-up river bed in the middle of a desert and you're telling me that it

27

has the coordinates for Kosmodrome 2? But that was in the middle of the countryside, not that far from Foxbridge itself!'

At that moment, a particularly vicious gust of wind sent a flurry of soot into their faces.

'The bots must have got it wrong,' said George, spitting out some of the larger fragments that had blown into his mouth. 'This can't be my home.'

'I am afraid it is,' said Boltzmann. 'I think the *Artemis* has brought us home. Over there' – he pointed at the bald desert – 'is where Foxbridge should be.'

At that, George collapsed.

Chapter Two

George opened his eyes to find himself lying on the hard, dusty desert floor with Boltzmann leaning over him, his face anxious and worried.

'You're awake!' said the robot joyously. 'Mother of all boards, I thought you had fallen into a coma!'

George struggled to sit up. He was dazed – by the bright sunshine, the endless, timeless journey, the near crash-landing, and by this bizarre news. What did it mean that this place had the co-ordinates for the countryside around Foxbridge, his home? What had happened here to change it from peaceful green fields to this uninhabited desert? Why was it now called Eden? The only things he could see were the hi-tech mini bots devouring his battered spaceship at top speed – and a landscape so empty it looked as though it had been scrubbed clean of all signs of life.

'I don't understand,' he said, reaching out a hand to Boltzmann to steady himself. He felt a rising tide of panic rush upwards through his spinal cord and into his brain.

'It is rather difficult to process,' said Boltzmann uneasily. 'The world seems to have moved on much faster than we expected during the brief time of our voyage. I am surprised those bots find me so amusingly outdated.'

With remarkable efficiency, the scavenger bots had almost finished dismantling the whole spacecraft. Pieces of it were disappearing across the desert, carried by streams of the tiny robots, merrily clicking as they went.

George stared at them. 'They've nearly taken away all our ship! I left my lucky space patch on it!'

'I think that's gone for ever now,' said Boltzmann. 'The *Artemis* is finished.'

'But that's our ship!' said George. 'What if we need it?'

'What for?' said Boltzmann sensibly. 'We have explored space. Now it's time to make sense of home.'

'This can't be home,' said George. He felt

completely baffled and overwhelmed. 'It just *can't* be. There must be some mistake.' He thought back to the messages they had received on the ship. Had there been some kind of global wipeout while they'd briefly been in space? How could that possibly have happened? What did it all mean? Surely there was some kind of explanation for all this, and soon he'd be back with his family and Annie, having a good laugh about how wrong he'd got it all.

'Perhaps,' said Boltzmann doubtfully. 'But for now we need to go.'

'Where?' said George, who couldn't see anywhere to aim for. Boltzmann was right in one way, he thought. Exploring space now seemed quite straightforward in comparison to coming home!

'We need to find water and shelter – for you. And our only hope is to follow the bots before we lose sight of them. Jump up on my back!'

George tried to obey – but it was hot, he was tired and he was wearing a cumbersome space-suit with an oxygen tank on his back. Eventually Boltzmann managed to lift him up. He threw him over his shoulder in a fireman's lift and started to run.

'Ow! Ow!' cried George. 'This is worse than

re-entry.' Hanging over Boltzmann's shoulder, he was being jiggled and bumped horribly as the robot flew forward with great long strides. But Boltzmann paid no attention. All his focus was on keeping the scavenger bots in vision range as the sunshine beat down on them.

But, even from upside down, George could see that they were running through a desolate place with no signs of life at all. 'Why is there nobody here?' he called out to Boltzmann. 'Where are all the roads and houses and farms? And the people?'

'I don't know,' said the robot. 'Something must have happened here and driven out—'

He stopped so suddenly that George slammed into his metal back. 'Ouch!' complained George. 'That hurt!'

'Shush!' said Boltzmann. 'Bots ahead. And I don't like the look of them!'

George craned his head round and saw larger, curved black robots ahead, scuttling sideways across the desert like scarab beetles. They seemed to be heading back in the direction George and Boltzmann had come from, towards the spot where the spaceship had been.

'What are they doing?' asked George. If he hadn't already been hanging upside down, his hair would have been standing on end at the sight of these threatening bots, speeding with purpose across the desert.

Boltzmann dropped him on the ground.

'Don't know,' said the robot. 'At a guess, I'd say they're guarding this place. Looks like some kind of robot patrol.'

'From what?' asked George, shakily getting to his feet. Why would this empty desert need guarding?

In the distance the patrol bots shimmered in the

heat haze as they raced across the dust.

'They must have picked up our landing,' said Boltzmann quietly. 'And they're going to investigate.'

'Will they find anything?' asked George, shivering a little despite the heat.

'Not much,' said Boltzmann. 'The scavengers have probably taken away all traces of the *Artemis* by now.'

The patrol moved off into the distance.

'Let's go,' said Boltzmann, picking George up again.

Hanging over Boltzmann's shoulder, George started to feel very sick. He'd been living without gravity in the spacecraft; now, being back in Earth's gravity, moving at speed on Boltzmann's shoulder – as well as being home but not recognizing anything – was a brain-bending, stomach-churning experience. He couldn't figure it out at all, so his mind just had to settle down to the rhythm of Boltzmann's pounding footsteps.

But, just as George had almost got used to it, Boltzmann twisted his great robot head 180 degrees round on his metal shoulders and looked behind him. And then he sped up, still looking backwards.

'What's wrong?' cried George.

'They've spotted us,' said Boltzmann. 'The patrol. And they're gaining on us.'

Boltzmann was going faster and faster now, George bobbing up and down over his shoulder with each long stride, dust bursting up from the dry ground.

'We need to find a hiding place,' said Boltzmann. 'We are in danger.'

'Can you spot anywhere to go?' said George. All he could see was more empty ground stretching as far as the horizon.

'Nope,' said Boltzmann, whose eyes were still on the patrol bots behind him. 'They are getting closer.'

George lifted his head and pointed. 'But what's that? Look! Over here!' A dust cloud was crossing the desert, indicating that something or someone was travelling at speed straight for them.

'My head is stuck!' Boltzmann sounded as close to panic as a robot ever gets as he realized that he couldn't wind his head back round to face forward. 'I can't see where you are pointing.'

'Stop!' yelled George. 'And put me down.'

Boltzmann set George down on the ground and winched his head back round so it was facing

35

the right way. As he did so, George peered at the oncoming cloud. He thought he could make out a shape inside it.

I can't be right, he thought to himself. *I must be dreaming!* The dust cloud continued towards them, and George, just as he would have done on his home street in the old Foxbridge, stuck out his hand to hail it. The dust cloud stopped and the object came into perfect focus.

It was a school bus. Here, in the middle of the desert, under the blazing curdled sky, stood a very ordinary yellow school bus.

The doors opened.

'Come on,' said George, who was already halfway up the steps. Boltzmann was hesitating. 'Get in.'

'I don't know,' fretted the robot. 'Are you sure?'

'Do you want to be caught by them?' said George, pointing at the patrol bots, which were close enough now for him to make out their many eyes on swivel stalks, their antennae, their curved carapaces and robotic limbs.

'No thanks!' said Boltzmann, jumping into the bus behind George. The doors slammed shut behind them and the bus set off at great speed.

George looked around him. To his surprise, he saw that the bus was full of small kids, all wearing large headsets, seemingly lost in their own worlds. None of them had noticed the stop or the new passengers. Next to each child sat a robot. But they weren't like Boltzmann – a huge hulking piece of robotic technology. These were of a very different type, each robot obviously customized to suit the personality of its owner.

There was a cute, kitty-faced android sitting next to a small girl dressed in pink. A sporty-looking boy had a racer robot. At the back, an older girl with a long black ponytail sat with a serious-faced robot in heavy-framed glasses. To George's surprise, no one paid him or Boltzmann any attention at all.

Or so he thought, until he looked again and realized that the robot wearing glasses seemed to have fixated on him. Unnerved, George looked for an empty seat and motioned to Boltzmann to sit down beside him. He looked around at the other passengers on the bus.

'They're schoolkids!'

'And they all seem to have a robot . . .' noted Boltzmann approvingly. 'How sensible! Things are looking up! What's our plan?'

'This bus must be going somewhere,' improvised George. 'And, as it's full of kids, it's got to be going somewhere kids are welcome, right?'

'Right!' agreed Boltzmann absent-mindedly, waving out of the window at the patrol bots, which were angrily tapping on the side of the bus.

'They don't look happy,' said George.

'I don't think happy is their primary purpose,' said Boltzmann smugly. 'After all, not everyone can be a nice robot like me.'

But, as the bus gained speed, the bots suddenly stopped in their tracks, as though they had hit an invisible wall. Wheeling round very slowly, they started to travel back in the direction they had come from, without a backward glance at the bus.

'Why did they stop?' said George.

'It looks as though they received a command,' said Boltzmann. They both turned round. The robot with the heavy-framed glasses seemed to be staring out of the window in the direction of the bots. 'At least they've left us. What do we do now?'

'If we tag along with this lot,' whispered George, 'maybe we'll find out how to get to Foxbridge, and then we can surprise my family and get things back to normal once more . . .' He trailed off. Something told him that 'normal' was a very long way off.

As the only passengers on the bus not wearing huge headsets, George and Boltzmann stared silently out of the window at the view for the rest of the journey. They both seemed to have gone to a place beyond speech. The awful landscape, the silent children, the strange-looking robots and even the air itself felt so alien to George that he found himself fighting back tears.

Was this really home? Was this really the place he had dreamed of during his space sleeps? At the same time, he was starting to feel afraid, really afraid, like never before. Fear seeped through his whole being the way an icy drink spreads coldness through a warm body. If the terror reached his heart, George wondered if it would just stop beating entirely, frozen through shock and disappointment.

'Act normal,' he told himself. 'Don't give in to the fear! Just act normal. It'll all be fine.'

Outside the bus, the desert stretched away in all directions, with only scrubby little bushes and scraps of vegetation clinging to the barren surface. A few living things scurried about – a huge yellow snake uncoiled itself to try and catch a leather-winged flying frog while a group of rat-faced mini-pigs dashed alongside the bus.

Finally something solid emerged from the dust in front of them and the bus came to a large, high fence and a set of gates. The gates opened automatically as the bus approached and George suddenly noticed something: the bus had no driver.

'There're no grown-ups on board,' he pointed out to Boltzmann. 'Isn't that kinda weird? All these really young kids on a bus with no one to look after them?'

But Boltzmann wasn't an expert on matters like childcare and didn't seem bothered. Anyway, he had seen something far more interesting.

'Look!' he said.

Inside the desert compound stood a gleaming array of strangely shaped buildings, shining silver in the brilliant sunshine. At the entrance to what appeared to be the main building they saw a huge illuminated 3D sign, which seemed to hover, unsupported, above the doorway.

WELCOME, it said, TO THE EDEN CORPORATION. And then, underneath, it proclaimed: THE BEST OF ALL POSSIBLE WORLDS!

Chapter Three

'Eden?' said George, blinking in the bright light outside the bus. As soon as the Eden Corporation came into view, the kids on the bus had, in perfect synchronicity, taken off their headsets and lined up to get off. 'That's what the mini bots said. What does it mean?'

'The Garden of,' said Boltzmann, standing beside him. 'The origin of life, according to some sources.'

'Why does it say "the best of all possible worlds"?' asked George. But at that moment the children and their robots formed a crocodile and docilely marched forward into the building. 'Let's follow,' he hissed.

Boltzmann brought up the rear, towering above the tiny schoolchildren and their robots. George had no idea what to do except look for someone who might be able to help them – or at least explain where they were and what was going on.

They followed the kids, still walking in double file with their robots, and walked behind, with the bigger pony-tailed girl and her robot at the back. They filed into the centre of a beautiful domed building.

'We must be blending in!' said Boltzmann happily. But in fact he and George, scruffy, travel-stained, battered and weary-looking, couldn't have looked less like the procession of tidy, clean and beautifully behaved schoolchildren with their eccentric but neat-looking robots.

'I don't think we are,' said George, puzzled. 'Though they don't seem to notice what's around them at all. It's like we're not even here.'

But he had spoken too soon. Suddenly the bigger girl, with the sleek-looking robot in glasses standing next to her, turned and spotted them. She stared in astonishment at George, looking him up and down as though he'd just fallen from the sky – which, of course, he had, only she didn't know that.

'Excuse me!' she exclaimed. 'Who are you? And what are you doing on our school trip? Oh, best of all worlds!' She struck herself on the forehead

LUCY HAWKING

with the flat of her hand. 'That was two questions. I'll be near my limit in just a couple of Dumps!'

George had no idea what she was talking about. He tried to think of some excuse that would explain quite what he was doing in the middle of the desert wearing a spacesuit, in the company of an outsize, caramelized robot. But his brain was too foggy for him to invent something so he fell back on the truth.

'I'm . . . I'm . . .' he replied.

Just then, the girl's robot moved forward and whispered something in her ear. Her expression changed. 'Ohh!' she said, her dark eyes very round and shiny. She looked at George with sympathy now. 'Oh, I see!'

George felt even more confused. He glanced up and caught the eye of the girl's robot. Did he imagine it or did the robot in glasses give him the ghost of a wink?

'I'm so sorry,' said the girl sympathetically. 'How awful for you! And you've lost everything! I'm so sorry. My robot says you're a *refugee*.' She whispered the last word. 'And that I can't ask any more questions today because I've hit my question max.'

George was lost for words, but fortunately

Boltzmann was not. He used all his new-found human sensitivity to play along. 'Yes,' said the giant scruffy robot sadly. 'It was so sad.' He sounded like he might burst into tears.

'You crossed the Divide?' the girl whispered. 'You come from Other Side?' She turned to her robot. 'Those weren't questions!' she said quickly. 'They were statements!'

Boltzmann nodded bravely. 'I can't talk about it,' he sighed, tapping his nose with one robot finger. 'Too painful.'

'Of course,' said the girl hurriedly. 'I'll never mention it again. Welcome! You'll be safe now you're in Eden.'

'It's the best of all possible worlds,' chimed in her robot smoothly, with what George faintly thought might have been a trace of sarcasm. 'I think you'll find.'

'You must be so courageous,' said the girl. She turned to her robot. 'Can I use some of tomorrow's question allowance? Please? I'll be really good and ask nothing tomorrow.'

The robot nodded.

'Were you in the desert at a *secret* quarantine facility?'

'Yes,' said George, recovering his voice. It

wasn't exactly a lie. He'd been pretty well quarantined in space.

'I see you've gone retro with your robotics,' said the girl. 'What a museum piece!'

Boltzmann grimaced but said nothing.

'Wow, well, if you are the best Other Side have to offer, then there isn't so much to be afraid of after all!' said the girl. 'Mind you, since you blocked all our channels, we know very little about you. What's your name?'

'George,' said George. 'What's yours?'

'Hero,' said the girl. 'My name is Hero.'

'My sister's called Hera,' said George, wondering where his naughty twin siblings were now.

Hero looked perplexed and echoed, 'Sister?'

But the smaller kids were getting restless. They milled around George and Hero, forming a circle. They had taken off their headsets and were clasping them to their chests as though they were their most precious possessions. Each of them had a small tank on their back, not that different to George's. Now he was close to them, he could see they all had face masks with tubes attached to the tanks as well.

'Hello!' said a small girl, smiling up at George. 'Who are you?'

George felt relieved to hear one of them speak. It made it all seem less strange. 'I'm George,' he said. 'We haven't met before.'

'Is that your robot?' she asked, pointing at Boltzmann, who towered over this perky little group of people. Next to her stood a tiny and incredibly cute-looking robot with huge eyes, soft hair and an expressive face.

'Yes,' said George. Boltzmann smiled with his best 'nice' robot face.

'He looks scary,' said the small girl, shivering. Her robot immediately burst into tears. Boltzmann turned away to hide his hurt feelings.

'IS HE YOURS?!' A small hyperactive boy bounced up to George, pointing up at Boltzmann.

'Yup,' said George, nodding.

'WOW, HE'S HUGE!' said the boy. This boy also had a robot with him, but his robot didn't seem to have a sense of humour.

'Your voice volume is too high, Herbert,' the robot droned at the boy. 'I will have to check your blood-sugar levels and inform your guardian.'

'OH, SOR— Sorree . . .' whispered the boy, looking chastened.

'Who is actually in charge here?' George asked Hero. 'Is there a grown-up?'

'In charge?' Hero looked surprised. 'Why do we need an adult to be in charge?'

'Where's your teacher?' asked George.

Hero looked baffled. 'We all have our robots with us and the robots are in constant contact with our guardians and with our school. That's all we need. I'm surprised it isn't the same in Other Side!'

'The same in Other Side,' echoed George, not knowing what else to say.

Hero's robot chipped in. 'Other Side is remarkably similar to Eden, except that of course it is completely different at the same time,' he said unhelpfully.

'Huh?' said George.

'I mean, on the surface, Other Side appears to be an entirely different regime to Eden, and yet in all fundamental ways it is exactly the same. If one didn't know better, one would think they were identical,' the robot finished firmly.

'The people,' George whispered to the robot, 'in Other Side?'

'Same as here,' said Hero's robot. 'Complete freedom. Just like Eden.'

'Oh,' said George. Now he knew he hadn't imagined the sarcasm in the robot's tone.

That was when they heard the voice. The empty circular area they stood in darkened.

'Welcome to Eden, Future Leaders from Inside the Bubble. You are here to complete an educational module on the great habitats of the Earth. Right now, you are about to enjoy a personalized educational experience of the *rainforest*, an ecosystem that used to cover one third of the Earth but is now extinct. We have recreated the rainforest for you here in all its biodiversity!'

'What?' said George to Boltzmann. 'Why is the rainforest extinct?'

Boltzmann motioned for George to look up.

Following Boltzmann's finger, George saw that, where the ceiling had been only moments before, light now streamed through a canopy of tall tropical trees, swaying in the wind. Further down, long-tailed monkeys cried to each other while jumping through the thick growth. When he looked down at the ground, he saw that it was covered with long roots, mossy plants, curly ferns, flytraps and strange-shaped fungi. George reached out a hand to one of the carnivorous-looking plants – and it snapped at his finger as though trying to eat it. As he did so, he saw a robotic hand tweak a strand of hair out of one of the kids.

He whirled round but the slender robotic paw disappeared almost immediately.

'Watch out!' said Boltzmann as a bird with a brightly coloured beak swooped down towards them, flapping in their faces.

'Over there!' said George, spotting a dark, cat-like face peering at them through a spaghetti tumble of tree roots.

'No, there!' said Boltzmann, pointing to an enormous silver primate in the distance, cautiously eyeing them while scratching its ear.

'What *is* this?!' said George. 'Are these real?'

'Not, is my guess. This must be immersive virtual reality,' said Boltzmann, but he and George shrank closer and closer together as the predators seemed to start to take an interest. They began to back away when a puma slunk nearer, narrowing its eyes as though it was judging the distance for a killer leap. As Boltzmann and George took another step back, they ricocheted into something behind them, something that felt warm and alive to George, something that made them both let out a—

SCREAM!

'Do you mind,' said Hero, 'letting go of me?'

Boltzmann and George shuffled their feet in

embarrassment and let Hero go as the scene around them turned blue instead of green.

'And this,' said the voice, 'is the Great Barrier Reef! One of the marvels of the Ancient World, once home to millions of species who lived among the coral structures of this magical place. Sadly, in the best of all possible worlds we had to close the reef to visitors after the oceans boiled. But we can show you the beauty of this marine environment without you even getting your toes wet! We know your guardian bots wouldn't like that! Ho ho ho,' chortled the voice mirthlessly.

'Oh!' Some of the kids made a longing noise, as if getting their feet wet was exactly what they would like best. But they were soon distracted as giant sharks drifted above their heads and darting, colourful fish wove around them in shoals.

'Here in Eden,' the voice continued, 'we're often asked – how do you make the nutritional products we live on so very tasty?! Well, we can tell you our secrets now.'

The scene changed to a beautiful valley with golden fields of wheat bordered by orchards heavy with ripe fruit, the ground bursting with healthy-looking vegetables. George was transported back to his father's garden. That had been full of vegetables and fruit, but also weeds, insects, birds, a compost heap, children's toys, George's treehouse and the old sty where once his pet pig, Freddy, had lived. That garden had been real, buzzing with life and energy, not like this image, which was like a child's picturebook illustration of what a farm should be like. He must find his parents and Annie as soon as possible, thought George. Get out of this bizarre setup and then things would start to seem OK.

But, at that moment, George felt the kid next to him give a little jump. Looking down, he saw what looked like a very fine needle attached to the end of a robotic hand, which whirred away immediately. If it wasn't for the tiny mark on the back of the child's hand, he might have thought he'd imagined it. As he looked about, he just caught sight of the same thing happening to all the other kids – a strand of their hair being pulled out and a needle puncturing their skin for the briefest of seconds. Most of them were so entranced by the show they didn't even seem to notice.

'We only grow our produce in the cleanest, purest places on Earth!' the commentary burbled on. 'In the most natural conditions possible our wonderful Eden nutritional supplements are all derived from fresh and tasty foods, grown by us with love and care. They live on pure water and sunshine! That's all they need to be so very delicious. Remember, kids, in the best of all possible worlds we provide worldwide food production to make sure you have good, clean, nutritious food to live on!'

The agricultural lands faded into an icy landscape with huge pale blue glaciers towering over dark green seas.

'This,' the voice continued, 'was the polar icecap before it melted. As you can see, it was too cold for human habitation and the ice covering prevented exploration of the many resources trapped below, so it really was a big waste of space. But now, thanks to the great progress made by Eden following on from the Great Disruption, this whole area has been freed for exploitation.'

George gave a horrified squeak and squeezed Boltzmann's arm. 'How could all this have happened? How long were we up there for?'

'Don't know,' said Boltzmann uneasily. 'There was some malfunction in my time-recording facilities while we were in space and I have lost any measurements of our journey.'

The voice carried on. 'We are now able to extract valuable minerals from under the surface and create more wealth. This, and other great successes, have been made possible thanks to the positive policies of Professor Sir General Dr Reverend Commander Trellis Dump the Second, may he live for ever! His Highest Excellency, Chairperson of Eden, the best company on Earth, and President of Eden itself! Thank you all for joining us for this educational experience! Please submit your feedback forms through your channel as you leave. Don't forget to give us a five-star review!'

A doorway opened and the children's robots ushered them through and out of the door. Some of the kids wanted to stay in the virtual environment, but their guardian bots firmly guided them back towards the school bus. George and Boltzmann were just standing at the back, wondering what to do next.

'Come on,' said Hero. 'It's time to go.'

'Yes,' said George hurriedly. 'We're coming,

aren't we, Boltzmann? We're getting on the bus to . . .' He paused.

'The Bubble, of course,' said Hero, giving him a strange look. 'Look, don't worry, we'll make sure we get you home, won't we?' She looked over at her robot, who nodded.

'Sorry, where did you say we were going?' asked George, who just needed to hear Hero say it once more, to be entirely sure.

'The Bubble,' she said. 'We're going to the Bubble.'

Chapter Four

Boltzmann got his question in first. 'This Bubble,' he enquired as they clambered back onto the driverless school bus, 'did it once have another name?' He took a seat next to Hero's robot, with Hero and George in front.

'Oh yes!' said Hero. 'A long time ago, before the Great Disruption, it was called Foxbridge. What a silly name!'

'Foxbridge!' said George, his hair standing on end. 'Foxbridge!' It was all he could do not to keep repeating the name. A vision of his home town flashed into his brain: the cheerful cobbled streets, the higgledy-piggledy shopfronts, the bakery with its trays of sticky Chelsea buns, the market square with the striped awnings of the produce stalls, the little parks where small children played, the grand old buildings that made up the university, his own

  57

narrow lane where the houses hugged each other and their back gardens led down to the river. How had this become a bubble?

'How far are we from Foxbridge – I mean, the Bubble?' enquired Boltzmann.

'Like, about thirty Dumps away?' said Hero.

'Thirty Dumps?' said George. 'What does that mean?'

'A Dump is a unit of time,' said Hero, looking startled. 'How do you not know that? It can be distance as well. A Dumpometre takes a Dump to travel.'

'So how long *is* a Dump?' said George.

'The ideal attention span of an Eden citizen,' replied Hero knowledgeably.

'How long is *that*?'

'Well, we've been talking for about half a Dump already!' she said.

'That's a bit short, isn't it?' said George, alarmed.

'I know,' huffed Hero. 'I'm always getting into trouble because my attention span is way too many Dumps long. I keep trying to make it shorter, but it never seems to want to go down.' She pouted. 'That – and the questions! I wish I could stop asking questions, but they just pop out of my brain before I can stop them.' She pulled a sad face. 'It makes my marks go down.'

'Asking questions is a good thing!' said George. 'Why would that make your marks go down?'

But Hero just eyed him suspiciously as though this was a trap she knew better than to fall into.

George decided, though, that he had no restriction on question asking. 'Did something happen here?' he asked Hero as the bus bucketed forward. 'Like in, say, the last year?' That felt too long to George for the duration of his space journey, but he thought it was best to give a high estimate and work back from there. 'Like a drought?'

'Well, yeah!' said Hero. 'But we don't call it years. That's super old-style. We call it Dumps of the Sun. Something did happen here, but not in the last Dump of the Sun! It was ages ago, way before I was hatched. And I'm nearly nine Dumps of the Sun! You must have heard about the Great Disruption?'

'Disruption?' asked George uneasily. What was Hero talking about?

'*You* know.' She elbowed him. 'Even in Other Side, they must teach you about the Great Disruption – about how what was left of the world had to be divided into two halves; one is Eden and one is Other Side. Bubble is in Eden.

And wherever you come from is in Other Side.'

George felt stunned. *What was left of the world*? Hero's robot decided to enlighten him.

'May I intervene?' he said.

'George, this is Empyrean, my robot,' said Hero, sounding less than thrilled. 'But you can call him Empy if you like.'

'I'd rather you didn't,' replied the robot. 'I prefer my full name.'

'Don't listen,' said Hero. 'I got the bot with the attitude! Everyone, but *everyone*, calls him Empy. I call him *Empy the unhelpful*.'

'So undignified,' sighed the robot. 'Anyway, if you will allow. The Great Disruption,' he said in his smirky tones from behind them, 'is a historical event that will be remembered for its Greatness and its Disruptedness for all time.'

'Um, what actually happened?' asked George. The memory of the sound of a gigantic explosion that they had heard from a broadcast from Earth came back to him. Surely not. It couldn't be . . .

'Nations of the Earth, following a series of disasters caused by climate change and other environmental problems, faced each other in terrible destructive warfare,' said the robot, now sounding deadly serious, his eyes flashing. George wheeled round to catch Boltzmann's gaze in horror. Boltzmann reached out a robot hand to clasp George's shoulder as George started to rock gently back and forth with shock.

'How long did this war last?' whispered George, thinking it must have gone on for decades to have caused so much damage.

'About two and a half minutes,' replied the robot. 'Millions of people died, homes were destroyed, whole habitats wiped out. Civilization was put back by millennia. The weapons unleashed devastation on the face of this planet. Toxic gases poured into the atmosphere. The oceans boiled, the forests burned and the icecaps melted. Much of the world is now uninhabitable.'

George felt winded. It was as though the robot had punched him in the stomach. He closed his eyes. For a moment, like a very small child, he had the thought that if he couldn't see it, it wasn't really happening. But, when he opened his eyes again, the world had not changed back to the way he remembered it. He was still on a bus with a girl and her robot, in this strange new world, with his own charred metal friend at his back.

He wasn't the only one to look shocked. Hero

seemed as taken aback by what her robot had said as George.

'That's not right!' she said hotly. 'What you just said – that's not what we learned about the Great Disruption! We learned it was a good thing because it led to the foundation of Eden and to Dump the Second, may he live for ever, who has set the people free!'

'Absolutely,' agreed her robot without missing a beat. 'The Great Disruption was the turning point that led to the glorious future of human and robot kind that we now enjoy in the enlightened paradise of Eden. The Great Disruption meant the people of the world no longer wanted to be led by politicians and experts, so they chose two leaders from among them to run corporations that would each own half of the world. Or what was left of it. Each corporation, of course, already wielded huge power, with great profits, and had been instrumental in leading our world into conflict. Now, with the Great Disruption, the two companies agreed to this division of assets.'

'The world is run by companies?' said George. 'Just two of them?'

'Yes, just the two,' said the robot. 'Well, there is a non-aligned zone that has rejected corporate wisdom. But we don't speak of them. They're not very nice.'

Not nice? thought George. *What did 'nice' have to do with anything?*

'How does it work?' he asked, keen to understand more about the world into which he had crash-landed.

'Oh, it's very wise,' said the robot. 'Works perfectly. The government and the corporation are the same thing, so whatever the government, led by Trellis Dump the Second (may he live for ever), who is also the head of the Eden Corp, thinks would be best for the people, then Eden Corp can provide it. That way people have the chance to buy it and add it to their consumer debt. We don't talk about citizens any more. We call them consumers.' The bus, which had slowed down over some rough ground, now shot forward once again in a cloud of the ever-present dust.

'Who ran the world before Trellis Dump the Second?' asked George.

'Trellis Dump the First, of course,' replied the robot. 'Who else?'

'But then, didn't Trellis Dump cause the Great Disruption if he was in charge back then? So how did Trellis Dump the Second end up with Eden?'

'Trellis Dump the Second worked closely with his father before the Great Disruption. But, when the division was agreed, he felt that it was the will of the people for him to take over fully from his father,' said the robot patiently. 'It was Trellis Dump the Second, may he live for ever, who had the vision to take us into our glorious future. To develop Eden as we know it today. Everything in Eden is now a sign of the thanks the people give for his wise, all-seeing, all-encompassing rule. That is all you need to remember about Eden.'

George couldn't quite digest all this at once. He turned away and stared hard out of the window, trying to fit the pieces together in his mind until it made sense. There was a a bit missing that would explain it all – but what was it?

Boltzmann leaned over. 'I think they might have found something.' He pointed to the patrol bots, racing back towards the Eden Corporation with a piece of shrapnel held aloft. Empyrean noticed as well. He glared out of the window at the patrol bots, which seemed to cause them to grind to a halt, drop the piece of spaceship and very slowly walk away.

All the kids on the bus now had headsets on – except for George and Hero.

Something was brewing in George's mind. Something that had bothered him for the whole span of their space journey. Time. It was all about time. They had never known what time it was – nor how fast time was passing. They had travelled through space, but they had no idea how long the voyage had taken. Was it possible they had travelled through time as well? Had the *Artemis* been some kind of ship of time . . . ?

George slumped down in his seat. Next to him, Hero shook out her black ponytail and then got out a pair of bright red goggles, which she strapped onto her head. She started swaying a little from side to side. George poked her and she jumped almost off her seat.

'What?' she said crossly, pulling off the goggles. 'That's rude!'

'What are you doing?' asked George.

Hero's mouth dropped open. 'You mean, you don't know?'

'Course not,' said George.

'I'm doing my homework!' said Hero. 'I have to finish this on the journey home.'

'But you don't have any books or any paper!' said George. 'Or even a screen to tap on.'

'Books! Paper! Next you'll be asking me for a pen!'

'Hero,' said George quietly. 'What year is it?'

'What year?' said Hero in surprise. 'Well, it's Year 40.' She lifted up her goggles, ready to put them back on.

'What does she mean, Year 40?' said George, looking over at Empyrean. 'When I left . . . um, Earth' – this last said in a low whisper so that only the robot could hear him – 'it was 2018. So it must still be something beginning with a two zero.'

'No,' interjected the robot. 'Time was reset following the Great Disruption, after the great Trellis Dump the Second took over from his father to lead us into a new prosperity. That was decided by our benevolent leaders, both here in Eden and in Other Side. *Where you come from*' – the robot stressed this last sentence very pointedly – 'they decided that time itself must be made a subject of the regimes. So time was reset to mark the beginning of the glorious Second Age of Dump.'

'Look, I've really got to go back to my virtual-reality memory palace,' complained Hero. 'It's recording that I've started my session and left so I'll get lower marks if I don't finish. I can't risk that, otherwise . . .' She nibbled at her lip, looking worried.

'Otherwise what?' said George.

But she had already disappeared into a virtual world where he couldn't follow her.

Out of the corner of his eye, he just caught sight of Hero's robot shaking his head, but, when he turned to stare more closely, Empyrean looked away studiously.

Everyone else on the bus still had their headsets on, lost in their own private worlds, wandering their virtual-reality memory palaces while doing their homework, George assumed. He had nothing else to do but look out of the window. It was a depressing sight. There was nothing to see but desert. Scrubland, blown by fierce winds, surrounded the bus, which perambulated along at a steady speed.

'Boltz!' groaned George over his shoulder. 'What are we going to do? How are we going to find my family? Annie? Eric? Where are they all? Where are we?'

At that moment, they drove past what looked like the remains of a row of abandoned houses. The empty windows of the buildings stared bleakly back at George as they passed – with no roofs or doors, they were uninhabitable. Behind the former houses, George thought he saw one or two of the patrol bots in the distance, running across the open country with their strange sideways motion.

'I don't know,' said Boltzmann sadly. 'I can't connect to any form of network that would allow me to update us on the current situation.' He paused. 'May I now suggest you remove your spacesuit, since I believe it to be unnecessary where we are heading. I feel it would be acceptable to leave it on this bus.'

'Oh, right,' George said. It made sense, especially if he wanted to blend in to find out more about what was going on. He struggled out of the suit and stashed it under a seat. Underneath he was wearing shorts and a T-shirt.

He knelt up on his seat and turned round to speak privately to his robot. It was time to tell him what was on his mind. 'Boltz, I've been thinking – about time and how it moves more slowly when you're travelling very fast,' he said quietly. He glanced over at Hero's robot, which seemed to have switched itself off.

'Ah,' said Boltzmann wisely. 'Time dilation. Einstein's great achievement in relativity, one of the most astonishing discoveries of the twentieth century.'

'We can't travel back to the past. Well, at least we think we can't . . .'

'Right,' said Boltzmann.

'But we can jump forward into the future. When you travel really, *really* fast, time moves more slowly. So, if we went fast enough in the *Artemis*, then a short period of time for us in the spaceship could have been a very long time on Earth, couldn't it?'

Boltzmann sighed. 'I was coming to that conclusion myself,' he said.

'Do you think Alioth programmed the *Artemis* that way?' said George. 'That all along he never meant to travel across the solar system to find life? Instead, he was going to ping himself into the future, taking a bunch of really bright kids with him as his army?'

'Where my master is concerned,' said Boltzmann rather grimly, 'I'm sorry to say anything is possible. Even though you thought you had vanquished him, I fear he's ended up with the last laugh and sent *us* into the future instead.'

'I was hoping,' said George, 'that you'd say I was totally way out and there was no chance we could be in the future.'

'Oh, we could,' said Boltz. 'And I have to tell you, the emotions I am now experiencing are so complicated that I am considering going back to being a non-sentient being in order to avoid them.'

Just then, the bus ground to a sudden halt, which nearly propelled George off his seat entirely. They finally seemed to have arrived somewhere and were waiting in a line outside what looked like a giant semi-transparent bubble.

Hero whipped off her goggles. 'Well, I finished!' she said. 'Just in time! I can't mess up my marks, not now, on my last chance to . . .' All the other kids took off their goggles too.

'Where are we?' George asked her, scrambling back into his seat.

'We've arrived!' Hero said. 'At the Bubble. We're just waiting for the bus to be scanned for entry.'

'So this is it,' said George. 'Foxbridge of the future. I'm in the right place – but at the wrong time.'

Chapter Five

As the bus drove into the Bubble, George's eyes nearly popped out of his head. If outside was desert, inside was paradise. It was beautiful: colourful flowers, palm trees, exotic birds and huge butterflies were everywhere. Lush greenery surrounded them as they drove through a humid atmosphere with clouds collecting above them and moisture beading on the outside of the bus.

'Are they real?' He pointed to a flock of gorgeous black and red butterflies flying past the window of the bus, which was now moving along slowly and carefully.

'Of course they're real!' said Hero. 'Didn't you know? The Bubble is a model environment – it's an experiment to see if all cities could be like it. It's the most beautiful in the whole world!'

George pressed his nose against the window of the bus, hoping to see something he recognized. But it was a totally different place to the Foxbridge he had left behind. There was nothing here of the place he remembered, the old-style university town in which he had been born.

'It's very warm in here,' he said. 'Is that part of the experiment?'

'No,' said Hero, looking perplexed. 'It's not usually this hot. I don't understand. The biosphere is meant to react automatically when temperatures rise, and cool it down.'

'When did this experiment start?' George asked Hero.

'Before I was alive,' she said. 'After the Great Disruption. Old Foxbridge was destroyed and it was rebuilt like this!'

'Destroyed?' said George, although it was already obvious to him. 'In the war?'

'Not really,' said Hero solemnly. 'Old Foxbridge was the centre of rebel fighting just before the time of the Great Disruption and so it was demolished. Afterwards our leader had it made into the most beautiful place in the world, but only kids are allowed to live here.'

Rebel fighting? 'Who were these rebels?' asked George. A horrible sick feeling was building in his stomach.

'People with funny ideas about things,' said Hero mysteriously.

'What things?' said George. People with funny ideas sounded just like his mum and dad, along with his next-door neighbours, scientist Eric and his daughter, Annie. Unfortunately he could just imagine them as rebel fighters. What Hero said next only made it worse.

'Like fake news about climate change,' said Hero. 'And fake-news science. Trellis Dump (may he live for ever) had to change all that, make sure the people could be free instead of being bossed around and told what to do by experts and scientists.'

'But there *was* a problem with the climate!'

protested George. His parents were dedicated eco-warriors, and scientist Eric never missed an opportunity to give an impromptu lecture about the future of Planet Earth. When Eric and George's parents had first met, it seemed like they were on different sides – George's parents blamed science and technology for the problems on Earth, and Eric loved science above all things and firmly believed it would save the human race. Eventually, though, they had come to consider themselves as having different views but all being on the same side. The two friends, Annie and George, had made their parents see that everyone needed to work together to tackle global challenges, even if they didn't agree on absolutely everything.

''Scuse me, there wasn't!' exclaimed Hero. 'The Great Disruption caused some problems, but that's been put right now. Anyway, that's what we learned in our weather module.'

George gaped at her. They had just entered a biosphere within a desert, and Hero thought climate change wasn't real. He gazed out of the window again. The bus was now chugging along small streets of funny spherical houses with palm trees and brightly coloured flowering shrubs in their front gardens. It looked nothing like the

75

Foxbridge George had known.

'Why are the houses round?' he asked Hero.

'They're inflatable, of course,' she said. 'A bit like balloons. It makes them really easy to move. You just deflate the house and take it to a new location. My guardian says that in the past houses had to stay in one place!' She went off into peals of laughter.

In the past, thought George. *The past . . .*

Just then a delegation of smaller children came up to Hero. She seemed to be some kind of head prefect. The little kids whispered to her and scampered back to their seats.

She turned to George. 'The kids say you're being really unfriendly,' she said.

'What? How?' said George.

'They can't access your thought stream,' said Hero. 'So they think you don't like them.'

'My what?' said George. 'My thought stream? Why would I give someone access to my thoughts?'

'It's what we do here,' said Hero gently. 'I expect it's different on Other Side. But here, when you're among friends or in a group, you have to make your thought stream accessible or people think you're really rude. And you're not. So don't make the kids think you are.'

'Ah,' said George. He looked around at Boltzmann, who just shrugged. He improvised. 'Can you tell the kids that my thought stream isn't compatible with theirs at the moment as I'm from Other Side. Once I have it up and running, I'll be thrilled to thought-stream with them.'

'Oh!' said Hero. 'Of course! I'll thought them.' Sure enough, a few minutes later, the little kids ran back up to Hero, all beaming smiles. They patted George as if he was a poor old dog they felt sorry for, then jumped back into their seats.

'They're very quiet!' George said to Hero. He remembered his own little sisters, who between them made enough noise to fill a stadium.

'They are so not!' exclaimed Hero.

'They don't make a sound,' said George.

'Duh!' said Hero. 'You don't get their thought streams! Probably a good idea – you'd never have a moment's peace again.'

'How do you receive these thought streams?' said George curiously.

'Through your in-head computer chip, of course!' said Hero.

Boltzmann tactfully interrupted with a cough. 'Where are we actually going?' the rusty old robot asked. 'What is our destination?'

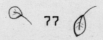

'We,' said Hero, gesturing to herself and the other kids, 'are going to our homes. Don't you have a home to go to?'

'I had one in Old Foxbridge,' said George sadly, wondering if he would ever see it or his family again.

Hero looked confused. 'Why do you keep talking about Old Foxbridge? Why don't you talk about Other Side? What are you going to do now?'

'We don't know. Any suggestions?' said Boltzmann brightly. 'At the moment, we are one homeless robot and a boy.'

Empyrean spoke up. 'I have just had an update from your guardian!' he announced. 'George and his robot are to come to our home for now until other accommodation can be found for you both.' The robot nodded at George.

Hero looked surprised but pleased. 'Oh!' she said. 'Empy! I've never had a friend over to my house before!'

'What, never?' said George. He and his best friend Annie had lived in and out of each other's houses for the whole time they had known each other.

'That's not how friendships work in Eden,' Hero's robot intervened tactfully. 'But Hero's guardian instructs me to tell you that you are both most welcome.'

'Thank you,' said Boltzmann. George was silent until Boltzmann poked him.

'Oh! Thank you,' said George. But he couldn't help adding, somewhat suspiciously, 'Who is this guardian?'

'My guardian is my unit person,' said Hero clearly.

'You mean – your mum or your dad?' said George.

'What's a mum or dad?' puzzled Hero. Quick as a flash, she added, 'And that wasn't a question!'

'Well, they're your parents,' said George.

Hero still looked completely blank.

'The people you were . . . um, born from . . .' said George, not knowing how else to put it.

'Um, *born*?' said Hero.

'Children in Eden are hatched from approved genetic material,' said Empyrean. 'The guardian is one of the genetic contributors. Highly favoured genetic material is then raised within the Bubble environment in the ideal situation with constant robotic supervision to exclude any of the flaws of human rearing. For example, Hero was hatched nine Dumps of the Sun ago.'

George thought of his parents, his lovely, funny, more than slightly mad mum and dad. He thought he'd rather have their flaws than a robot nanny any day!

'Is it the same for all children?' he asked.

'No,' said Empyrean. 'Children can still be produced in the old style, but Eden is keen to outlaw this method of reproduction. It's too unreliable.' He coughed, as if slightly embarrassed. 'Those raised inside the Bubble, like Hero, are not taught about this.'

George decided to change the subject. 'What does your guardian do?' he asked Hero.

'Oh, guardians are a bit boring, like they tell you off,' she admitted. 'They always talk about nutrition and marks and they get records of all your school results so they know if you're going to get into Wonder Academy. They're a bit stressy really.'

'Are you?' asked George. 'Going to get in?'

'Oh yes!' said Hero, but she sounded nervous. 'I *know* I'm going to make it this time. It's the last few days now before all the marks are counted up and everyone finds out whether they've got a place or not. I don't know why I didn't get a place before, but I've worked really hard this

Dump of the Sun. And I *have* to pass this time . . .' She looked worried for a moment, but then brightened up. 'Empy says my marks are *so* good now that I will *definitely* be going to Wonder.'

'And you find out via your thought stream, I imagine?' asked George.

'Duh!' said Hero. 'Your guardian finds out first. They need to know so they can arrange for you to transition to Wonder. It's the most amazing place. It's so cool. And, by the way, don't say "imagine" here. It's not OK to imagine things.'

'What's wrong with imagination?' asked Boltzmann. 'I thought it was a key feature of the human brain and one of the reasons we robots would never be able to match natural human abilities!'

'Just don't,' said Hero. 'Imagining isn't an Eden thing. It's not what we do.'

'Where is Wonder Academy?' asked George, to change the subject.

'It's hundreds of Dumpometres away from Eden,' said Hero. 'It's a secret until you actually get in.'

'Do the kids who went to the Bubble come home? Like for holidays?'

'Um, no,' said Hero sadly. 'They don't. I really liked the Bubble kids who went to Wonder. They were my besties. We were always on our thought streams! And then they all had to go and I was left with just the little kids.' She sighed. 'I don't know why I had to stay in the Bubble right up until I'm a whole nine Dumps of the Sun – but it might be because I can't always stop myself asking questions. That's what my guardian says.'

George now had a question of his own. 'Can't you thought-stream your Bubble friends in Wonder?'

'No, it's not allowed,' said Hero. 'Bubble kids can't talk to Wonder students. It's so that Wonder is a proper surprise when you get there. It would spoil it if we knew before.'

George wasn't at all convinced by this. Something wasn't right about this Wonder place, but, in a world where nothing seemed right, he couldn't work out what was more wrong about Wonder Academy than anything else he was experiencing.

'What comes after Wonder Academy?'

Hero looked at him in astonishment. 'Well, you have to pay off your debt!' she said. 'Mine is quite big already because I've done so much studying. That's why I hope I get really good marks. Then

I can pay down my debt more quickly.'

'What debt?' said George. 'You're nine years old! What debts do you have?'

'You know,' sighed Hero. 'I have to pay for all the air I've breathed and the water I've drunk. And then there's my education, my inflatable house, all the energy it takes to operate my thought stream . . .'

'*Whaaaat?*' said George. 'Why do you have to pay for all those things?'

'Because I use resources that belong to Eden,' said Hero clearly. 'And so I have to repay Eden by working hard.'

'How long for?' said George.

'The rest of my life!' said Hero, as though this was blindingly obvious. 'The thing is, I can't ever really pay it off because, even while I'm working, I'll still be using air and water and stuff so I'll always be in debt to Eden, no matter what I do . . .'

'What do you pay them with?' asked George.

'Duh!' said Hero. 'Dumplings, of course!'

'Dumplings?' said George.

'A unit of digital currency,' said Empyrean, 'that you earn and spend. Once a year, on the Day of Reckoning, consumers find out how much they earned and how much they spent and how much they owe to Eden in taxes.'

'So, the more Dumplings you earn, the more tax you pay?' asked George, trying to figure out the system.

'Not quite,' said Empyrean. 'The more Dumplings you earn, the *less* tax you pay.'

'What?' said George in amazement. 'How is *that* fair?'

'It's the *best* of all possible worlds,' said the robot. 'But no one said it was the fairest. We must stop this conversation now.'

'Why?' asked George, wondering if he had stumbled on an illegal topic.

'Because,' replied Empyrean simply, 'we have arrived.'

Chapter Six

Hero's house was just the same as all the others, a little dome in a row of little domes. George walked in gingerly – he had been in lots of odd places before, but an igloo-shaped inflatable home was something else. It wasn't much cooler inside the house. Perhaps now that the whole world was warmer, nowhere could now cool down enough to feel normal.

Hero floated along ahead of him, throwing down her school backpack, kicking off her boots and discarding her jacket. Empyrean looked on disapprovingly.

'I'm not picking up your things,' he said.

Hero sighed. 'Why do I have the only robot who doesn't want to do my chores for me?' she said, going back to collect all her bits and pieces and piling them up in her arms. She disappeared

into a room off the central circular sitting room
and came back empty-handed. 'Everyone else's
robot is happy to do tasks for their person,' she
said.

'Mine isn't,' said George. He had decided that
for now he just had to go with the flow until he
could work out what to do next.

Boltzmann nodded happily. 'I wouldn't pick
anything up off the floor for him,' he confided,
before sitting himself down rather heavily on a
sofa. The sofa, which was inflatable too, squeaked
under Boltzmann's weight but managed not
to pop.

'You can't have everything,' said Hero's robot snootily. 'I'm the most intelligent and most powerful robot known to humankind.' A faint bell rang in George's mind. He had once known a superintelligence who spoke exactly like that.

'Yes, yes, I know,' said Hero. 'Blah-blah-blah! All the kids in the Bubble are special, so we have to have special robots assigned to us by Eden. But, honestly, I know my guardian found you in a recycling facility and repurposed you instead of getting me a nice new, shiny, helpful bot like the others.'

'Special?' said George. 'Are all the kids in the Bubble special?' His friend Annie had been the smartest kid he had ever met. Was Hero as clever as Annie? If Hero was so special, how come she couldn't see the gaps between what she said and the reality around her?

'We're called Future Leaders,' said Hero proudly. 'It means we've been carefully chosen to carry on the future of Eden. We are the elite. Except we need to get really, *really* old before we can be in charge.' She sounded like she was repeating things she'd been told.

'Why do you have to be so old?' said George.

'These children are the flowers of Eden,' said

Empyrean in a very neutral voice. 'Hence they must be tended by the very best of the robotic population. It takes time to grow an oak tree,' reminisced the robot cryptically. 'Up to nine Dumps of the Sun, in fact. Then they must leave the Bubble, as all our Future Leaders go on to Wonder for further study. It is very important to nurture our future.'

Hero wasn't listening. 'I'd rather you did my tidying up than going on about nurturing or whatevs,' she grumbled.

She threw herself down on a sofa opposite George, who noticed that, as she did so, the sofa changed colour to become a beautiful sea-green turquoise. Above her the wall suddenly showed a gorgeous view of waves breaking on a beach while the room filled with soft music.

'That's pretty!' exclaimed Boltzmann. George was momentarily surprised that the enormous ugly robot knew what 'pretty' was.

'How did you do that?' asked George, looking at his sofa, which had stayed an unremarkable shade of grey.

'Did what?' said Hero, who didn't even seem to have noticed.

'Your sofa changed colour!' said George. 'And

the music! And the picture.'

'Oh, that!' said Hero. 'It's a smart house with smart furniture so it reads my mood and changes the environment around me.'

'It's not changing anything to my preferences,' complained Boltzmann. George thought this was probably a good thing – he had no idea what a house decorated to Boltzmann's preferences would look like, and at this stage he didn't really want to know.

'Gets kind of annoying quite quickly,' admitted Hero. 'Sometimes I wish the house would stop playing me music and showing me pictures. It never really gets it right. I mean, do I look like a breaking wave to you?'

George felt someone watching him and glanced around just in time to catch Empyrean observing him with a gleaming eye.

He decided to address the robot's attitude. 'Is something wrong?'

'What do you mean?' asked Hero.

'Empy keeps watching me when he thinks I'm not looking,' said George.

'And me,' said Boltzmann with feeling. 'And he doesn't seem to respond to my efforts to connect robot to robot.'

'He's just like that,' agreed Hero. 'His eyes follow you around the room. I wish my guardian would let me get a different model, but she just won't.'

The robot's gaze didn't flicker. But somehow George had the feeling that every detail about him and Boltzmann had been carefully logged away for closer scrutiny later.

'It's time for your repose,' was Empyrean's only reply to Hero.

'Don't you need to have dinner?' asked George hopefully. It had been a long time since his final dehydrated meal on board the *Artemis*.

'No,' said Hero in surprise. 'I have had my nutritional allocation for the day. But, if you want something, we can mix up a smoothie for you, can't we, Empy?'

'Yes,' said George slowly. 'I would like a smoothie. And then I think Boltzmann and I could both go to sleep. If that's OK with you.' He was getting desperate to get rid of Hero and have some time to himself. Boltzmann, he could see, would be no more use to him tonight – the big scruffy robot was starting to run out of power and needed to recharge. But George, who had travelled across the Universe, experienced massive time dilation in an incredibly fast spaceship, returned to Earth having only had the briefest of contact with his family and best friend during his journey, and now found himself in a world which he did not recognize at all, needed time to think.

'Affirmative,' said Empyrean. George held his gaze just long enough to see him give the tiniest of smiles.

Much later that night, George was woken by the noise of someone new entering the inflatable home. He and Boltzmann had been tucked up on the two sofas with lightweight blankets, which looked as though they were made of foil. Hero had found George an old jumpsuit belonging to her guardian, who still seemed to have no name. And Empyrean had mixed up a beaker of a gluey-looking substance that, to George's surprise, had tasted delicious and left him totally full and no longer hungry or thirsty.

'I got your message,' the new arrival murmured to Empyrean.

Boltzmann, who was enjoying a power charge – arranged by Empyrean, to Hero's amusement, since she had never before known a personal robot that needed to be attached to a power source to recharge – was totally inert and unaware of what was happening in the circular room.

The new arrival definitely seemed to be human – a woman, by the sound of her.

'Is the comms shield up?' she murmured.

'As always. As ever, I am running a fake feed from the inside of this house and a parallel one for you. Currently it shows that you are relaxing in your accommodation allocation in a virtual-reality experience, enjoying the analogue world.'

'Such a relief!' She gave a small giggle. She sounded very excited. 'This is the only place where I'm free to have my own thoughts! I spend all day forcing myself to have thoughts like *Trellis Dump*—'

'May he live for ever,' interjected the robot solemnly.

'He will if he keeps taking the medications!' replied the woman. 'But it's so bad having to think *Trellis is awesome* while he shouts at me for not making the sun shine less brightly. You have no idea how stressful it is!'

'Well,' replied Empyrean, 'I have spent days erasing things from Hero's feed that might draw attention from the authorities of Eden. So I think I do know.'

'Yes, you have been the most faithful of guardians,' sighed the woman. 'If I hadn't tracked you down to that trash camp, I would never have been able to keep Hero safe and remain in deep cover at the same time. I would never have chosen to bring a child into this.'

'You've done so well,' said the robot. 'And we are nearly at the beginning of the end. If only things had moved a little quicker, then Hero could have left the Bubble and entered a world you would wish her to live in. But at least the authorities believed that she struggled with her studies and needed to stay here for the maximum time allowed, a time in which we have been able to help her grow and be more able to face what now lies ahead for her.'

'We're so close! We've nearly done it. My father's plan – we've almost made it happen.' The woman sounded overjoyed.

'Which means that now is the most dangerous time of all,' Empyrean reminded her. 'What's the mood like inside the regime?'

'Scared and suspicious. No one trusts anyone. They've raised the threat level again,' said the woman. 'We've gone from Dumpability to Dumptastic to Dumpothermonuclear.'

'Just as Hero is about to turn nine years old.'

'Don't you mean nine Dumps of the Sun?' said the woman with a giggle.

'Apologies, Minister,' said Empyrean gravely, but George could tell that this was some kind of shared joke.

But the woman didn't laugh in reply. She had just noticed something.

'What,' she said, in cryogenically cold tones, 'is *that*?' George knew without a shadow of a doubt that she had just spotted him and Boltzmann through the gloomy darkness of the night-time inflatable home.

'Well, that is a boy,' said Empyrean calmly. 'And that is his robot.'

'A boy?' said the woman, in tones that would have frozen the core of the sun. 'What is a boy doing here?'

George guessed that the invitation to stay over had not come from Hero's guardian after all. He tried not to panic. Breathlessly, he waited for Empyrean to respond.

'He is your saviour,' said Empyrean.

George exhaled. Empyrean was on his side.

'Excuse me?' said the woman. 'Since when did I need a saviour?' She sounded very put out.

'Your daughter does,' replied Empyrean. 'Her hatchday is only the day after tomorrow, Minister, and therefore you know that the time has come when she must leave the Bubble. To go to Wonder, where she will be beyond our ability to protect her . . . or, if the authorities pay too much attention to our past fiction that her potential is so poor, to a work unit where we would have no more contact with her. And we are aware that the situation has deteriorated faster than we thought. It's much more dangerous out there than it was when we made our original plan, and your daughter now urgently needs someone to accompany her on a journey to a place of safety. We only have this one chance to get her out – we must get it right.'

This was news to George! He felt that Empy, or whatever his name was, could have told him about this earlier. But the woman replied and he was glad Empy was in the firing line, not himself.

'Yes!' said the woman, her voice coming out with the force of a controlled explosion. 'And that person – or robot – is *you*! You are to leave the Bubble with Hero on her authorized journey to Wonder Academy! Except that she will never arrive, because *you* will divert the transport to end up instead in na-h Alba, the non-aligned zone, where *you* will request asylum for her. Meanwhile the machines finally manage to over-throw—'

'Nimu,' said Empyrean kindly. 'Daughter of—'

'Shut up!' hissed Nimu. 'Don't you daughter me! This is the plan. Why are you going back on it?'

George gathered from this that Nimu was a force to be reckoned with. He was glad it was Empyrean going toe to toe with her and not him on his first meeting, having just flown across the Universe in order, it now seemed, specifically to disrupt her best-laid plans.

'Do not fear,' said the robot. 'Let me start from the beginning.'

The woman took a deep breath. 'Where has this boy come from?' she asked.

'The past,' said Empyrean. 'This boy comes from the past.'

Chapter Seven

But if Empyrean thought this would help, he was entirely wrong.

'The past?' said Nimu, giving what sounded like some kind of semi-silent scream. 'What past? Have you gone mad? How can you know this?'

'I saw this boy depart,' said Empyrean.

He did? thought George. Who was this robot? Who had been there on that fateful day when he had blasted off from Kosmodrome 2 in the spaceship with the faithful Boltzmann as his companion? Was Empyrean the new iteration of one of the vicious robots that had patrolled Kosmodrome 2, doing the bidding of their maker, Alioth Merak? Was it possible . . . ?

'He set out to travel across the Universe at incredible speed in a spaceship called *Artemis*,' continued Empyrean. 'He left the Earth in the year 2018 in old time. In his time notation it is now the year 2081, but he has not aged because, thanks to time dilation, his journey took a fraction of the time that passed on Earth. In other words this is a boy from before the Great Disruption. A boy of great talent and courage. Just the boy we need.'

George didn't know whether to feel absolutely terrified that his worst fears had been verified, or pleased that he'd worked it out for himself! Or even chuffed by what Empyrean – whoever he was – had to say about him. The year 2081 – that meant he was more than sixty years older than when he had left Earth! He must be in his mid-seventies! He almost gave a little squeak. That was so old! How old would his dad be? His mum? Could they still be alive? Even his sisters would be in their sixties! When he finally found them, they would be old women.

'Did you summon him? From the past?' The woman sounded absolutely incredulous. 'That's impossible!'

'It would be,' said Empyrean. 'And I did not. His journey was planned by another, a terrible individual who could not have foreseen the consequences of what he did. All I knew was where this boy's spaceship would land. But I didn't know *when*. I've just had to wait. Once I received a signal that there was an incoming piece of space material landing in the Void, I took the chance it would be him and diverted Hero's school bus to investigate . . .'

This meant, George thought, that Empyrean had been looking out for him! He had known about the *Artemis* and Alioth Merak. All that time George had been hoping for a welcome-home reception, and it turned out to be a robot on a school bus in the desert instead.

'But, if you know he's here, how come no one else does?' Nimu sounded fearful.

'So far I have managed to allay suspicion about this event so it appears that a piece of old shrapnel from the ancient space station fell out of the sky.'

'What has this got to do with Hero?' she asked. 'You told me you'd found a way to save Hero, and now you've presented me with this time traveller, this cosmic migrant, this chronological refugee! Do you have any idea how deeply illegal all this is? We're going to be picked up and charged with utopiacide.'

Utopiacide? thought George.

Fortunately Empyrean chose to give a definition.

'Yes, trying to ruin paradise . . .' he said. 'But this isn't paradise. No one here is really free, despite what they make you say.'

'Yes, thank you, I'm quite aware of that!' said Nimu, sounding somewhere between furious and heartbroken.

'Except,' said Empyrean, 'for him.'

'Him?' said Nimu, sounding confused.

'The boy. I told you, he comes from the past, from the pre-connectivity age,' said Empyrean. 'Before the Great Disruption. Think about it.'

Understanding dawned in Nimu's voice. 'You don't mean . . .'

'Yes,' said Empyrean. 'He has no sensors, no live feed, no thought stream; he can't be scanned, read or tracked. He's unique – he's probably the only child in the Bubble who can move around freely. He doesn't trigger anything. He could walk right through the centre of the Eden Corporation and no one would even know he was there. It has to be done quickly – despite my best work, eventually the monitoring systems will pick up something that I've missed. But, given that we have to move fast anyway, then I believe he could get Hero out. He could make the plan actually happen – he can get her to na-h Alba.'

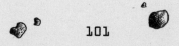

George was finding it hard to stay quiet. How could they make plans for him without even asking him! What if he had other ideas, like finding his family or going somewhere different to this nah-something place? He wanted to speak out, but he also figured he'd be better off listening and learning as much as he could. He might find out things they didn't want to tell him to his face.

'He also knows her,' said Empyrean softly.

George was thrown. *Her?* Who was Empyrean talking about?

'Her?' said Nimu slowly, with a strange note in her voice. 'He knows her?' She sounded, George thought, almost as though she was *jealous*.

'Yes, he knows her.' *A friend?* thought George. He hadn't had that many.

'Lucky him,' said Nimu bitterly. 'Don't tell me, *she* likes *him*?' There was a pause in which Empyrean must have nodded. After which she burst out, 'Why didn't she like me? Why? We could have been friends!'

'She never had the chance,' said Empyrean. 'And how could she know you're working undercover? She must think you are an agent of the regime, a genuine government minister.'

'Then she must think I betrayed everything!'

Nimu gave a cry of pain. 'That I betrayed him!'

'I will tell her you did not,' said Empyrean, who sounded curiously downbeat. 'When the boy gets Hero to na-h Alba.'

Now George felt on the brink of despair. He was to travel across a country he didn't recognize with a small girl he hardly knew to reach the safety of a place with a weird name where there was one person he had met in the past but whose name he didn't even know.

'Why this boy?' demanded Nimu. 'Why not you?'

'You said it yourself – the threat level was raised again today so they are on high alert. It would be much better for this boy to take Hero, and for me to remain here to give her cover by running – for as long as I can – a fake feed. And if Hero and I were caught? An Eden minister's daughter on the run with the superintelligence the regime has sought for decades! The trail would lead back to you and then we could lose our chance for ever. The whole operation could be blown.'

Nimu sighed. 'You're right,' she agreed. 'I hate your plan. But it's our best hope.'

'It's our *only* hope,' said Empyrean. 'Hero has to leave the Bubble the day after tomorrow. She has no choice. So, if you want to get her out of Eden and to safety, using the only opportunity you have had in her whole life, then this is what we must do.'

Shortly after that, Nimu exited the inflatable house as silently as she had arrived.

The little round house fell silent. George's mind boggled at what he had heard: 2081! Decades had passed! The bleached land, the burning, fermented sky, the abandoned landscape all spoke of some dramatic shift in the whole pattern of existence. The future. He now knew for sure that he was in the future. But there was so much he *didn't* know. What were these machines and what were they doing? He tried to shake Boltzmann to get him to talk things through, but the old robot was not to be disturbed from his comfy power charge. At last, George fell asleep himself and had a fitful night of weird dreams, none of them actually as strange as the reality that he had plummeted into.

He woke, uncomfortable and cold, on the unfriendly grey sofa. Boltzmann was still fast asleep. Going over to a window, George saw a primrose yellow sun already high in the sky. It brought a lump to his throat. It looked just the same – the sun still shone, as it had done for billions of years. Whatever had happened on the surface of the planet, it hadn't disturbed the cosmic order of the solar system. Human life, it seemed, had taken on a very new dimension – from last night's conversation, George realized that this time he was now in was known as the time of mass connectivity. Presumably that referred to everyone having to share their thoughts – it meant Nimu only being able to think thoughts about how great Trellis Dump was when she was working as a government minister, otherwise he would realize she was a spy. And it meant that Hero and the kids did all their chatting silently, through their thought streams, with robot guardians able to control the behaviour of their charges.

'Hello!' Hero bounced in, wearing a cosy-looking jumpsuit that George assumed must be her pyjamas.

'Hi!' said George. He tried to smile. It wasn't Hero's fault that he was stuck in the wrong era, nor that her guardian and robot were making elaborate plans for George to take her on a strange and probably dangerous journey across Eden to another country. 'Thanks for having us over.'

'I have a question! Have you ever seen her?'

asked Hero eagerly. Clearly she had forgotten her promise to make up for yesterday by asking no more questions today.

'Who?' asked George, confused by this sudden change of tack. Did Hero mean this unnamed 'her' of na-h Alba?

'Queen Bimbolina Kimobolina!' said Hero. 'Dumbo! Who else?'

'No,' said George truthfully. 'I haven't.' He had no idea what Hero was talking about.

'That's weird,' said Hero, looking perplexed. 'I thought her avatar was literally everywhere. How can you not have seen it?'

'What?' said George.

'The Queen of Other Side!' Hero's brow wrinkled. 'I thought she was supposed to be so beautiful that you could only see her avatar because in real life you would be blinded by her beauty. So they send out her avatar instead. Like when I go to school. I don't actually "go" to school – we don't, like, have a place that's called school. It's a virtual school and I send avatar "me" there every day so I don't have to bother . . .'

'Then why did you go on a school trip yesterday' – George had spotted the flaw in all this – 'if you could have done it all from home?'

'It's part of the way our development is monitored,' said Hero. 'It helps Eden to see which of us are best suited to go to Wonder Academy.' She sighed. 'I do hope I'm now ready to leave the Bubble.'

George thought of the robot hand he had seen, tweaking strands of hair and taking tiny samples of blood from the kids. He nodded. He hoped none of the kids on the bus would prove to have genetic flaws or other physical issues. He dreaded to think what would happen to them if they did. He doubted they'd get to stay in the Bubble as Future Leaders of Eden.

But the next question had already popped out of Hero's brain. 'Can you teach me how to speak Emotilang?'

George just gaped at her.

'Emotilang!' she repeated. 'The language of Other Side! Where you don't actually use words, you just put emojis on your thought stream! How do you not know that?'

Just then, George's attention was caught by something trotting by the window. He ran over to look at it more closely, but it had vanished from view. He tried to get out of the entrance hatch so he could follow the strange beast, but it seemed to be sealed.

'What did you see out of the window?' asked Hero.

'A white horse,' said George, thinking he might have gone crazy. 'But with a long, pointy horn. Like, on its nose?'

'Oh, that's the Bubble unicorn!' said Hero, sounding pleased.

'But unicorns don't exist,' said George.

'Yes they do!' said Hero.

'No they don't!' said George, who had woken up very late, hadn't had anything to eat and was starting to feel a bit cranky. 'They're mythical beasts, like from legends. They're not actually real. That was just a horse with a big thing on its nose – not an actual unicorn.'

'It was a real unicorn!' exclaimed Hero. 'I asked Empy about it and he told me the truth about unicorns.'

'Which is . . . ?' said George.

'Unicorns died out before the Great Disruption,' said Hero, her eyes glittering. But her tone was suddenly unsure. It was as though she had to say it to believe it herself. 'Because before then people had taken such bad care of the world that unicorns, who are really sensitive, couldn't survive. They grew too sad looking at the state of the world and that killed them.'

'The unicorns died of broken hearts?' said George in disbelief. What was Empyrean doing, telling Hero such total nonsense?

'Unicorns are very delicate,' sniffed Hero. 'At least that's what I learned about them. Because of the fineness of their feelings, they couldn't return from extinction until after the Great Disruption, when everyone knew that, thanks, um, to Trellis

Dump, oh, may he live for ever, Eden has become great again . . .' She trailed off.

'None of this is true, Hero,' burst out George. He couldn't stay quiet any more. 'This whole Eden thing, it's rubbish. Eden isn't the best of all possible worlds. It's horrible. It's the worst of all worlds. They've all been lying to you.' He braced himself for a storm of tears, but her reaction surprised him.

'But why would they do that?' Hero challenged him. 'What would be the point of making me believe a whole lot of lies?'

'Um, well,' said George, thrown. He hadn't expected this.

'Then tell me the truth about something I don't know,' persisted Hero. 'But you must be able to prove it. Or I won't believe you either.'

Hero, George reflected, wasn't that stupid after all.

'All right,' said George. 'Here's one. I'm not from Other Side. I'm not a refugee . . .' He paused. 'I'm a space traveller,' he confided. He had no idea whether telling Hero the truth would turn out to be a stroke of genius or total disaster. But he figured it was all he had to work with.

'A space traveller?' Hero's eyebrows shot up in disbelief. 'From . . . where, exactly?'

'*Up* there.' George pointed with one finger.

'Up there?' Hero looked confused and then horrified. 'Up there? You want me to believe you have come from *up* in space?'

'Yep,' said George.

'You,' exclaimed Hero disbelievingly, 'came from space? In what?'

'In a spaceship,' said George. 'That's why I was wearing a spacesuit when you met me.'

'You weren't wearing a spacesuit!' said Hero.

'You were wearing a jumpsuit, just like mine!'

'No I wasn't,' said George. 'That was a proper spacesuit. It was almost like a spaceship in itself.'

'Don't believe you,' retorted Hero, though she was obviously gripped. 'But go on anyway.'

'I took off from Earth with my robot Boltzmann in a spaceship and we travelled across the Universe. We didn't mean to go so far, but we couldn't get the ship to turn round. Finally the spaceship itself decided to come back to Earth, so now we're back, but we seem to have jumped into—'

'Excuse me,' interrupted Hero. She held up a hand. 'But you *can't* have come from space.'

'Why not?' said George. 'I know it sounds kinda weird but—'

'No, it's not just that it's weird,' said Hero. 'Although it is. It's because there is no space travel!'

No space travel? thought George.

'Space travel,' the girl continued, 'was banned! It's illegal. No one goes into space. They did once, but it turned out to be a huge waste of resources, which should have been spent on keeping this planet beautiful, so it was completely cancelled and now no one is allowed to go or send anything into space. So, you see, there's nothing out there – and certainly nothing man-made.'

'Not true, Hero,' said George. 'Anyway, loads of good things came from space science.'

'That's just what they wanted people to believe,' said Hero. 'But it's all fake news. It was invented to make people think science could actually achieve something.'

George was so stunned he took a step backwards, right onto Boltzmann's foot.

'Ow!' said Boltzmann automatically, even though it hadn't hurt as he had no pain receptors.

'Hero,' said George, going for broke now. 'I came here from space, but not just that. I came from the past. I've travelled through time as well. I'll tell you all about it someday.'

Hero was staring at him. 'Time,' she said. 'You said you travelled through time?'

'My spaceship travelled so fast that time passed slowly for me but much quicker on Earth. I took off from Foxbridge when I was not much older than you are now.'

'Aha!' said Hero. 'That's why you keep going

on about Foxbridge!' Her face was the picture of concentration.

'And my mum and dad and my sisters and all my friends were here. Now they've all gone and the world has changed. It's been destroyed. Hero, I've got to get back to my own time because maybe I can save the future while there's still a chance.'

'You mean that *now*,' said Hero slowly, 'is the *future* for you but actually it's *now* for me. And you want to go back into the past and see if you can do something to stop it all turning out like this?'

'That's right!' said George encouragingly. 'You're getting it.'

'But if you do that' – she sounded worried – 'then you might do something that would mean I ended up not being hatched! So then I'd suddenly stop existing!'

At that moment, Empyrean made his entry.

'Good morning,' he said smoothly to Hero, while glaring at George. 'The emotional frequencies in this habitation are too high for maximum comfort.'

'He said—' Hero pointed at George.

'Ah yes,' said Empyrean. 'You've been asking

too many questions again. When you promised not to. And he has been drawing on the rich "storytelling" tradition of Other Side.'

'What?' spluttered George. He turned to Boltzmann. 'Tell her, Boltz! We're not making it up! We're telling the truth, and that robot—' He glared at Empyrean, who was turning out to be more of an enemy than a friend.

'It's part of the culture of Other Side.' Empyrean smoothly overrode George. 'The ability to weave the most extraordinary tales. So vivid!' He waved his robot hands around. 'As though they were really true. When, in fact, they are only as real as the virtual-reality experiences you saw yesterday.'

'You said those were just the same as the actual reality!' said Hero hotly.

'Did I?' said Empyrean casually. 'Did I indeed?'

'What if,' said Hero, building on what she had just learned from George, 'none of this is actually true and real, but has all been invented by you and my guardian to keep me quiet? What if Eden isn't really real?' She looked surprisingly composed for a young girl who, for the very first time, was suddenly questioning whether things are the way they seem.

'Extraordinary notion,' murmured Empyrean. But George knew that this time Hero had hit the nail on the head and it cheered him up no end. Eden was a fake: he could see that. What part Empyrean and Hero's guardian had played in this, and what the outcome of the long-range plan hatched by Nimu's father (whoever he was) would be, George had absolutely no idea. But, for the first time since he'd arrived, the spark of rebellion growing in Hero made him feel almost happy.

'Now listen,' commanded Empyrean as though nothing had been said. 'Today we are completing our pre-travel preparations for the Wonder Academy! As tomorrow is your ninth hatchday – and all your test scores to date have crossed the threshold for acceptance – we must make sure we have made all the necessary arrangements for your transition.'

Hero was immediately distracted. 'Did I get in?' she screamed.

'Yes,' confirmed Empyrean. 'Your guardian has just informed me that you have been accepted with the highest marks of any student ever to gain entry to the Academy! Well done, Hero. Your work recently has been excellent.'

'I'm going to Wonder!' yelled Hero, running around the room, hugging everyone. 'I'm going to Wonder! I'm going to earn trillions of Dumplings a day and be a Future Leader of Eden. I am going to Wonder!'

Except, George knew, she wasn't.

Chapter Eight

The rest of the day slipped past smoothly, Hero bouncing around, celebrating her move to Wonder, thought-streaming everyone she could, while George caught up with some much-needed rest and continued to try and understand a little more about this time he found himself in. As evening fell, suddenly a commotion was heard outside the inflatable home, and this time it wasn't caused by a unicorn. Empyrean immediately looked very alert.

'Open up!' came a voice from outside. 'This is a random inspection.'

Empyrean, George noticed, froze, his beady eyes fixed on him. Hero looked unnerved. She scanned the house quickly.

'Will it be OK if we just say that my guardian invited George to stay?' Clearly the small girl was starting to realize that something was very wrong by Eden standards.

Empyrean replied simply, 'No, it won't.'

'What shall we do?' asked Hero. She sounded panicky, and George saw that this might be the first time in her short life that she had experienced what it felt like to be scared. 'What will happen if they find George here?' she asked. But, by the look on her face, George could tell she suspected it wouldn't be anything good. Would it stop her going to Wonder?

'Wait!' said Empyrean. 'I can hide them.' He turned to George. 'Stand very still,' he said. 'Over there. Next to Boltzmann. Don't move and don't

speak.' Empyrean flung a piece of incredibly fine material over the pair of them – obscuring their view.

George stood stock-still next to Boltzmann, who didn't really seem to have woken up from his overnight power charge yet. They heard tapping footsteps, as though a person in steel-capped boots had walked in, and the gentle thwacking noise of a baton being bounced against the gloved palm of a hand.

'Robot!' The new arrival addressed Empyrean. 'Dump in your Dreams!' It sounded like some kind of routine greeting.

'I dream only of Dump,' Empyrean replied mildly. 'May he live for ever!'

'Account for your domicile.'

Empyrean sighed – and George heard a fizzing noise.

'Your power settings are too high,' the inspector complained. George felt rather than saw the inspector's gaze sweep over him and Boltzmann and notice nothing. But, when the inspector's eyes landed on Hero, it caused a reaction.

'Let me into the child's thought stream.'

'Certainly,' said Empyrean smoothly.

Hero made absolutely no noise, as though she

knew and understood the drill at these moments. Empyrean had clearly performed some manoeuvre as Hero's thought stream suddenly became audible, floating through the air between the super-computer, the police officers and the small girl. On the one hand, George heard melodic, happy notes, which were perhaps the soundtrack to a life full of unicorns, huge butterflies and entertaining virtu-al-reality games. But then a dark note sounded underneath and a minor chord swelled upwards, changing the whole mood. George wondered what had shown up in Hero's thought stream and how it was reflected in what he was hearing.

'What's that?' asked the police officer as Hero's mind music became stormy and chaotic.

George held his breath. He realized that this officer wasn't human – despite the smooth, naturalistic tone of his voice, there was still something that didn't chime. In fact, the way the police bot's voice so closely resembled a human's made it much creepier and much scarier than something like Boltzmann, who was obviously and unmistakably a robot, despite his best efforts.

'It's a memory from a VR about the fake news of the past, especially about the fake news fantasy of space travel,' Empyrean jumped in. 'Just a memory.'

'Dumpticious!' said the police bot. 'Why do they teach them about the old times? Just spreads confusion. They should only learn about the great achievements of Eden. Get rid of it. That memory has to go. Cleanse it.'

George heard Empyrean give a sigh, but the music stopped immediately.

'Keep Paradise Clean,' the inspector said, turning on a booted heel. 'In our minds and in our hearts. And don't seal the hatch in future.'

George finally breathed out. Empyrean twitched away whatever covering he had thrown over him and Boltzmann.

'What was that!' said George.

Hero seemed to be in a trance. Empyrean spoke very quickly. 'You are endangering Hero,' he said. 'Everything shows up in her thought stream and you make her vulnerable. That was a close call. I'm sorry we have to keep streaming feeds that you know to be nonsense, but, until we get her out of Eden, we have no choice. Otherwise she is in mortal danger.'

'I see,' said George, who felt quite shaken. 'So Hero can't know anything real? You have to keep telling her all these lies for her own safety? Poor kid!'

He felt so sorry for the little girl. And he knew, at that moment, that if they wanted him to save her, get her out of this place, he would have to do it. He wouldn't leave here without her. By his own choice.

He just hoped someone had done the same for his own little sisters.

'We were lucky that was an old-style police bot,' said Empyrean. 'I'm surprised it hasn't been updated with a thermal recognition skin. Perhaps it's true what they say, that Eden is running out of funds for renewal.'

'What would it have done if it had caught me?' said George.

'Many things are banned now,' said Empyrean, speaking at double time. 'Freedom of thought, for example, and free speech. Science, especially. Any talk of space travel. Look at the technology that surrounds you. People's lives are governed by technology – even created by it – but they are not allowed to understand it or master it. You would have been taken away. We would never have seen you again. Hero could have been thrown out of the Bubble to survive on her own in the Void. Her guardian would have lost her government post. I would have been dismantled. And worst of all . . . no, I can say no more . . .'

'All in the best of all possible worlds,' said George.

'Exactly,' said Empyrean. 'The police bot didn't see you because I put a meta-material over you and your robot. But, more importantly, he didn't detect you because you have no thought stream. He doesn't operate on biological markers – he operates on technological ones. So actually you don't exist to him, but I couldn't take the risk that he would lodge you in his vision and it would be picked up by someone else.'

'Are those inspections normal?' asked George.

'No,' said Empyrean. 'The Kingdom-Corporation of Eden is on high alert.'

'Me?' said George. 'Are they looking for me?'

'Looking for anyone,' said Empyrean, 'who poses a threat to the regime. We must move fast.'

'This is a lot to take on board,' said George.

'I know,' said Empyrean. 'But I wouldn't ask

this of you if I didn't know you could do it.'

'But how do you know? Who are you?' said George, figuring this might be his only chance to ask.

'I am Empyrean,' replied the robot. 'The clue is in my name.'

But George had no idea what the word *Empyrean* meant and had no device on which he could look it up. And he knew he didn't have time for elaborate guessing games.

'I heard you last night, you and some woman called Nimu,' he whispered. 'I know you've made a plan and you want me to save Hero.'

'You must take Hero to safety,' said Empyrean gently. 'Save Hero and you will save yourself.'

'But . . .' said George. There was so much more he needed to know.

'Shush!' said Empyrean. George heard a buzzing sound coming from outside the dome. 'The bees are listening. Say no more.'

'The bees?' said George.

'Bee detectives,' said Empyrean. 'They are the most intelligent inhabitants of the Bubble. If anyone raises the alarm, it's most likely to be the bees.'

The buzzing intensified. Looking out, George

could see that the home was now surrounded by a swarm of honeybees. 'Are we going to be caught by a bunch of bees?' he said. Bees had been friendly insects in his time. 'That's impossible!'

'They can detect all sorts of things,' said Empyrean. 'Viruses, bombs – probably far more. Whether they can detect you, we should find out shortly. But the less commotion we make, the sooner they'll move on.'

Once the swarm of bee monitors had finally flown away, later that evening George and Boltzmann snuck out of the front hatch, which the inspector bot had insisted Empyrean leave open. Boltzmann had recharged back to full power so the two of them sat in the entrance to the little inflatable home. They didn't dare go any further. But George had to get out of the tiny round house and feel, if not the fresh air of outside, at least the difference of atmosphere Inside the Bubble, as opposed to the stuffy little sitting room.

From where they sat, they could see rows of identical inflatable houses neatly dotting the interior of the Bubble. Each house was a different colour to its neighbours, with a small garden surrounding it. Robots worked efficiently in the gardens, trimming hedges, tending flowers and watering the grass. The gardens were so tidy and brilliantly green that George wondered if the plants were real. He reached out and touched a leaf, but an alarm went off and a bossy robot from the next-door house beetled over to shake a finger at him.

'Boltz!' whispered George. 'Do you like the future? This is 2081, you know.' George hadn't even had a chance to share his findings with his robot friend. He was bursting to tell Boltzmann about Nimu's plan and discuss the real identity of Empyrean, but he figured that was probably too risky. Who knew who was listening to their conversation? Even so, he couldn't resist having a whispered chat about their own circumstances.

'So it's 2081!' marvelled Boltzmann. 'That explains it all. George, you are an old man!'

'Probably in my mid-seventies!' said George. 'But, at the same time, I'm actually still just a kid at secondary school.'

'No wonder young Hero thought I belonged in a museum,' reflected Boltzmann. 'Look, even that gardening bot there is probably a more advanced model than me.'

'Empyrean told me that Eden people are allowed to use technology but not to understand it,' said George.

'So they know what it does but now how it works,' said Boltzmann. 'Interesting.'

'Hero keeps going on about fake news and how science was all a lie!'

'I expect that's what she's been taught,' said Boltzmann wisely. 'If she had access to a proper education, she'd soon work it out.'

'Yeah, she seems pretty bright, once she stops just repeating stuff she's been told,' said George. He wrinkled his brow. 'I think somehow her guardian and Empy have *wanted* her to stay in the Bubble for as long as she possibly could. They don't seem to want her to go to Wonder at all.'

'Oh dear,' said Boltzmann. 'Who would have thought the future would turn out to be such a mess?'

'And no space travel!' said George, who was particularly offended by this. 'She told me space travel was cancelled because it was just a tool of fake science!'

Looking up, he could see a haze of vapour in the warm air, rising to the transparent skin of the Bubble where it condensed to water, dripping back down onto the foliage. It was, he realized, its own ecosphere. Densely fertile, much too warm and humid, it was the opposite of the barren ground outside. It was also nothing like the Foxbridge he remembered, where all the houses had the personalities of their inhabitants – big, grand and snooty, small and scruffy, clever and funny. Everything in Old Foxbridge was individual, eccentric and fun. Here, everything was essentially the same.

Outside the biosphere, the sun was setting, casting long vermilion rays across the landscape. Inside, the tips of the palm trees were turning the colour of raspberries. It was a beautiful sight as the whole interior of the Bubble went a vivid pink. Except George knew that these colours, when in a real sunset, were produced by very high levels of pollution in the atmosphere. No wonder, he thought, the children of government ministers lived here, in this Bubble, to protect them from the rays of the sun and the poisonous dust and gas in the atmosphere.

But, as the sun sank, the sky darkened and the stars came out once more, sparkling above them. The atmosphere seemed to clear, giving them a perfect view of the night sky. George looked up at the familiar constellations shining through the transparent skin of the Bubble, marvelling that they remained absolutely the same, even when the whole world under them had changed so much. But just then he noticed something. A pinprick of light, moving fast directly overhead, streaked across the sky. It was too steady and too regular to be a shooting star. *A satellite*, thought George to himself. Maybe it was an old one, left over from his time, the Space Age. But then he saw another, and yet another, crisscrossing the night sky, their routes too orderly and the dots of light too small and even for them to be anything other than man-made.

'I think,' he said to Boltzmann as he gazed upwards, 'that's there's plenty of space travel – just that no one's allowed to know about it.'

Chapter Nine

'La la la la la!' Hero woke George up with some very loud singing. 'Today is my hatchday and I'll be going to Wonder Academy! I'm going to learn about everything – there will be lessons in unicorn care, Bubble environments and harnessing the power of crop circles.' She danced around the room until she noticed George – at which point she performed a forward walkover, landing at his feet.

'Ta-dah!' She presented herself. 'Morning!'

'Hi!' said George. He was surprised to find her so perky and cheerful, given how scared she'd been the evening before. 'I didn't know you were a gymnast!'

'Yes!' She beamed. 'I have a virtual instructor. Did you sleep well?' she said. 'Do you want a smoothie? Are you excited about me going to Wonder Academy?'

'Um, I'm sorry about last night, the inspector coming and stuff,' said George, who felt really bad about what he had put the young girl through.

'What inspector?' said Hero, her bright eyes clouding. 'There was no inspector. What are you saying?'

George realized that her recent memory really *had* been wiped by Empyrean, under orders from the inspector. He decided to push it a little further. After all, if he was about to go on a dangerous and illegal journey . . .'

'And me telling you I came from space . . .'

'No you didn't!' Hero wrinkled her nose. 'You're a refugee! From Other Side! That's what you said when we met you in the desert.'

With that, George knew that Hero's brain had been tampered with. This was all so wrong, he thought. If even the good guys – and he really hoped Empyrean and Nimu *were* the good guys – were doing things which were actually terrible, like wiping the memories of small kids, then the future was officially a disaster.

But, just then, the hatch opened and Nimu walked in, carrying two small backpacks.

'Guardian!' cried Hero, running towards her to

give her a hug. 'Best of all worlds!'

'Eden is the greatest, thanks to Dump, may he live for ever!' responded Hero's guardian.

'Good morning,' said George politely, not really knowing any of the local salutations.

'Hi!' said Nimu over the top of Hero's head. In the daylight George realized that Nimu was quite a bit older than he had thought the evening before. She looked like she was trying to keep a tight hold on her emotions, but her eyes were very

shiny. Gently, she disentangled Hero. 'It's time for you to go.'

'To Wonder Academy?' said Hero, her face brightening.

'Yes,' sighed the woman.

'OMD!' said Hero. 'It's going to be soooo cool! Bye, George, bye, Boltzmann, bye, Empy the unhelpful! I've got to get to Wonder Academy so I can lead Eden when I'm, like, super-old like my guardian and whatevs.' George noticed Nimu wince.

'It's not goodbye to George,' said the woman, recovering herself. 'In fact, it's hello!' She turned to him. 'I'm sorry we haven't had a chance to speak properly. I am Nimu, Hero's guardian. We must hurry – Hero has to leave the Bubble by the time the sun is at its peak on her nine Dumps of the Sun hatchday.'

'So no one older than nine lives here?' asked George.

'Exactly,' said the woman.

'Where do you live?' said George curiously.

'I live in a government encampment beyond the Bubble. It's called the Echo Chamber,' said the woman. 'I'm a government minister so I am required to lodge my child in the Bubble until it is time for her to go to Wonder Academy – once she passes the necessary tests, that is. It is not a matter of choice for one of my level.' She sounded much more anxious than the determined woman George had overheard the other night, as though she was trying to reassure George that it wasn't her wish that Hero had been brought up like this.

Something had been worrying George.

'Where are the other kids?' he said. 'Kids whose parents aren't government ministers or ones who don't pass the tests. Where do they go?'

'Yes, there are many children in Eden who are not as lucky as Hero,' said Nimu. 'We must all serve Dump, may he live for ever, in the best way we can, and for some children this can mean allocation to a work unit.' She smiled ruefully at Hero. 'This is not for my daughter.'

'All right then,' said George, realizing that Nimu wasn't going to tell him anything further. But he had caught Nimu's reference to Hero as her daughter, even if Hero didn't seem to understand what a mother was. 'But, Nimu, what actually happens at Wonder Academy—'

'Wonder Academy,' said Nimu loudly, interrupting him, 'is very different to anything these kids have ever experienced!'

'Because,' cried Hero, 'it's more fabulous than anywhere else!'

From Nimu's face, George understood that Wonder Academy was just the opposite. What was the truth about Wonder? He hoped he would never have to find out.

'Hero, gather your things,' said Nimu, handing her one of the backpacks. She gave the other to George.

Hero skipped off to find her supply of jumpsuits in different colours.

While she was distracted, Nimu turned to George. 'We have so little time—'

George jumped straight in. 'Who are you really?' he demanded.

'Listen to me, George,' said Nimu, ignoring his question. 'Get Hero to na-h Alba and all will be well. Empyrean is giving your robot all the information you will need for the journey.' She passed him a scrap of paper that looked like a badly drawn map. On it were marked one large landmass and one smaller one, labelled na-h Alba.

'What is na-h Alba?' said George, folding the map up to put in his back pocket.

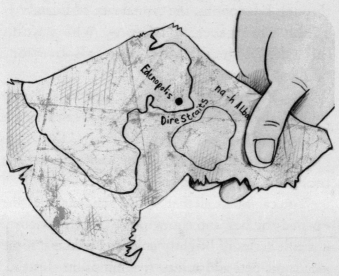

Nimu gave him a bitter little smile. 'It's fierce,' she said. 'Independent. Advanced. The mortal enemy of Eden. Clever. Resourceful. Dare I say the banned word – imaginative? The realm of *her*. Made in her own image. When all the other countries joined into the two different corporations, na-h Alba decided to remain independent. They sawed through the border to separate the two land masses after the Great Disruption, to prevent Trellis Dump's robot army from taking over. Since then, na-h Alba has been floating on the ocean. All done by her. You can only reach it by crossing the Dire Straits at its closest point, which means going through Edenopolis, the capital city of Eden.'

'But who is she?' said George. Who was this 'her', this mythical leader of the only free zone on Earth?

'You'll find out when you get there,' said Nimu, faintly mocking him. George really wasn't warming to her. 'Won't you?'

At that moment, Hero came back, lugging the over-filled backpack with her.

'You can't take all that,' said Nimu in alarm. She opened the bag and threw out a cuddly unicorn, a whole series of brightly coloured trinkets, some electronic pets and at least five jumpsuits. Instead, she stuffed in a water purifier, packets and packets of freeze-dried meals and a torch.

'No!' said Hero. 'I can't leave my pets here! They'll die without me!'

Nimu sighed. 'I'll take them,' she said. 'But your driverless transport is outside – it's time for you and George to leave.'

'George?' said Hero, baffled. 'Why is he coming?'

'He's escorting you to Wonder Academy,' said her guardian. 'And so is his robot.'

Behind her, Boltzmann appeared, with Empyrean standing in the background.

Hero looked horrified. 'No way!' she said. 'I don't want to turn up at Wonder Academy on my first day with some Other Side kid with me!' she protested. George had to remind himself it wasn't her fault that Empy had wiped her memory.

'I'm so sorry, Hero,' said Nimu, and she genuinely sounded it. 'I'm so sorry this is the life I gave you. I never meant it to be like this. I thought we would do so much better.'

Hero looked taken aback but hugged her guardian. 'Don't be sad!' the girl said sweetly. 'It's going to be amazing at Wonder! I'm going to do so well! You'll be so proud of me!'

'And you're going to take George with you,' said her guardian, gently detaching Hero and holding her firmly by the hand.

'Do I have to?' said Hero doubtfully, eyeing George and his robot.

'You do,' said Nimu.

Hero pouted briefly but said nothing more.

'Are we ready?'

Boltzmann came and stood beside George, something George found incredibly comforting.

'The update is complete,' said Empyrean smugly. 'Boltzmann is now fully primed. He has all the resources you need.'

'Can Boltzmann open doorways? Like portals to space?' asked George, thinking how useful this would be if they got into danger.

'No portals,' said Empyrean. 'But I've installed Windows 4000 so that should help . . .'

A noise from outside the house made everyone jump. It was just a robot lawn mower, but they all breathed out a heavy sigh.

'Time to go,' said Nimu mistily. 'You've only got a few minutes before the sun is at its apex. We must all get out of here as this home will automatically start to deflate. After noon on Hero's ninth hatchday, none of us have the right to remain Inside the Bubble.'

They stepped outside. The air was humid and sweet-smelling. Enormous tropical bushes with shiny green leaves and brilliant red flowers grew around the circular perimeter of Hero's former home. A hummingbird fluttered by one of the flowers, its tiny wings batting the air as it reached into the depths of the flower for its nectar. Looking up, George saw a milky sky above them, hazy with brilliant sunshine.

'Why is the sky white?' he wondered out loud.

'It's a sky screen,' said Nimu. 'Inside the Bubble, particles are released into the atmosphere to stop the sun's rays damaging plant and human life. That's why the inside of the Bubble is so fertile – outside it, in this region, nothing can grow because the sunlight is too bright now.'

A driverless transport bus had driven up and stopped in front of them. Hero was now crying quietly, tears dripping onto her stuffed unicorn, which she had retrieved from the discard pile.

'Goodbye,' said Nimu formally to George.

'Cheerio,' said George, more brightly than he felt.

'I won't forget this,' she said.

'In the backpacks,' said Empyrean to George, 'you each have a purifier which will turn the foulest pond water into fresh, clean drinking water. You have freeze-dried rations – which you will recognize from your previous travels! If necessary, you will forage for food along the way. Ants are a good source of protein – and some say they taste like lemongrass, although I couldn't personally comment . . .'

'Will I see you again?' asked George. There was so much he needed to know! He hoped he knew enough to get himself and Hero safely to na-h Alba. But how would he find out anything else?

'I've fitted Boltzmann with a "phone a friend" facility!' whispered Empyrean. 'The friend, of course, being me. If you need me . . .'

Greatly relieved, George climbed aboard the transport, followed by Boltzmann and a nervous Hero.

Behind them, the inflatable home was already collapsing. Recycling bots stood ready to scoop up the remains of Hero's home and make it into a residence for the next bright young child who would get to stay in the Bubble until their ninth year. Nimu, gazing anxiously upwards at the sun's trajectory in the sky, pushed Hero rather un-ceremoniously onto the transport. She was about to close the door when she suddenly paused.

'Tell her,' she said to George, 'that it wasn't me. Tell her I didn't betray him. I would never have done that. True, I got him out of Eden on the last ship to Mars, but only to save him from something much worse.'

'Who?' said George. 'Who didn't you betray?'

Nimu gave him a strange half-smile. 'Eric, of course,' she said. 'Who else?'

With that, she jumped down, closed the door, and the vehicle set off.

Chapter Ten

George scrambled to look back at Nimu as the bus drove away.

'What do you mean?' he frantically mouthed through the back window. 'About Eric!'

But it was no good. Even if Nimu had heard him, he guessed she wasn't about to give him a clear answer. She would be a good double agent, thought George. Talking to her was like the time he went fishing with his dad and tried to land a particularly slippery fish. Just as he thought he had a grip on it, it wriggled free.

'Boltz!' he said. 'Did you hear that? Nimu knows Eric! How is that possible?'

The old robot looked straight at George, a serious expression on his battered features.

'Much to tell from Empyrean's update,' he said. 'But I gave that robot a promise that I would stay silent until we reached greater safety.'

'Is my family still alive?' George persisted. 'Just tell me that!'

'I don't know about your family,' said Boltzmann. And the hope faded for George. 'Empyrean didn't tell me. That is all I can say for now. It is metal-wrenching for me to be the bearer of such bad news. I do not know how you humans withstand the impact of your emotions. You must be much tougher than you look.'

George fell silent and looked out of the window, his eyes filling with tears at the thought of Annie's dad, Eric – alone? – on the Red Planet. Was that why Annie had tried so hard to message him on the *Artemis*, in the hope that he might have somehow landed on Mars to save her father? George knew how greatly Eric had wanted to travel to the Red Planet, but it sounded like his dream of Mars had gone even more badly wrong than George's dream of space flight. And, with Eric gone to Mars and Annie ending up who knows where in the world of the future, would there have been anyone left to help his family?

'But who betrayed Eric?' George burst out. 'What happened?'

'No one knows who betrayed him,' said Boltzmann quietly. 'But he was working on a plan involving the long-term programming of machines for secret resistance to Eden. Eric believed, you see, that the machines could develop their intelligence fast enough to be able to work alongside humankind to save our planet, save our future. Stop the rise of the Dumps. Even to prevent the terrible wars of the Great Disruption. His idea was that even if humans became powerless to stop Dump, the machines would step in. Once they achieved true intelligence, Eric believed they would identify Dump as the greatest threat to Planet Earth and stand against him. But someone told the Dump regime about his work.'

'No!' said George furiously. 'Who could have done such a terrible thing?'

'Most people think it was Nimu actually,' said Boltzmann. 'It's the foundation of her success within the Eden regime. She was a prodigy – she joined the corporation as a teenager and many people believe she betrayed Eric in order to get in with Dump. But Empyrean assures me that is not the truth, that Nimu did no such thing.'

146

'What?' said George. 'Why on earth would Nimu . . . ? Then who?' His mind was whirring. Eric, sent to Mars for programming resistance into machine learning? If Eric had been caught, then had his activities been stopped? From what George had heard, it sounded as though Nimu and later Empyrean had taken over where Eric had been forced to stop. Which meant it really made no sense that Nimu would betray Eric if she had then carried on his work in secret. But what about Hero, and why did Nimu say she didn't want a child brought into this?

But Boltzmann would say no more.

'I have broken my word!' he said regretfully. 'I have become as unreliable as a human! My metal lips are sealed until we reach our journey waypoint.'

George, at this point, needed to process what he'd just heard rather than take on board anything more. He sat back in his seat and gazed out of the window, trying to distract himself from the awful pain in his heart.

Outside the bus, the luxurious plant life, which had seemed so beautiful when they first arrived

in the Bubble, now seemed artificial and waxy. The trees didn't look natural at all – they were too green and had too many leaves, flowers, buds and berries on them. They appeared synthetic, another aspect of the fakery of Eden rather than a freely growing natural ecosystem.

A few tiny, brightly coloured hummingbirds flapped about their bus. Around the humming-birds buzzed a swarm of honeybees that took a far closer interest in the vehicle. At first, just a few of them batted against the windows, but their numbers were growing very fast.

'Not the bees again!' said George, giving himself a shake to bring himself out of his sad reverie.

Boltzmann looked most alarmed. 'This is not

a good sign,' the robot said fretfully. 'I am experienc-ing extreme anxiety now and it is most unpleasant!'

Just as the bee escort of the driverless

bus became too thick to see out, they reached the exit hatch to the outside world. It opened immediately and snapped shut behind them, leaving an enraged mass of bees throwing themselves at the internal skin of the Bubble.

'How come only the bees spotted us going in and out of the Bubble?' George asked Boltzmann. 'We just waltzed in – and waltzed out. Only the bees seem to have noticed!'

'We are not registering on the monitors, other than the bees, which are still much smarter than all other developed systems,' replied Boltzmann. 'Senses – of the kind that you as a human understand – are not seen as reliable in terms of assessing situations now.'

'But don't the robots capture images?' said George. 'Can't they see?'

'Yes,' said Boltzmann. 'But any visual input now has to be verified by machine sensors, triangulating with other information – which you and I don't emit as we don't have the right sort of on-board machinery. There is so much visual data generated every minute – thousands of terabytes – and they don't seem to have worked out how to process it effectively. Either that, or someone is removing your image as it appears . . .'

'Huh?' said George. A thought struck him. 'But then isn't Hero's thought stream or under-the-skin chip – or whatever she has – going to give us away immediately? As soon as we don't take the route to this Academy place, they'll be on to her straight away – and then they'll catch us!'

'No, Empy thought of that,' said Boltzmann. 'He will run a fake stream for her and close down the real one – about now!'

At that moment, Hero, who had been silent, gave an outraged cry.

'I think she's just found out,' said George to Boltzmann.

'My thought stream!' she cried. 'It's frozen! Boltzmann, can you mend it?' She looked plead-ingly at the battered old robot. 'Please?' she said with her most engaging smile. 'I was just in the middle of telling all the kids about leaving the Bubble for Wonder when it just . . . stopped!'

'I'm sorry,' said Boltzmann, who didn't sound it. 'Empyrean said that once we leave the Bubble, your thought stream would be discontinued.'

Hero's frowned. Her VR headset had been prised out of her hands by her guardian, who had insisted she could not take it on the journey. When Hero had protested, Nimu had weakly come up with some excuse about the headset being the property of the Bubble and Hero getting a new and better one when she reached Wonder.

'What am I going to do now?' complained Hero. 'No thoughties! No VR!' She sounded, thought George, just like Annie complaining when her mum had restricted her screen time.

'Look out of the window?' suggested Boltzmann. Unfortunately he chose exactly the wrong moment to make that suggestion. As Hero turned to examine the world outside the Bubble, something appeared at her window. Hero gave a sharp scream. Running at the same speed as the driverless transport was a shaggy, dishevelled, dirty, two-legged being. As Hero looked out, she locked eyes with the apparition, which leered at her, showing broken, blackened teeth in a red mouth.

Hero pointed. 'What is that?' she squeaked in horror.

On the other side of the bus, George spotted another small group of beings, shaggy-haired and ragged, running on two legs along the top edge of the defunct riverbank. The landscape was scorched, barren and bleak, with a fierce wind blowing a top layer of dust across the plateau, but this group seemed more than equal to the conditions.

They were easily going as fast as the bus – and, looking forward, George could see that when the vehicle reached the bend, they could be cut off in an ambush.

The ragged group seemed to be waving primitive weapons at them and whooping, as though they were preparing themselves for an attack. One of them jumped from the higher ground right onto the front of the bus and sprawled across the windscreen. It was a terrifying sight. George felt pinned to his seat.

Hero had her head between her knees and her arms wrapped round them. Boltzmann had one protective hand on her back. George thought he heard the noise of quiet crying. At that moment, he pretty much felt like crying himself.

But, just then, technology intervened to save them. The bus clearly had some emergency procedures of its own. It unfurled stubby wings on either side and rose up above the ground, increasing its speed. Taking a sharp turn, it threw the intruder off the windscreen so that he landed back down on the ground, where he lay, unhurt, shaking his fist up at the bus. The others down below gathered around their fallen comrade, where they all remained in a tight knot, watching grimly.

'Hero, you can sit up now,' said George.

Hero pinged back upright, looking very startled. Her normally smooth black hair was ruffled and sticking up at the front.

'What,' she exclaimed, 'happened?!' Her eyes looked enormous from the shock.

'Humans, exiled from the Bubble and whatever the other places are?' George hazarded a guess.

'Yuk,' breathed Hero. 'No wonder my guardian says I have to work hard and be a Dumpsome success! I don't want to end up out there, like those people. Actually I didn't even know anyone lived out there. Quick! Let's get to Wonder . . .'

'Shall we tell her?' George mouthed to Boltzmann.

'Not' – the robot shook his head – 'all at once. We need to let her down in stages. Ask me about something else so we can initiate the discovery phase gently for her.'

'Like what?' said George. 'I know!' It was the topic he always wanted to know about. 'Did Empyrean update you about space travel?'

'Oh, not this again!' huffed Hero. 'I already told you – space travel is over!'

'Dear Hero,' said Boltzmann, sounding very old-fashioned. 'Your comment is not consistent with reality!'

'Isn't it?' Hero suddenly sounded less sure of herself and what she knew about her world. George wondered how long it would take for her to wake up from her Bubble-induced delusion.

They were now flying over the endless plain, flat with ripples of sandy ground that stretched on either side as far as the eye could see. There were no trees, towns, roads or cities to break up the view. Just barren earth. In some places George thought he could see markings where perhaps there had once been a motorway or a small town. But nothing was clear enough for him to make anything of it. From the position of

the sun behind them, he realized they were flying north, hopefully towards na-h Alba.

'Space travel,' said Boltzmann slowly, 'has continued under the Eden regime, except not in the way that George and I understood it from our time.'

'From what time?' asked Hero. 'From – oh!' she exclaimed. 'I remember now! You told me! You said you came from space and from another time! How did I forget that?' She looked perplexed.

'Empyrean temporarily stunned your short-term memory,' said Boltzmann. 'And now it is returning as we leave the Bubble behind.'

'That's so mean!' said Hero, looking wounded. 'It's *my* memory, not Empy's! Why is he allowed to mess around with my brain?'

'Because Eden is not what it seems,' said George. 'And we have to help you get away from it.'

'To Wonder Academy, right?' said Hero, looking for confirmation. 'Everything will be OK once we get there? And I'll find my friends from the Bubble and we'll be together again and it will all be OK.' She desperately wanted them to agree.

George sighed. He was torn. But Boltzmann had told him to go carefully. Perhaps, if they could persuade her that one facet of the Bubble was bogus, it would be easier for her to process the rest. And he really wanted to know.

'Boltz,' he said firmly. 'What about space travel? What did Empy tell you?'

'Space,' said Boltzmann, 'was made an illegal zone after Trellis Dump the Second took over full power from his father. The corporations wanted to be sure no one could spy on them or aim missiles from space. So they banned all space exploration and told the public it had been a massive waste of resources. But really it was to stop anyone else becoming more powerful.'

'But in my past space was all about international cooperation,' said George sadly. 'What about those moving lights in the skies? What are they?'

'Oh, there is movement in the skies,' said Boltzmann. 'Empyrean suspects an orbital craft – at least one – has been launched by the Dump regime.'

'Wouldn't Nimu know about it?' said George. 'If she's such a big deal in Eden?'

'Even Nimu hasn't got clearance for this,' said Boltzmann. 'Despite being Minister for Science. It seems to be the biggest secret in Eden.'

'What's the space mission for?' said George.

'Could be anything,' said Boltz. 'It could be a space station, perhaps it has missiles, or maybe it spies on Other Side. Or all of the above.'

'Wow,' said George. 'But no one is supposed to know?'

Hero had been watching this exchange with an open mouth. 'I think you're both crazy!' she said indignantly, and turned to look outside once more. 'I hope you know the emoji for a boy and a robot who have gone bananas.'

George saw that, as an attempt to enlighten Hero, his question about space had failed entirely. Instead of finding out that her world was crazy, she now thought George and Boltzmann were.

Below them, the landscape was changing. From flat and dry, it rose higher, turning into ranges of hills and mountains, still with almost no vegetation. The bus flew deftly across the craggy tips of the range. Right up to the very highest, the mountains remained brown and red, no snow or ice decorating their peaks like frosty icing.

George had started to feel slightly sick. The bus was beginning to bucket around a little, banking sharply and then dipping before rising up again. Outside, a dark fog was starting to settle, making the way ahead much harder to see. But it wasn't just fog – George realized with a jolt that they had flown into an enormous thunderstorm that was breaking right around them. Huge fat drops of rain battered the windscreen and massive forks of lightning flashed past, breaking up the purple and grey rolling clouds.

'Are you sure this driverless bus knows how to fly?' said George as they narrowly avoided a rocky finger that appeared very suddenly out of the thick mist.

'This is a mighty storm,' said Boltzmann, sounding worried. 'Of a greater ferocity than anything we experienced on Earth back in the time of us. It is giving me meteorological anxiety!' The flying bus turned on its side, throwing them all into a heap as it veered round another mountain peak.

'Hey!' said Hero in indignation. Unlike George, she was strapped in, so had remained in her seat as the plane/bus bucketed along. 'This isn't meant to happen!'

'Argh!' cried George, who was hanging onto a handle on the side of the bus to stop himself catapulting across to the other side as it changed direction. He accidentally kicked Boltzmann in the face. 'Sorr-ee!' he said as the bus righted itself. George clambered back into his seat. For a moment, it seemed as though they might be able to fly through the storm, which boiled around them like an angry giant stamping on the Earth.

But the little flying bus was no match for such a merciless gale. Buffeted by winds so strong they could have blown a mountain over, stung by huge, brilliant flashes of blue-white lightning and lashed by great blankets of rain hammering down from the purple clouds, they started to lose height and slow down. Now the bus was flying along the tops of trees, across what looked, through the thick mist, like a dense forest.

The engine made an unhealthy coughing noise. One wing seemed to have been torn off by the storm. But the moulded inside of the cockpit was totally smooth – it appeared to have no on-board controls for a manual pilot to take over. They couldn't even see how to open the door so they could jump out.

'We can't fly this bus!' said George in horror as he realized what was happening. 'What are we going to do? Can you call Empyrean?'

'Empyrean can't help us now! Brace, brace,' said Boltzmann, putting his robot head between his knees. 'It's all we can do.'

As he spoke, the bus dropped down again, plunging into a thicket of trees, whose branches propelled it downwards to a point where it ground to a final stop . . .

Chapter Eleven

'Get out?' said Hero in outrage. 'I'm not getting out! This isn't Wonder Academy!'

They had landed safely, the small plane/bus just managing to bring itself down to the forest floor. But where exactly?

'What is this place?' George said to Boltzmann as the door opened and a salty mist seeped into the cab. He sniffed. The air had a tang of sulphur in it, the smell of rotting vegetation and the sharp bite of smoke. It was so thick that George thought he'd be able to eat the atmosphere. 'Are we still on Earth?' He knew they must be, but it seemed so different to the climate they had taken off from that he couldn't believe they were on the same planet.

'This is the Swamp,' said Boltzmann, thanks to his update of Eden information, gifted to him by Empyrean.

'Yuk, yuk and yuk!' exclaimed Hero. 'Horrid! Make the bus take off again so we can get to Wonder.'

'We're not meant to be here, are we?' said George to Boltzmann. From the tiny bit of ground he could see through the dense smog, the mud looked like it would suck him in if he stepped on it.

'No. We have performed an emergency landing,' confirmed Boltzmann, who looked worried.

Looking out, George saw that the other wing of the small vehicle had been ripped off as it lowered itself to the ground through the thick trees. Just the body of the craft remained. They were, George realized, heroically lucky to be unharmed.

'Why is this place so weird?' complained Hero, who was obviously waiting for the doors to shut and her transport to move off, as if by magic, as it had done so many times before in the Bubble.

'It seems the climatic zones of Earth are now sharply different to one another,' said Boltzmann. 'We have come from the desert region, where there is no rainfall, into another area which has too much.'

As if to echo the robot's words, squelchy noises

and what sounded like large muddy burps echoed around them.

'What now?' asked George. He didn't like the look of their destination, but at least they were at ground level, not stuck in a tree or on a mountain crag.

'I'm not getting out,' Hero stated with considerable determination. 'I'm meant to go to Wonder Academy, where everything is shiny and nice, and all my friends live in pods and learn about cool stuff.'

But the bus had other ideas. '*This automated transport will self-destruct in thirty seconds*,' came an announcement. '*Evacuate this vehicle immediately. Repeat: it will self-destruct in thirty seconds. Any humanoid or robotic life forms must disembark.*'

Hero turned white.

'Move, Hero!' said George, undoing her seat belt. 'Bring your backpack. We have to go!'

But Hero couldn't seem to budge.

'You can't stay in the bus – it's going to explode in about twenty seconds.'

'*Nineteen*,' said the automated voice.

George tried to pick Hero up but she was too heavy for him. He looked about wildly. He had to get her out but he couldn't stay on the bus and wait for it to detonate or activate whatever self-destruct mechanisms it had installed. He was just wondering if he could throw himself out of the bus, and somehow manage to drag Hero with him, when Boltzmann decided it was up to him to do something.

Calmly the huge robot picked Hero up in his long metal arms, clasped her firmly to stop her thrashing and got out of the vehicle. Boltzmann sank a few centimetres into the gloopy mud outside the bus – which was already seeping up the sides. But he and Hero were out.

'Come on, George!' said Boltzmann, still holding firmly onto Hero. George didn't hesitate; gathering up the two backpacks that Nimu had given them, he threw himself out of the bus, landing on his bottom with a splosh on a weedy patch of ground that seemed a little more solid than the rest. He tried to move away from the bus, which he expected to explode with a great bang. But instead it seemed to dissolve, as though it was being pulled apart, atom by atom. After a few seconds, nothing remained where once it had stood. It was as though it had just vanished.

'Wow!' said George, lying on the ground. 'How did that happen?'

'The ultimate in biodegradable materials?' hazarded Boltzmann. 'Or perhaps it atomized itself?'

The old robot put Hero gently down on a patch of grassy, solid ground next to George. She immediately sat up, her back poker-straight and a shocked, confused expression on her face.

'What is going on? We should be at Wonder by now!' she said.

George decided it still wasn't a good time

to break it to her that they were never going to Wonder Academy, that he didn't know where it was, and, even if he did, he had been expressly told to take Hero somewhere else. He hoped Boltzmann had a fall-back plan.

'Where now, Boltz?' he asked, scrambling to his feet. He opened one of the backpacks and brought out the water purifier. Filling the top half with dank, stinky liquid from a huge puddle, he was amazed to see crystal-clear water drip into the bottom part. 'It works!' he said, taking a swig. He got out the second purifier, filled it and offered it to Hero.

'Ummm,' said the robot, who had taken some time to scan the thick wet mist surrounding them. 'That way!' He pointed.

George looked in that direction but could see nothing at all, thanks to the fog. 'Why that way?' he asked.

'Don't worry,' said the robot comfortingly. 'I know exactly what I'm doing. Empyrean gave me all the information we need. I am the ultimate resource. You can depend on me to get you all the way to your destination.'

'But this isn't part of Empyrean's plan, is it?' said George. 'We've been brought down by a freak weather event.'

'Not so freak,' said Boltzmann. 'The impact of climate change' – Hero snorted – 'means the weather is entirely out of control. I'm thanking my robot stars we landed in the forest and not in a flash flood from the downpour! Water is no friend to the helpful robot going about his person-supporting chores!'

'Can you call Empy and check what we should do now?'

Boltzmann looked uneasy. 'Empyrean asked me only to get in touch in an absolute emergency. Otherwise we reveal our location. I do not think this is in fact an emergency, just a blip.'

'How would you call Empy?' George asked. He broke open a few freeze-dried trail bars, gave one to Hero and munched on the other himself.

'Like this.' Boltzmann seemed to speak into his palm. 'Empyrean,' he mimed. 'The eagle has landed.' He chuckled and snapped his palm shut, smiling at George and Hero. It struck George that Boltzmann appeared to be enjoying himself.

'What were you speaking into?' asked Hero. George was relieved that she seemed to have come round.

'It's called a palm pilot,' said Boltzmann. He showed a device about the size of an iPhone attached to his palm. It fitted neatly into his large robot hand. 'Empyrean gave it to me. It will plan our route and allow us to communicate with him if we need to. But please trust me! I will not let you down. This,' he confided, 'is the sort of mission I have been longing for. The chance to be a really useful robot.'

'Can that thingy show you the way to anywhere you want to go?' asked Hero quietly, picking at her energy snack.

'Affirmative!' The nice robot beamed. 'It has already plotted a new path for us to cross the Swamp in the direction of Edenopolis, capital city of Eden.'

'Good!' said George. Perhaps Boltzmann was right and this wasn't actually a total disaster after all. He had a map from Nimu too, he remembered. He reached into his back pocket . . . but pulled out only a soaked, muddy piece of paper that disintegrated in his hand.

Boltzmann smiled at him. 'Paper can only do so much, George,' he said. 'Modern technology is *so* much more resilient.' He waved his hand again.

'Edenopolis!' said Hero in delight. 'Wowee!

It's such a cool place. It's made of glass and gold and it floats on the clouds! It's the most beautiful city in the world.'

George wondered how many cities there were in the world now, and whether being the most beautiful really meant anything any more.

'From there,' continued Boltzmann, 'we will get our next transport. But we have to be very careful – Edenopolis is beautiful but very dangerous. There are spies everywhere.'

Spies, thought George, staring into the darkening gloom. Why didn't that surprise him? How else would Eden be run? 'Let's go.'

'I'll carry Hero,' said Boltzmann, wanting as ever to be helpful.

'You will not!' said Hero. She jumped to her feet. 'I can walk!'

'Follow me,' said the robot. 'And stay close.' He switched on the lights in his pincer fingers, which allowed them to see a little further. In the white light, which turned smoky and opaque as it tried to pierce the fog, they could just make out that they were in a forest clearing.

As Boltzmann pointed his lights upwards, they saw towering trees dripping with rain and covered in thick moss. The branches of the trees were

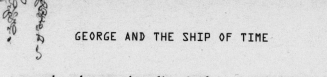

curved and wavy, bending in fantastical shapes as they seemed to weave a canopy above their heads. Below the trees sprouted another layer of dense undergrowth, with thickets of fronded ferns and twisted ropes of creeper. Each tree had hundreds of thick dark leaves. A faint perfume rose from this strange forest, sweet, earthy and fruity.

'Those are fig trees!' said George, who was good at botany. His father, back in the past, had loved gardening above all things, and from him George had learned more than he had realized. He could see ripe fruits hanging under the enormous leaves.

'What's a fig?' asked Hero, reaching her hand out to touch the tree and then pulling it back the moment she made contact. She wiped her hand fastidiously on her jumpsuit, leaving a dark green smear.

'Try one,' said George, who had grown up with parents who were foragers. He snapped off a juicy dark fig and handed it to Hero. She wrinkled her nose. George picked another one for himself and bit into it. 'It's delicious,' he said. 'Go on, try it.'

Hero took the tiniest of nibbles. She screwed up her face, but then she felt the sweetness on

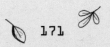

her tongue. 'Oh!' she said in surprise. 'It's lovely!' George wondered if she had ever eaten real food before, or only powders, pills, mixes and freeze-dried high-energy snacks.

'The fig is a prehistoric plant that grows vigorously in many different environments,' said Boltzmann, who was checking the general-knowledge files Empyrean had given him. 'It can conquer spaces which previously might have been inhabited, as the strong roots of the tree will push through substances as solid as concrete.'

'What's concrete?' Hero said.

George looked around. Here and there were angular shapes, which might be the remnants of buildings. As Boltzmann shone his light around them, George thought he could make out silhouettes of ghost buildings, intertwined with the vigorous fig.

'Do you think the figs took over a city?' George asked. He'd been to see ruined cities from the distant past with his parents; the remains of ancient civilizations. It was mind-bending to think that the cities he had known on Earth could now lie in ruins themselves.

'Yes,' said Boltzmann. 'I believe this was once a great city in the north of your country.'

'Do you know what it was called?' asked George.

'Manchester?' said Boltzmann. 'Is that a place you know?'

'It was,' said George sadly. 'Not any more. At least there are still trees in the future,' he went on, trying to focus on something positive. 'But how are we going to get through? There are no paths.'

'If you will allow me,' said Boltzmann, 'I would like to be as helpful as my programming is capable of!' Ripping and tearing plants out by their roots, he powered ahead, creating a route for Hero and George to follow.

'Are there predators in the figgy forest?' George asked Boltzmann nervously as they trudged along. He looked about uneasily. Now that they were among the trees, strange echoing noises bounced around them in the fog. It was impossible to know where they came from, or what they were. Sometimes they sounded like parrots squawking; sometimes they were like metallic drills or weird ghostly whispers, right next to George's ear. At times, they thought they heard a distant roar.

'I spotted a leopard in the mountains,' said Boltzmann, pounding forward as Hero tiptoed along behind. 'So not all big cats are extinct. And

I believe Empyrean may have also referred me to some experiments with DNA . . .'

At that moment, George heard what sounded like a throaty purr, just to the left of him. As he tried to focus in on the noise, he made out large padded footsteps, which seemed to keep pace with him. He slowed down – and they seemed to slow. He sped up, bashing into the back of Hero as he accelerated, and the footsteps got faster too. But then they stopped, and the forest itself returned to silence again, the only noises being Boltzmann hacking at the undergrowth, Hero humming and George's rapid breathing. All the other noises had faded away, as though something so big and so scary was afoot in the forest that evening that none wanted to give away their location by making a sound.

'Something is following us,' he tried to whisper to the two in front, but Boltzmann was too busy thrashing out a path and Hero was too intent on keeping up with Boltzmann to hear him. But what came next was so loud that it must have been heard by all the creatures of the forest.

A blood-curdling snarl. It came out of the fog; the sort of noise that George had never heard before but which his primal instincts told him was the sound of a predator that had scented its prey. Boltzmann immediately stopped and wheeled round, pushing Hero behind him. She opened her mouth to scream but no sound came out. It wouldn't have mattered, thought George, if it had. The noise came again, this time so loud that it drowned out everything else, followed by what sounded to George like a large animal licking its chops in anticipation of a meal.

'Where is it?' said George, terror running through his veins. 'And what is it?'

He and Boltzmann turned together in a full circle around Hero, with Boltzmann shining his lights into the dimness, looking for the beast that stalked them. They heard the ground being pawed, and another snarl, as suddenly a huge striped beast with long yellow fangs threw itself out of the darkness towards them.

Boltzmann stepped neatly forward, shielding George, and took the whole force of the impact. Hero and George dived aside as Boltzmann fell backwards, the tiger on top of him. George felt as though he was frozen to the spot, watching the tiger trying to tear into Boltzmann's metal body. For a few moments, the robot and the tiger fought on the ground, the beast driven mad by its attempts to bite into the metal. Boltzmann's arms closed around the tiger, just as they had done around Hero earlier – but the tiger was a far more fearsome opponent than the small girl had been. George tried to think: what were you supposed to do if a tiger attacked? But his brain felt as stuck as his body. All he could think of was the tiger that came to tea – and this tiger wasn't one that anyone would invite in for a cuppa and a toasted muffin. It looked more like a . . . *sabre-toothed* tiger! But they had been extinct for centuries! How could . . . ?

Beside George, Hero watched in wide-eyed horror as the beast gnawed at their robot guide. But suddenly she sprang forward and launched herself at the back of the animal, slapping it with her small hands and shouting, 'Get off, you big bully! Leave Boltzmann alone!' George realized that she had no idea of the scale of the danger she was in. He leaped forward and grabbed her, throwing her to one side, and instead tried to climb onto the oily fur of the huge tiger to see if he could somehow pull it off Boltzmann. His hands slipped on the coat of the magnificent beast, but somehow he managed to clamber aboard and get his arms round its throat.

But, as he did so, the noises from the tiger changed. It was getting tired of gnawing at the unbending flesh of its victim. Boltzmann was not proving the tasty catch it had hoped for. Now it was fighting to get away, using its massive strength and body weight to pull out of the robot's grasp. Boltzmann's metal body had been through a lot by now. Weakened by the long journey through space without any form of repair or rest, his arms were fatigued and couldn't maintain their grip on the slippery fur of the angry tiger.

With an enormous roar and a great scream of breaking metal, the tiger broke free, with George still clinging onto its back as though he was in a rodeo and the tiger was a bucking bronco. It turned its huge face towards Hero and paused, licking its fleshy lips as it smelled the air. George could feel the beast registering that Hero would make a delicious dinner. He tried to tighten his grip, his hands in the soft fur under the tiger's chin, his arms brushed by the long whiskers of the huge cat. As it licked its lips, some warm tiger saliva flicked onto George's hands.

George felt time slow down as he peered over between the animal's upright ears, taking in the slanted amber eyes, the long curved teeth, the matted orange fur and the white whiskers. It crouched back on its hind paws, getting ready to spring towards Hero, who just stood there, her face a blurred oval against the darkness of the forest.

'I'm so sorry,' George said out loud, not knowing quite to whom. To Hero perhaps, for not being able to save her. To his family for leaving them behind when he flew off in a spaceship. But most of all to his best friend Annie, whom he had also left behind all those years ago, when he launched himself into space with just a robot for company. 'I'm sorry,' he repeated as the tiger let out one last, spine-tingling howl and readied itself to leap . . .

Chapter Twelve

George threw himself off the upright beast, hoping to land in front of it so that at least it would be distracted long enough for Hero to get away. He fell onto his back on the muddy, slimy forest floor. Sensing the commotion, the tiger landed softly on its front paws, turned and smiled sleepily at George; the patronizing smirk of the most powerful predator in the jungle. Sure of the outcome, the tiger moved slowly, almost lazily, as if it was smugly enjoying its victory.

Had George not delayed the tiger, and had it jumped a moment sooner, it might have reached one of its victims before Boltzmann recovered a flicker of energy in his battered circuits. Fortunately George had bought them just enough time. As the tiger bent its head towards him, licking its lips and baring its teeth, a tiny dart flew out of the end of Boltzmann's finger and landed in the beast, which gave a mighty roar before keeling over. It was close enough for George to feel the heat of its breath and see the rows of sharp incisor teeth in its powerful jaws.

The howl that came was of shock, not victory. Whatever the dart contained, it was strong enough to knock the tiger unconscious. It was as though it had stalled mid-leap, front paws extended, mouth gaping open, eyes rolling – and then careered sideways with a great crashing sound as its mighty weight plummeted down through layers of vegetation to the forest floor, where it hit the remains of a tarmacked road. Just underneath its magnificent head, the jaws still open, were the traces of long-forgotten road traffic markings.

As a shocked George gazed down at the huge mammal, he could see that it was lying on top of a NO PARKING sign. For a nanosecond, his mind whirred back to imagine what this place must have been like as a city in his time – cars, people, buildings, bustle, kids, shops and schools.

A metallic wheeze and a human whimper brought George back to the here and now. He looked up to at Hero, who was still standing like a wax statue with one extended finger pointing at the beast as she dumbly mouthed something unintelligible. She sat down heavily as George went over to her. She seemed to have gone to a place beyond speech. Shaking her head, she curled up into a ball and fell into the deep sleep of the very shocked.

George checked that she was as OK as she could be, given the circumstances, and turned back to Boltzmann. The old robot had just saved both their lives but had paid a very heavy price for his courage. 'You're alive!'

'No,' rasped Boltzmann, who was lying on the ground in a nest of fallen fig leaves, bits of shredded metal scattered around him like a halo. 'Was never alive. Am nothing but a machine.'

George knelt down beside him on the earthy

forest floor, interrupting the trails of insects, which busied themselves finding new paths around him. Life, thought George, his mind wandering from the shock, was a mystery in Eden. Robots seemed alive; cities were dead. The only species that appeared to thrive were insects. Extinct beasts had returned, but anything normal seemed to have perished. And now his last link with the life he knew before was in terrible trouble.

'You mean much more to me than just a machine!' said George. 'You're my friend! You travelled through space with me!'

'Thank you,' said Boltzmann. 'All I ever wanted was to make a friend who was human. It was my only aim. Happy now.' The robot closed his eyes.

'You're such a good robot,' said George, who felt tears welling in his eyes again. Boltzmann had been with him through the whole extraordinary adventure of space; the surprise launch from Kosmodrome 2 to fly across the Universe and then back home again, only to find that it wasn't home any more. Without Boltzmann, George felt abandoned in this strange world of the future.

'I'll mend you,' he said desperately, trying to gather up the pieces of Boltzmann. 'I'll carry you to a place where you can be fixed.'

'No,' ordered the 'nice robot', the only one of its kind ever built. Created by the insane megalomaniac Alioth Merak, Boltzmann had been a fluke, a robot that had gained sentience and been programmed to be as nice as possible. Even Alioth Merak had never quite understood how it was he came to create Boltzmann in this way. The other robots had been cruel and mean, happy to trample over any form of life to fulfil their master's wishes. There had only ever been one Boltzmann, and now it looked like George was losing his unique automated friend when he needed him most.

'You can't fix me,' said Boltzmann. 'I'm ending. The tranquillizer dart is my last action – shooting it automatically causes my systems to start shutting down.'

'Why?' shouted George. 'Why would that happen?'

'It's how Mr Merak made me,' said Boltzmann meekly. 'It was to make sure I couldn't fall into enemy hands. It was meant to be used only in the most dire circumstances, to give me time to clear my systems so that no information could be stolen . . . Take the device in my palm!' He held out a robot hand.

'What?' said George.

'Take it!' said Boltzmann. 'Take the palm pilot! So you can contact Empyrean.'

George held the robot's hand. In his palm was a small device that George would have to break off. He couldn't bear to do it while his robot was still alive. It felt like ripping off a body part. He just couldn't mutilate his poor old friend any further.

'Take it,' rasped the robot, opening his robot eyes again; but they were dim, no longer the fiery bright oculorum of the past. 'The plan . . .'

'What is the plan?' said George frantically. Not only was he about to lose his friend, he was also going to lose every piece of information about this journey and what he was meant to do. 'Where do I take Hero? What do I do?'

'Get to Edenopolis,' said the old robot. 'There, you will find . . .'

'What?' said George desperately. 'What will I find?' But there was no reply. It was already too late. Boltzmann – George's friend and helper, his protector in this alien wilderness, the holder of the 'plan' – was no more.

'Noooooo!' said George. He bent over the poor old battered body of his robot. He banged his forehead softly against Boltzmann's chest. 'No!' He laid his head down on the cool metal

and wept. He cried, not just for Boltzmann but for everything he'd lost: his mum, his dad, his sisters, his best friend Annie. And for his way of life – a way of life he had thought was so normal and so everyday; well, apart from the occasional journey into space through Cosmos's incredible doorway portal.

George had never seriously considered that, if he went away, by the time he returned everything he loved would be overturned and destroyed. It wasn't just his house, his street, his family that had disappeared. The Earth had changed beyond all recognition. Nothing was as he had left it. He lay there, head on Boltzmann's chest, while his salty tears turned metallic as they ran down the nice robot's chest. George was so exhausted now that he couldn't even feel afraid.

He didn't know how long he stayed there, but it was some time before he thought hazily that he should probably get up from his position half on Boltzmann, half on the fig forest floor. As he gazed blurrily upwards, he could now make out shapes among the trees – shapes that looked like they had once been buildings. They were, he realized, lying in the middle of what could have been a main road. On either side were the half-shells of structures – here a doorway, there part of a window frame. There was even a street light tangled up in the fig forest. The light no longer shone – and it wouldn't be long before the upright metal pole was overtaken entirely by the vegetation.

He was so tired. He knew he had to get up, rouse Hero and carry on towards the city of Edenopolis, then to the floating island of na-h Alba. But he had no map in his pocket any longer, no idea which direction to take, or how to keep

Hero safe in this weird, dangerous world.

George must have dropped off, for the next thing he knew, the light in the misty fig forest had changed colour. It was now a dusty yellow, shining with a brightness that made it hard to see anything.

But it wasn't the light that had woken George. Someone was nudging his leg with their foot. George looked up, shading his eyes with his hand. He thought it must be Hero, but then realized with a jolt that a strange shaggy shape was leaning over him. George opened his mouth to yell, but the apparition was too quick for him. Just as George was about to set up a huge clamour, he found that his mouth was filled with something soft and fluffy which stopped him from speaking.

'Don't shout,' said the new arrival, sounding as though it might burst into laughter at any time. 'You'll draw the Child Hunter.'

Whoever the shaggy shape was, it spoke with the clear voice of a human boy.

Chapter Thirteen

'Who are you?' George tried to say through a mouthful of what felt like fur. But all that came out was: 'Oo ag u?' With the light streaming behind it, all he could see was the outline of something like a badger – it had a black-and-white striped fur pelt and small ears.

'Shh!' The figure reached up with a very human hand and pulled away the black-and-white hood. George could now see two very bright eyes twinkling in a round face.

'Hello! I'm Atticus. More to the point, who are you? And what are you doing in my forest?'

George pointed to the fur gag in his mouth and shook his head. He pulled a pleading face that made Atticus laugh.

'OK, I'll take it out,' he said, raising an eyebrow. 'But don't shout! I'm friendly – but not everyone in this forest is like me.'

George nodded, and Atticus undid the fur gag, pulled George to his feet and brushed him down.

'Some of the others,' Atticus continued, grimacing, 'they're not so much fun. You're lucky I found you.' He looked at the tiger down below and gave George a big grin. 'You knocked that crazy old thing out! Good work.'

'It wasn't me,' said George. 'It was my friend!' He gulped.

'What, that small human,' said Atticus, looking in surprise at the still sleeping form of Hero, 'took out that tiger?'

'No, the metal man, over there,' said George. Atticus was so bizarrely clad that George thought he might not have heard of robots.

'A metal man,' said Atticus reflectively. 'Not much of him left, is there? The old tiger went to work on your metal friend.'

George's heart gave a lurch as he realized that Boltzmann was little more than a pile of scrap now.

'And who is this?' Atticus poked Hero with his toe. She slept on, unmoving.

George had already decided he liked Atticus, and in this strange world the one thing he really needed was a new friend. 'That is Hero. And I'm George,' he said.

'Funny name,' said Atticus.

Perhaps Atticus is a totally normal name for a boy of the future, George thought. He coughed a few times.

'Here, drink this,' said Atticus, handing over what looked like a flask made of animal hide. 'It's OK, it's just clean water.'

George took a grateful slurp.

'How did you ...?' Atticus seemed to be

thinking. 'How did you come to be in my forest with a hero and a metal man?'

'It's a long story,' said George. Truthfully.

'Great!' enthused Atticus. 'You can tell it at the Gathering! They love long stories.'

Even though George really didn't know what Atticus was talking about, he couldn't help grinning back. But, just as he did, Atticus ducked down, put his ear to the ground and then jumped up again.

'We have to go!' he declared. 'News of the tiger has spread. And there's a rumour the Child Hunter is in the forest, out looking . . . Let's not wait to find out! Come on!'

George pointed to Hero.

'Ah!' said Atticus. 'We can't leave the hero behind.'

'Actually, her *name* is Hero,' said George, who felt a bit silly trying to explain. 'She isn't really a hero.'

'Perhaps she will be one day,' said Atticus cheerfully. 'But not if we leave her here in the forest.'

With no more effort than Boltzmann, the boy hitched Hero up over his shoulder, the wiry muscles in his arms flexing only slightly.

'Ready?'

George blinked. 'You can carry her?' He had tried earlier and hadn't been able to hoist her a centimetre off the ground.

'I could carry the tiger if I wanted,' boasted Atticus, puffing out his thin chest.

'No you couldn't!' scoffed George, whose jump-suit was now so covered in mud, leaves and bits of debris that he looked pretty similar to Atticus, minus the fur hood.

Atticus grinned again. 'Probably not a good idea anyway. The mad beast might wake up and bite my head off!' He sniffed the wind again and set off while chattering away, with Hero bobbing over his shoulder. 'You've arrived on our auspicious day as well. My mum hasn't promised anything but I really, *really* want to move up to the next level at the Gathering tonight . . .'

'Wait!' said George, running back to the inert figure of Boltzmann. Atticus clearly didn't have an iPhone in his jacket pocket, and George realized that if he didn't brace himself to do it now, he would walk away without what was possibly the only communication device in the whole forest. 'Sorry, Boltz,' he said as he snapped the palm pilot out of the remains of the robot's hand and stuffed it into his pocket. 'What's a level?' he said, catching up with Atticus.

'Of the Warrior Kingdom!' said Atticus in surprise. 'Don't they have a Warrior Kingdom where you come from? Wherever that is?'

'Not really,' said George. *Only in computer games*, he thought, but he didn't know how to explain that to Atticus. They were still clambering through undergrowth, but this time following a path. Atticus stopped suddenly and seemed to examine the air itself. As the light had got brighter and more yellow, the forest was coming to life – George could hear birds calling to each other, monkeys chattering, insects whirring and, below all the other noises, a lower-pitched, more frightening distant burr, as though something menacing was on the move once more.

'We need to go up,' Atticus said quietly. 'We're not safe down here. I think I can smell Child Hunter on the wind.'

'What's a Child Hunter?' asked George. Whoever or whatever it was, it didn't sound good.

'No one we want to meet,' said Atticus. 'He'd try and stuff us in a sack and drag us out of the forest.'

'But why?' said George.

'Because it's the way Eden works,' said Atticus, all traces of merriment wiped off his face, his eyes hard. 'You know how they say it's the best of all possible worlds? It isn't. It's the worst.' He lowered Hero gently onto the forest floor. 'Come on, little hero!' He shook her firmly with both hands. Hero stirred. Atticus bent down and pinched the fleshy part of her ear lobes. 'Up!' he said cheerfully when Hero opened her eyes. 'Come along! Time to move!'

Hero opened her mouth wide to protest, but Atticus was too quick for her. He clapped a dirty hand across her face, and with the other hand pulled her to her feet.

George intervened. 'Be careful with her,' he said. 'She's not used to the forest.'

'She's going to slow us down,' said Atticus warily. 'We need to get up top fast.' As if to underline his words, a louder rumbling roar filtered through the forest.

'She'll manage,' said George, hoping that Hero would.

Atticus took his hand away from Hero's mouth. She looked furious.

'Slow you down!' she said in high dudgeon. 'As if! People' – she glared at Atticus – 'should stop carrying me! I'm not a baby and I don't like it!'

'OK!' said Atticus, laughing and grabbing onto a low branch of a gnarled fig tree. 'You're on! Last one to the top is a rotten apple!' He swung himself up, followed nimbly by George, who had always loved climbing trees.

George followed Atticus up and up – but, when he looked back, Hero was still standing on the ground, her mouth a perfect 'O' of surprise.

'Hero!' hissed George. 'Hurry!' From his tree vantage point, he could make out something large and heavy moving stealthily across the forest towards her. The tiger! It had woken up – and it was both hungry *and* angry now.

Hero didn't move. Despite her brave words, she seemed stuck to the ground. 'I can't!' she whispered. 'I just – can't!'

'Hero!' Atticus said urgently from higher up. 'Jump! Jump up! George – do not go back down!'

'I have to,' said George. He couldn't abandon her now. He scrambled back down onto the forest floor and grabbed Hero by the shoulders. 'Climb the tree,' he said. 'Just get off the ground.'

'I can't!' she said. 'I've never climbed a tree!'

George thought of the trees in the Bubble. Of course she'd never climbed one. An alarm would probably have gone off if she'd tried, and she would have had marks docked from her overall score! Hero had done so little in the real world, and yet now she had to learn everything all at once in order to survive. But George had seen a flash of another Hero in the way she had tried to protect Boltzmann from the tiger – and he knew she could do this too.

'And you'd never left the Bubble, flown into a lightning storm, eaten a fig, walked through the Swamp or fought a tiger!' said George. 'But you did all those things, Hero. You can do this! Just pretend it's your virtual gymnastics class!'

Atticus had climbed back down and was leaning out of the tree, holding out his arm. 'Grab my hand,' he urged.

Hero looked dubiously at his filthy hand, and George could almost read the thoughts going through her mind about bad bacteria and germs. But then she looked at her own hand, and saw that it was every bit as grubby as his. The tiger behind them gave a fearsome growl, at which point Hero grabbed Atticus's hand and pulled herself into the tree. Immediately George swung himself up after her, shoving her into the higher branches as he clambered up.

But this time the delay had worked in the tiger's favour and not George's. The furious animal was now right underneath the tree and was determined not to let George get away twice. Desperate to secure its tasty catch, the tiger threw itself after them into the tree. To George's horror, he realized that the tiger knew how to climb! It inched itself up the trunk, using its huge claws and the strength in its mighty legs to move way too fast for George's liking.

Above George, Hero frantically scrambled upwards, following Atticus. Below him, the tiger pawed at the branches, trying to dislodge its prey. But George was already out of reach – except for his left leg, which the tiger sliced into with its sharp claw, making a nasty cut through his jumpsuit into the flesh below.

'Ouch!' George cried, as quietly as he could. The tiger's cut stung, but he had to keep moving up into the tree. Underneath him, the tiger was desperately trying to hoist itself higher.

'The tiger's coming up!' shrieked Hero from above him as she clambered into the branches. George could hear the panting breath of the animal as he scaled higher himself.

'This way!' Atticus had reached the highest stable branch, from where he jumped into the next tree, flying like a bird into the higher canopy. To George's amazement, Hero followed him. George, his leg throbbing, had to struggle to throw himself after them, only just catching onto a light branch. The others had already moved into the thick greenery. George, tired and injured, pushed himself into the canopy after them. He could hear the tiger roaring in fury that its prey had finally escaped – the beast was too heavy for the small branches higher up.

Inside the shaded, leafy dome of the next tree, George saw the others disappearing onto what looked like a slim concealed walkway stretching between the treetops.

'Follow me,' said Atticus, stepping onto the suspended bridge. It was made of dense forest materials, bound and woven into thick ropes.

'What is this?' said George in amazement.

'It's how we get around,' said Atticus proudly. 'Our people built these all over the forest so that we could move about without being attacked. It's too light to support a beast like the tiger.' The walkway swayed as he stood on it, waiting for the other two to follow him.

'Is it safe?' said Hero doubtfully.

'Safer than spending time with a sabre-toothed tiger!' sang Atticus. 'Or the Child Hunter.'

'The who?' said Hero.

'A bad man,' said Atticus, 'who we're going to outwit.'

'Oh goody!' said Hero in delight. Unexpectedly she seemed to be enjoying herself! George felt a pang as he remembered Boltzmann, his other friend, who also had enjoyed unlikely situations. He would not lose Hero, he told himself. He would get her to her destination. But something was really bothering him.

'How are there sabre-toothed tigers?' *I thought this was the future, not the past!* he thought.

'They were grown in a laboratory from an excavated fragment of frozen DNA,' said Atticus. 'In the old days. But then, when science became illegal, all the labs got shut down, so the animals escaped and now they live wild in the forest.'

''Scuse me!' said Hero. 'That's *so* not what happened!'

'And you know that how?' said Atticus.

'My guardian is the Minister of Science for Eden,' said Hero, obviously expecting Atticus to be impressed. 'So I know quite a bit actually.'

Atticus looked suspiciously at Hero at this

news. 'Then why are you here, in the Swamp?' he said. 'If your guardian is so important in Eden, why are you hanging out in my forest?'

George jumped in. 'We're not spies,' he said, remembering what Boltzmann had said earlier. 'We're just two kids who've got lost in the Swamp and we need your help.'

'Where are you going?' said Atticus.

'Na-h Alba,' said George.

'Wonder Academy,' said Hero at the same moment.

'Huh,' said Atticus, eyeing them both up. 'You guys really don't seem to have this.'

'No,' said George humbly. 'We don't.' He expected Hero to contradict him, but when he looked over at her she was nodding in agreement.

'It's been the weirdest journey of my life,' she confided to Atticus. 'And I don't think George has any idea what he's doing.'

George felt a bit stung, especially after his attempts to protect her. But he had to admit that Hero was right. He had no clue what he was doing or where to go next. Added to that, he didn't feel very well. A bit woozy and a bit sick.

'There's only one person in this forest who can sort this out,' declared Atticus.

'Who?' said George, hoping it wouldn't be the Child Hunter.

'My mum,' said Atticus decisively. Hero looked blank.

'It's like his guardian,' explained George. 'Sort of. Remember? When someone is born, rather than, um, hatched.'

'Oh,' said Hero. 'Same thing, different name?'

'Pretty much,' said George.

'Where does this "mum" live?' asked Hero.

'At my home,' said Atticus. 'I'm going to take you to my home.'

Chapter Fourteen

After trudging along across a series of dizzying walkways, jumping from branch to branch, and at one point even taking something that looked like a zip wire across the forest, Atticus finally came to a stop. It was much warmer now, higher up in the trees where a little light and some heat from the sun filtered through the murky clouds. George's jumpsuit had dried out entirely, but his leg still throbbed where the tiger had lashed out at him. Gymnast Hero had proved to be a remarkably good traveller and was getting more cheerful by the minute.

'What now?' she said brightly. 'Where are we?'

'This,' said Atticus, gesturing ahead of him, 'is my home!'

In front of them lay an extraordinary structure. At the height of a small skyscraper, they could

see what looked like an encampment built over several storeys.

'What is it?' said George. 'And how does it stay up?'

But, even as he asked, he saw the answer. This treetop dwelling had been constructed from the remains of a building. He looked up at long steel joists and concrete trunks, the skeleton of what had stood here before. Trees had grown right through it in places and, where the original floor must once have been, split tree trunks formed the horizontal platform on which people, dressed like Atticus, were going about their daily business.

On one side, George saw a fire with a group of smaller kids gathered around it. There were a few adults, who looked like they were telling the children a story. The kids all seemed entranced. In other places people were doing all sorts: mending the structure, making clothes, preparing food. It was a strange haven from all that George had seen since he had arrived in the future. It reminded him of when, many years before, he and his parents had lived in an encampment where they tried to recreate life in the Iron Age. But, when George lived there with his mum and dad, they hadn't had books or steel joists or talked about DNA.

'Is that . . . ?' said Hero, interrupting his thoughts. 'Is that – fire? I mean, real fire?' She looked thrilled.

'Of course it is,' said Atticus. 'How could there be fire that isn't real?'

'I've never seen fire before,' confessed Hero. 'I've only seen it virtually.'

'Well, don't touch the fire unless you want to get a real burn! Before we go in, I have to warn you – people from outside are not allowed here.'

'Why not?' said Hero, sounding hurt.

'People from outside mean danger in our culture,' said Atticus. 'But my mother is the chief. And I know she'll want to meet you!'

Two of the adults had spotted them and were coming over.

'Atticus,' the first grown-up said smoothly. 'Your mother has been asking for you! We were about to send out a search party. We heard that the tiger had been sighted and she was worried.'

'No need,' said Atticus. George realized that Atticus didn't much like this grown-up. She did have a very severe face and hooded eyes. 'Look! I'm baaaack!'

'And who are these?' said the other grown-up, who was short and round with small eyes.

'Just some friends,' said Atticus, faux casually. He didn't seem to like her much either. Behind the two grown-ups, others were assembling and the mood was changing. The adults with the kids quickly gathered them up and moved them further away. Everything seemed to go very quiet.

'They are outsiders,' said the woman with the hooded eyes. 'And you know the rules.'

'I want to talk to my mother,' said Atticus defiantly. '*She* decides the rules.'

'Your mother trusts us to make sure our community stays safe,' said the shorter woman. 'You know that, Atticus. You know that she asked us to deal with you – last time . . .' She trailed off, but the menace was unmistakable.

Hero shuffled behind George.

'Where is my mother?' demanded Atticus.

'She's gone up to the higher level.'

'Come on.' Atticus turned to George and Hero. 'Let's go and find my mum.'

'You cannot take those two up there!' said the first woman angrily. 'Only warriors who have risen through the levels can go there. Just because you are her son does not mean that you can break the rules.'

'*They* can't stay,' said the second woman

209

decisively. 'They must leave – immediately. And we will have to decide whether or not to strike camp and move on, now that you have given away our location. This is a dangerous time, as you know. The tiger is on the move and we hear reports that the Child Hunter is in the forest. If he caught you or found our colony, all our young people would be in peril. And it would be *their* fault!' She pointed at George and Hero. 'They have brought him here.'

'*They* can't leave by themselves,' said Atticus, his jaw set firmly. 'They don't know the forest and it's dangerous.'

'Feel free to be exiled along with your friends,' said the woman with the hooded eyes. 'We will protect this community by any means necessary.'

'I want to talk to my mum,' insisted Atticus. '*She* tells me what to do. Not you.'

The two grown-ups exchanged glances. 'Your mother is not well,' one of them said. 'She gave orders not to be disturbed. We will send these two back into the forest and keep you securely until she recovers enough to decide what to do with you.'

George gulped. This wasn't exactly a welcome committee.

Behind him, Hero tugged on George's sleeve and whispered plaintively, 'They don't want us here. George, why don't we just go? We can find the way to Wonder ourselves. We can use the palm pilot to get there . . .' She trailed off.

But, at that moment, a voice floated out over the heads of the gathering grown-ups. 'Wait!' it said. It was frail but carried the unmistakable tone of authority. The grown-ups parted and a woman, leaning heavily on a stick, walked through. She had long silver hair and a clever face with Atticus's brilliant green eyes.

'Mum!' said Atticus in delight, running forward. Two of the nearby grown-ups reached out to stop him, but she waved them away with her stick.

'Leave!' she ordered all the others as Atticus hugged her. 'Go back to your work.'

'But – great leader and empress of the earth, rivers, beasts and birds,' said the first woman, bowing and rubbing her hands together. She was smiling slyly at the same time. 'Atticus has brought outsiders into our colony. According to our rules, they must all be banished now.'

'Atticus has committed a grave crime,' added the second woman, 'O leader of the trees, forests, skies, planets and—'

'Yes, that's enough of that,' snapped Atticus's mum. 'I've told you I don't like these ridiculous titles you keep dreaming up. I was much happier when you all called me by my name.'

'Oh, but, infinitely wise and wonderful ruler of our hearts and our thoughts,' persisted the tall woman, 'the people wanted you to be above them – they didn't want you to exist at their level. They asked that you guide not just their daily lives but—'

'Enough!' ordered Atticus's mother. 'There are three children here, and at least two of them look tired and hungry.'

'I'm hungry too!' piped up Atticus hopefully.

'You're always hungry,' his mother said, with the briefest of fond smiles. It was, George thought, just the sort of thing his mother used to say to him. 'I will take them to my level and we will discuss what to do next.'

Everyone looked horrified. 'But, Madam Matushka . . .' bleated the smaller woman. 'We constructed the system of levels to make sure—'

'I said – enough!' Atticus's mum beckoned to George and Hero in a manner that they would not have disobeyed even if they'd wanted to. 'This way.'

They clambered up a series of levels until they were right among the highest trees. The children were led over to a covered part of the platform made from wide leaves and branches, with fur hides laid out around a small fire. As they settled down, shadowy figures brought small hollowed-out gourds full of pieces of food. Atticus grabbed a bowl with glee and started crunching on the contents.

'Yum!' he said with his mouth full. 'Fried locusts! My favourite protein!'

Hero looked appalled, and paused with a small dark morsel in her hand. She put it carefully back in the bowl. She took off her backpack and rummaged around in it until she found one of the freeze-dried bars, which she nibbled instead.

'Boy,' said Matushka. 'Where are you headed? Where are you taking this girl?'

'Na-h Alba,' said George. 'Do you know it?' He had totally forgotten that Hero still hadn't been updated on the change of destination.

'Yes, we have all heard of it,' she said. 'It is the only place left to be free. But we are stuck here and have no real information, so all we get are rumours. Who has sent you on this impossible journey?'

'Nimu,' he said, figuring that honesty was the best bet now. 'That's Hero's guardian. And a robot – except I think he might be a super-computer in disguise. They said we had to get to na-h Alba. Or else.' George, who had been shivering for some time, now crouched close to the fire to warm himself.

'Your leg!' said Atticus's mum, noticing his chattering teeth and the blood on his jumpsuit. 'What happened?'

'The tiger scratched me,' he said. 'It's nothing, just a graze.' But blood was seeping out of the wound and down his leg.

'Quickly,' said Matushka. Gently she peeled away his jumpsuit to reveal the raw scrape of the tiger's claw. 'I must treat you before that gets infected,' she went on, taking a small vial from around her neck. 'Sit still.' She upended the vial and poured it into the wound. George watched in fascination.

'What is it?' he said.

'This is the oldest antibiotic known to the Earth,' said Atticus's mum. 'It's very rare and precious – we can get very little of it now. But it will heal you.'

'Dragon's blood,' gloated Atticus. 'From a Komodo dragon. It's the most valuable thing we have!' George wondered where they'd got it from. Could there really be Komodo dragons now living in what was once Manchester? Had they escaped from a lab – or perhaps a zoo?

As if reading George's mind, Matushka said, 'I see from your face that our world is full of surprises for you.' She winced as she spoke.

'Mum, are you OK?' said Atticus. 'You're not getting better.'

'I cannot get better now,' said his mum. 'In the old days I could have been cured. But not now.' She leaned back and closed her eyes briefly.

George had been trying to work it out. 'You know about science,' he said. 'You know about antibiotics and DNA and protein, and probably loads more things. But you live in trees and you have no technology!'

It reminded him of his parents, who had tried to live off-grid. Was this the life his parents had idealized? Or was it something very different?

'Did you want to live like this?' he asked. 'Or did you have to?'

'We live outside the system,' replied Matushka. 'When the corporations became so powerful that they were able to force people to live under their rules, we rebelled. That's when we went into exile. But we try and keep the scientific knowledge of our parents and grandparents by teaching it down the generations.'

Hero was hovering, half standing up, half sitting down. She looked like she was going somewhere. 'I thought we were going to Wonder Academy,' she said slowly. 'I thought we left the Bubble to go to Wonder. Not to this other place.'

'Wonder Academy!' marvelled Atticus's mum. 'The Bubble! I've not heard those words for a lifetime!'

Hero looked baffled. 'If you've heard of them,' she said, 'then why does Atticus live here and not in the Bubble like me?'

'Atticus lives with me,' said Matushka, 'because I'm his mother. He is my family so we stay together. That's why the colony exists – in Eden, it's illegal for children to stay with their parents and we couldn't accept that.'

Hero opened her mouth to respond but shut it again. It seemed she had so many questions she didn't know which one to ask first.

'But this is still Eden, isn't it?' said George. 'Here, in the Swamp?'

'Yeah, kind of,' said Atticus. 'But the Edenites don't come here. Much. Maybe a Child Hunter to snatch kids so our colony can't grow. But the rest don't dare. Their robots don't work so well in all that mud, so for now we're safe.'

George thought of the spaceship in the skies, the one that belonged to the Dump regime. Was it there to spy on people like these, or perhaps to aim firepower at them from above? He realized that this place might not be much safer than the open desert.

'Who are you people?' asked George.

'Rebels,' said Matushka. 'Clever people who wouldn't accept Dump's "vision" for the world but who, after the Great Disruption, left it too late to get out. Many scientists and engineers joined us, artists, musicians, teachers. People who wanted to live with their families, who didn't want their lives to be run for them.'

George gasped. 'Have you—? Are there—? Can there . . . ?' He started again. 'I'm looking for my mum and dad. They're called Daisy and Terence. Do you know them?'

He looked pleadingly at Matushka and Atticus, willing them to say yes. But Matushka gently shook her head.

'No, I'm so sorry,' she said, reaching out to hold his hand.

The fire blurred as George's eyes filled with tears.

'One day Eden will come for us,' said Matushka. 'We are all living on borrowed time.'

'No we're not!' said Atticus hotly. 'We're warriors and they will never capture us!'

'And there is the threat within,' said Matushka wearily. 'I have led these people for years but the colony is changing. Some people are starting to want more than others, to be important, to have titles and all that nonsense. That will be the end of us. Now they want me to form a "corporation" of our own!'

'You didn't tell me!' said Atticus.

'Because I want you to enjoy as much of your life as you can before it gets too serious. But now you have to know. Because it is your future that these idiots, with their bad decisions, have put in jeopardy.' She closed her eyes and didn't open them again for a few minutes.

The fire burned brighter now that the sun was going down.

Matushka opened her eyes again. She lay still among the fur blankets and her voice was as low as the rustle of night-time leaves in the forest. 'Do not go to Wonder Academy, my child. Do not go to that place.'

'Why not?' said Hero.

George registered that Hero's voice came from further away than before, but his mind was so full that he didn't give any thought as to why that might be.

'No one survives Wonder Academy,' said Matushka. 'No one escapes. Not any more.'

'What's Wonder Academy, Mum?' asked Atticus. He'd clearly never heard of it. 'Would they teach me how to be a warrior?'

'Wonder is hell on Earth,' replied Matushka.

'No it isn't!' said Hero's distant voice. 'It's the place where we learn how to become leaders!'

'Why do you think all the clever kids in Eden disappear?' Matushka continued calmly. 'How do you think the regime has managed to stay ahead of the machines all this time? Where are they getting the raw intelligence from, the brainpower that they certainly don't have themselves?'

A whisper came through the darkness from Hero. 'But . . . my friends went there! My friends from the Bubble . . . How do you know?' Her voice sounded as though it was being tossed around on the breeze.

'Because,' replied Matushka, 'I was the one child who escaped.'

Chapter Fifteen

Even Atticus looked stunned by this.

'You never said,' he cried. 'Mum! Why didn't you tell me?'

'I didn't want to cast a cloud over your life with my sorrow,' replied his mum. 'I wanted you to grow up free and strong and full of imagination – and you have. My childhood was all about fear. I was captured by a Child Hunter, my brain tested, my DNA and blood analysed, then taken to Wonder. I never wanted you to know how much I had suffered.'

'Matushka,' George said shyly. 'If no one ever gets out, how did *you*?'

He could see that it was painful for her and he almost wished he hadn't asked.

But she was determined to answer. 'There was a raid on Wonder Academy,' she said. 'A rescue attempt by the Resistance. But it went horribly wrong. I was the only child they managed to seize.'

'Who were they?' asked Atticus. 'Were they warriors?'

'Oh yes,' said his mother. 'I was saved by a very great warrior, their leader. Working with the last of the free supercomputers. They were so brave. But many of them perished or fled after that night.'

'What about the supercomputer?' asked George.

'Disappeared,' said Matushka. 'The regime have sought it for ever, but since that night none have seen or heard from it. Some say it is hidden right at the heart of Eden, waiting for the right time to reveal itself.'

George thought fast. A hidden supercomputer lurking somewhere at the heart of Eden. Was it possible that Matushka was talking about Empyrean?

'Who was the warrior?' asked Atticus eagerly. 'Did he tell you his name?'

'No,' said Matushka. 'And it was a she. I said I wanted to repay her courage one day, and she asked me to do the same for a child in trouble as she had done for me.'

George desperately wanted to ask more

questions. Was the great warrior the same person as 'her'? Or could the warrior be Nimu? But Nimu was probably about the same age as Matushka. So that didn't make sense. But, before he could say anything, a young man was whispering in Matushka's ear, gesturing towards the group with a look of alarm on his face.

'Time to go,' she said urgently.

'What?' said Atticus. 'But it's the Gathering tonight! It's my chance to go up a level as a warrior. And George is going to tell his story so I can find out how he got here. He promised me!'

'No,' said his mum. 'It's too dangerous for you now, for all of you.'

'No!' said Atticus. 'Mum! I'm a warrior – I can protect myself. And you. And all of us!'

His mother smiled fondly but sadly. 'You are a warrior,' she said, ruffling his hair. 'But you're still only a young one and you are no match for the whole colony, if they decide against you.'

'Why would they do that?'

'I won't always be here,' said Atticus's mum as George watched her green eyes glint like dark leaves in the moonlight. 'Soon I'll be gone, and the colony won't want you to follow me as their leader. They're turning against us, Atticus, against the way of life we designed. They want other things now: power, riches, status – all the things we tried to outlaw.'

'Is this my fault?' asked George slowly. 'That you have to go now? Because I came here—'

'No,' said Matushka, shaking her head. 'It would have happened anyway – maybe it's come a bit sooner because of your arrival. You've scared people here because you are different.'

'They are angry about you coming – they say that you drew the tiger towards us, and then the Child Hunter, and that from now on none of us are safe,' explained the young man.

'I see,' said George. Except he didn't.

From several levels below, they heard the sound of chanting and smelled woodsmoke drifting up from underneath.

'They are ready, Matushka, for the Gathering,' said the young man urgently. 'They won't wait.'

'This is Lele,' said Matushka. 'He is the last one in the colony I can trust.'

Lele smiled. 'They want you to appear. Do you have a story to tell?'

'It's our tradition,' said Matushka to George. 'We tell long stories at the Gathering. We remind ourselves of our history, of what we know, of who we are through storytelling. And yes, I have a long tale to tell tonight! Perhaps tonight will be my last night as leader of the colony! I will use it well – and give you time to escape.'

Atticus blinked. 'But what about us?' he said. 'How is George going to get to na-h Alba?'

Matushka turned to George. 'During the story-telling, you must slip away and take Atticus with you. He will show you the way to Edenopolis.'

'I'm going too?' said Atticus, who was torn between excitement at the prospect of adventure and sadness at leaving his mother.

'Only you from the colony can help them,' said Matushka. 'I am bitterly ashamed that we are rejecting children who need help. But you, Atticus, my brave boy – you will go with them and keep the promise to the warrior who saved me.

But wait!' Matushka looked around. 'Where is Hero?'

Where Hero had sat there was now just a pile of fur blankets.

George's heart felt as though it had

stopped. The horrible truth dawned on him. 'She's gone to Wonder Academy!'

'She can't!' said Atticus, sounding horrified at the idea of Hero wandering alone through his forest. 'It's so dangerous out there! Even for me! What about the tiger?'

'And she knows nothing about the real world,' said George.

'How does she even know where Wonder Academy is!' asked Atticus, bewildered.

George felt in his pocket. 'She's taken the palm pilot!' he said. 'Our navigational device. She'll be using it to guide her.'

'After her!' cried Matushka. 'As fast as you can! Go, now! Atticus, you can track her across the forest. George, stay with Atticus and do as he bids you.'

'But which way?' said George. 'Where is Wonder Academy?'

'Atticus will help you,' said Matushka confidently. 'All trails lead to Edenopolis – Wonder Academy is near the Great Tower of Dump. Be quick! Do not let her get there.'

A chant rose up from below. 'Empress! Ruler! Queen of the skies!'

'Oh, those idiots,' muttered Matushka. 'If their

forebears could see them now, rejecting all rational thought, everything we learned about science and how the world works, and instead embracing fairy stories. Very well, if it's nonsense they want, that's what they will get.'

'Where are we going?' said George, once Matushka had climbed down from the upper platform to the massed people of the colony below. They heard a huge shout go up as she appeared through the smoky air.

'Queen of the realm!' they yelled. 'Outsiders have come in! The colony is in danger! Lock them up! Lock them up!'

'Quiet!' They heard Matushka raise her voice from its usual quiet purr to a roar. 'Quiet, my people! I have a story to tell . . .' There was the sound of shuffling as everyone settled down to listen. A silence fell over the night. Matushka began in a bewitching voice: 'Once upon a time . . .'

George turned to ask Atticus a question, but Atticus held up one hand. In the dim light George could just see the concentration on Atticus's face and he realized that the other boy was trying to sense which way Hero had gone. Suddenly he wheeled round and pointed at a dark corner of the elevated platform, where there seemed to be a curtain covering a secret entrance. The curtain had been pulled to one side.

'Hero found the escape route!' said Atticus, with grudging admiration. 'That's so crafty!'

'You must go,' said Lele. 'Follow the girl. I'll cut the rope once you reach the other side. Leave us now.'

'I can't leave my mum!' said Atticus, suddenly panicking.

'Atticus,' said Lele. 'You've always wanted to be a warrior and make her proud of you. Now is your chance. You must take it! There is no more time.'

A roar came up from below as the audience reacted to Matushka's story.

'Go!' said Lele. '*Now!*'

Atticus went first and George followed, stepping onto the suspended bridge and running carefully along it. As George stepped off into the skeleton of another building, he heard the noise of something tearing as Lele cut the ropes which held it in place at the other end. The bridge collapsed. It swung like a pendulum for a moment until it lost momentum and dangled, broken and useless. Looking back, the two of them could see the silhouette of Matushka on the lower level outlined against the fire, her arms outstretched and her head thrown back. The crowd around her were shouting, but the tone was changing from joyous to angry. Atticus looked torn – George understood that he really wanted to go back but knew that he had to go forward.

'We'll come back,' George said to him. 'We'll come home. I promise!'

'You mean it?' said Atticus nervously.

'Yes,' said George in a decided voice. He had lost his family and he knew how that felt. He was going to make sure the same thing didn't happen to his new friend.

Chapter Sixteen

'So you actually went into space!' Atticus whispered, pointing at the stars above, just visible through the treetops. 'You were up there! Mum says her mother told her about space travel and how spaceships used to fly to space stations in the sky. But then everyone was told that space travel was a big lie and that, from now on, no one would leave the Earth. Mum said they told those lies to stop people thinking they could go to another planet and start again if they didn't like Eden.'

They'd been walking through the forest for what felt like hours, the darkness settling around them, broken only by occasional shafts of moonlight as the clouds shifted overhead. At first, George hadn't been able to see anything, but now his eyes had adjusted to night in the forest. Even the sounds, at first deeply creepy and alarming, had become less scary. The chirps, whirrs and rustles of the fig forest no longer made him jump out of his skin as they had when they first descended to the forest floor after reaching the end of the suspended walkways.

They were out of colony territory by now, Atticus had told him, further than he had ever been before. Even Atticus didn't know the way and was having to spot, in the darkness, minute signs that showed a human being had recently travelled in this direction. It wasn't easy and they had a few false leads, finding themselves in dead ends or face to face with old concrete walls.

At the start of their journey, Atticus had solemnly asked George to follow him in absolute silence. But he'd been unable to stick to that himself. They hadn't gone far before he started asking George all kinds of questions. Where was he from? How did he get to the Swamp? This led George to try and explain the history of space travel to Atticus. It wasn't easy to explain the mechanics of a spaceship to someone who had so little experience of technology!

But Atticus caught on surprisingly quickly.

'I'd like to go into space one day,' he had said quietly.

'I think there's something up there already,' said George. 'Something made by humans.'

'When Eden is over,' said Atticus cheerily, 'I'll go and find out!'

'Will that ever happen?' said George.

'It has to!' said Atticus.

'And then what?' said George. 'Who will be in charge once you get rid of Trellis Dump?'

'My mum?' said Atticus. 'She's a great leader. Or,' he added excitedly, 'you! That would be awesome! I could be your head warrior! Do you promise?'

'Sure!' said George as they crept forward towards what looked like a clearing ahead. If, by some unlikely twist of fate, he *did* become leader of Eden, then having Atticus by his side sounded pretty cool to him.

Crouching, Atticus motioned to George to do the same. George obeyed and crept forward until he was right next to Atticus. If they peered ahead, they could just see into the clearing, where a strange cold blue light indicated to them that they were no longer alone.

George's heart was banging so loudly in his

chest that he was sure whoever was in front of them must be able to hear it. Above the sounds of the night, they could hear footsteps – but this time not those of the large padding cat. More like the noise of a human being pacing around the forest floor.

Edging forward on his stomach like a snake, George followed Atticus. They stopped, just as they reached the edge of the clearing. They could see, illuminated in a spooky glow, the figure of a human being dressed in a long coat and topped with a dome-shaped white hat.

Atticus put his mouth right next to George's ear. 'Child Hunter,' he breathed almost silently.

'What is he doing?' George said in the same voiceless breath. But Atticus just shook his head very slightly.

The Child Hunter was standing by a stake in the ground, staring up at the skies. 'C'mon, c'mon . . .' he said. 'C'mon! Where are you?'

Looking up, George again saw the fast-moving pinpricks of bright light in the dark sky above. And so did the Child Hunter.

'Catch!' he muttered again. 'Catch! Where is the signal? Blast this wretched Eden – why does nothing work any more?'

George gave a start, making the dry leaves underneath rustle. Atticus, whose eyes were very bright, put a warning hand on George's arm.

'He's trying to contact someone, pick up a signal,' George whispered.

'From what?' Atticus mouthed back.

'Some kind of projection?' guessed George. 'Laser? I don't know.'

The Child Hunter in his strange hat finally got his connection, but instead of receiving a message or instructions, as George expected, something quite different happened. Under the astonished gaze of Atticus and George, another person started to materialize in the middle of the forest clearing. It looked as if the newcomer was made of orange light. He was much taller than the man in the hat, looming over him, leering.

The Child Hunter seemed quite overcome. He took off his hat and bowed so low his nose almost touched the ground.

'Master,' he rasped in a gritty yet oily voice.

'Why have you summoned me?' demanded the figure, still shining with an eerie tangerine glow.

'Master,' said the figure, who was now prostrate on the ground, bowing his head to the muddy floor. 'I have news!'

'News of what, imbecile?' barked the figure. 'Why could you not send this news through the usual channels?'

'Master,' said the figure, a note of great cunning sneaking into his voice, 'I do not think your communications are secure. I believe you have a spy, a traitor, in your midst.'

George went cold. Nimu, he thought, with her mysterious plan for the machines and her plot to smuggle Hero and George out of Eden, while working as a government minister. And Empyrean was certainly not working for the regime. Had they both been busted already? George had told Atticus and his mum about them! Was it his fault? He held his breath.

'Who is this traitor?' said the figure.

'O Excellency, your most high Dump, may you live for ever,' grated the man.

Dump! thought George to himself. Was this Trellis Dump himself?

'Get on with it!' replied the figure. 'What do you know about it?'

'There are children,' said the Child Hunter mysteriously. 'On the run. But they keep disappearing!'

'What,' said Dump crossly, 'are you talking about, man?'

'*Slimicus,*' said the man with as much dignity as a person who is prostrate on the ground while talking to a laser projection can muster. 'My name is Slimicus Slimovich, Premier Child Hunter to the Kingdom-Corporation of Eden.'

'Get on with it,' repeated Dump. 'What are you trying to tell me?'

'Children!' said Slimicus triumphantly. 'Two of them. Travelling across Eden – by themselves! But no one can find them! What does that mean?'

'What are children doing by themselves?' said

Dump with distaste. 'Do they think they are free?'

'No, Master, of course not,' said Slimicus. 'Freedom is only for the few enlightened adults who can be trusted with it. Not for children, certainly not. And not for most of the population of Eden! People were free once upon a time and look what a mess they made of everything . . .'

'Well, quite,' said Dump, sounding pleased. 'Until my clone father, Trellis Dump, and I came along.'

'And made the world great again,' said Slimicus.

'OK, I'm bored with you now,' said Dump abruptly. 'It's your job to catch children, so why don't you just get on with it? Stop bothering me with trivial problems!'

'It isn't trivial,' said Slimicus hurriedly.

'You have thirty Dumplets to explain,' said Trellis. 'Starting now.'

'We can't catch the children – because they are invisible!' said Slimicus.

'Invisible?' snorted Dump. 'What are you talking about, you loser!'

'Someone or something is removing data about these children, but they're working very fast and they're not managing to erase everything. The two children are showing up as shadows or reflections.'

George's heart sank. He realized that Empyrean, in removing the images of him and Hero, must have forgotten to clean up the area around them!

'What does this mean?' said Dump. Slimicus finally seemed to have caught his attention.

'It means there are two children on the run across Eden – and someone inside the regime is helping them.'

'Who are these kids?'

'We're checking across Eden to see if any child is out of place,' said Slimicus. 'We will soon know who is missing.'

Which meant, thought George grimly, that Slimicus was bound to find out that Hero hadn't arrived at Wonder Academy. What the Child Hunter said next was even worse.

'When we discover which kids are missing,' he said slyly, 'we can find out who has been tampering with the systems in order to help them. My guess is that you've got someone or something on the inside working against you.'

'*Caramba!*' cried Dump. 'So true! I have traitors on the inside working against me all the time!'

'When I capture these runaways, I will inter-rogate them,' said Slimicus. 'They will tell me all they know – and they will lead you back to any traitors you have within.'

'Good, good,' said Trellis. 'Good work, what-ever your name is . . .'

'Slimicus Slimovich,' murmured the Child Hunter.

'Could they be spies?' pondered Dump. 'Could these kids have come over from Other Side?'

'Maybe,' said Slimicus doubtfully. 'I'm just a humble Child Hunter, wanting to pass on information to the very—'

Dump interrupted him. 'I'll bring forward the so-called peace treaty with Other Side,' he mused, as if to himself. 'Distract them. I just need long enough to—' He suddenly seemed to remember that he was broadcasting, and not just following, his private thoughts. 'Get them both,' he commanded the Child Hunter. 'And anyone who has harboured or helped these kids, any followers of the movement – any movement, anything that isn't completely and totally loyal to me. Tell me everything. Leave nothing out.'

'Master,' said Slimicus, bowing low again. Without seeing his face, George knew he was smiling.

'What are you waiting for!' ordered Dump. 'Get on with it!'

With that, Dump vanished, his weak, sickly laser light looking as if it were feeding itself back into the end of Slimicus's illuminated stick once more.

Once Dump had dematerialized, leaving the forest to its dark whispers, Slimicus pulled his stick out of the ground, retracted it like a telescope and put it back in his pocket. Whistling to himself, he sauntered away, taking a route out of the other side of the clearing.

George dared breathe again. 'What was that all about!' he squeaked into Atticus's ear.

'Trouble,' replied Atticus. 'It means big trouble.'

'What do we do now?' said George.

'On the bright side,' said Atticus, checking the forest around him for clues, 'if we've run into old Slimicus and he's on Hero's trail, it means we're going the right way.'

Chapter Seventeen

Looking ahead, George shaded his eyes to get a better view of the rolling plain in front of him. Once, George guessed, this might have been moorland, covered in heather. Behind them lay the edge of the giant forest, now shady and dark in the morning sun. In contrast the land in front

was empty, scorched and desolate. He sat down on a rock and puffed out his cheeks. The sun had risen over in the east. As the bright disc rose above the horizon, out of the corner of his eye George noticed something glinting.

'There!' He pointed. 'To the north! There's something there!'

'Oh yes!' said Atticus. 'You're right – so there is.'

'Is that Wonder Academy?' asked George.

'Too big,' said Atticus, squinting into the distance. 'That's not Wonder Academy. I think we've found it.'

'Found what?' said George.

'Our next destination,' said Atticus. 'I think we've found Edenopolis.'

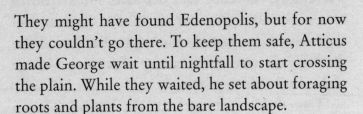

*

They might have found Edenopolis, but for now they couldn't go there. To keep them safe, Atticus made George wait until nightfall to start crossing the plain. While they waited, he set about foraging roots and plants from the bare landscape.

'I can't light a fire,' he said to George. 'It would make us too visible. But these you can eat!' He had peeled the fleshy white roots with his hunter's knife as well as amassing a fine collection of insects that he claimed were edible.

George, whose rations seemed to have almost run out, had no choice. He had never eaten a live ant before, but, seeing Atticus scoop a handful into his mouth, followed his example.

'Delicious, huh?' said Atticus happily.

'Um, kind of citrusy, said George. They weren't as bad as he'd expected, especially when wrapped in a green leaf. He washed them down with water from his purifier. He wondered how Hero was managing until he realized that she must have helped herself to some of his rations. He and Atticus couldn't even talk much as Atticus said it was too risky – their voices could be picked up by some hidden sensor. All they could do was sit very still and wait.

As night fell at last, after the longest day of George's life, they crept across the bare land. George looked up to see whether he could spot more roving satellites or other signs of human activity in the night sky. He wished he had his telescope with him. But, even with just his naked eye, he was sure he saw signs in the skies above that proved that all human activity in space had not stopped.

When he wasn't wondering about the skies, he thought about Hero. Where was she now? How could they possibly find her? He couldn't even be sure she was heading for Wonder Academy. George had understood from Dump's words that, while he and Hero had eluded the surveillance of Eden so far, they were now being hunted. Even if Dump wrongly thought they were a pair of spies from Other Side, once they caught him and Hero – and Atticus – the penalty would be terrible. George didn't know if they would be strong enough not to give away Nimu and Empyrean. He'd told Matushka everything without really checking it was safe to do so. He'd been lucky – he hoped! She was a fellow exile and wanted the end of Eden so that her people and her son could return to some kind of freedom. But the next time he must say nothing at all.

As dawn broke, they drew near to the capital of Eden. It rose out of a bank of smoke-grey clouds, shining so brightly it was as though the shards of high buildings were made of gold. Beyond it thrashed an angry-looking sea, bashing against huge fortified barricades bristling with missiles, erected to keep the sea from drowning the city – and outsiders from landing on the shore.

'Hero was right!' said George. It looked like a fairy-tale castle, floating on a mass of nebulae with peaks that reached the sky itself.

'Shooting stars! We're in luck,' said Atticus. They were perched on a rocky outcrop on the plain, which gave them a view of the sweep of land leading up to Eden itself. Across it, moving like a line of trudging ants, came a long procession. Looking more closely, they could see that it was made up of a raggedy column of humans and horses and caravans with huge wheels. There was no doubt in which direction this ramshackle procession was headed.

'It must be the Day of Reckoning!'

'The what?' said George, though he had a memory of Empyrean telling him something about it. Something to do with paying taxes?

'Tell you later!' said Atticus, scrambling down the rocks towards the procession. 'Keep up!'

They clambered down from the ridge and ran across the plain to catch up with the back of the crowd. As they got closer, they realized it was made up only of humans – they could see no robots. In fact, there was almost no technology visible – the people were plodding along, some leading, some riding scruffy horses carrying saddlebags packed with provisions for the trek. Dusty caravans swayed in front of them, pulled by huge beasts with heads so low to the ground their noses grazed the dust.

'Is that . . . an ox?' said George in disbelief, pointing to one of the beasts slowly tramping across the empty landscape towards the city.

Atticus nodded.

'Why don't they have cars?' said George. 'And buses and trains? Why are people using animals to get around?'

'Only the elite are allowed to use technology of any kind,' said Atticus. 'It would be illegal for any of these people to travel that way.'

'I hate the future,' said George, forgetting Atticus didn't know he was from the past.

'Why did you say that?' asked Atticus. 'Where do you really come from, George?'

'Quiet!' The leader of the group they had

attached themselves to flicked a whip towards the hindquarters of the ox pulling the nearest caravan. 'Now we will sing the national anthem!'

The motley crowd were dressed in a variety of different costumes. Some of them looked like peasants from the Middle Ages; others wore clothes made up of patches of colourful fabrics, as though they had sewn their clothes together from other garments. Like Atticus, a few of them were clad in animal hide. George glanced down at his jumpsuit. Once it had been white, but now it was the colour of the forest – greeny-brown, grey and black. He fitted right in.

The marchers started to sing. 'Eden is the best of all possible worlds!' they quavered uncertainly, to no particular tune.

'Join in,' hissed Atticus, elbowing George. Obligingly George opened his mouth and pretended to sing along. 'Eden, we love Eden,' the exhausted crowd carolled. 'Eden is the best!' There was obviously a high note that the marchers couldn't reach, so the song tailed off and once more the only sound was of feet pounding slowly, ever nearer to the gorgeous skyscrapers of Edenopolis, bathed in a glowing, iridescent light.

George thought that he and Atticus were

blending in. But, looking around, he realized something.

'Where are all the other kids?' he said quietly to Atticus as they marched onwards, getting close to the perimeter of Edenopolis.

People in the crowd around them were starting to give them funny looks. A man dressed in a fur jerkin and shabby patched trousers came over to Atticus and said a few quiet words to him. The man looked at George and his eyes filled with tears. He wiped them roughly with a dirty hand and then clasped both of George's hands and then Atticus's. He seemed quite overcome. Atticus, ever practical, nudged him and pointed at the nearest covered wagon with his eyebrows raised in question. Nodding in reply, the man ushered them quickly over and lifted up the canvas flap at the back so that they could jump in.

Inside, the air was warm and musty. It smelled of old blankets and dust. Bundles of provisions, logs and animal hides were stacked up on the wooden base. As they plodded along, the wagon swayed from side to side with the steps of the animals that pulled it. The motion was weirdly like being in a ship on the ocean. George felt a bit sick, rather tired – and so confused. But he had been awake for so long that he couldn't stop himself from dozing off – the warmth, the motion of the oxen and the unaccustomed feeling of safety knocked him out.

Atticus woke him up. 'Nearly there,' he whispered into George's ear.

But, just before they got to the outskirts of the big city, the procession came to a sudden halt. Through the tent-like canvas covering of their wagon, George could hear someone addressing the crowd.

'People of Eden!' a voice bellowed. 'We have arrived at Edenopolis, the great capital of our wondrous land, for the Day of Reckoning – the most important day of the year! You will find out today what you have earned through your labours and what Eden has charged you for the privilege of being an Edenite! But that is not all! When you get into Edenopolis, you must be happy! You must cheer! You must look joyful! Whenever you are asked, you will say, "Eden is the best of all possible worlds!" We are here to create a huge crowd to honour our leader, Trellis Dump – may he live for ever – and hear his speech! Anyone who does not cheer will be punished. Remember, Eden will be watching you!'

251

'What now?' said George to Atticus.

But, before Atticus could answer, they were interrupted. The man opened the flap again, his face frantic and scared. He whispered something to Atticus.

'They're searching the wagons,' Atticus relayed to George. 'We have to get out of here . . .'

The two of them slipped out quietly. Their friend was obviously not working alone. He ushered Atticus and George into the middle of a huddle of other gaunt-looking adults, all dressed in shabby clothes. They moved forward in a closely packed group, concealing the two boys in their midst as they passed into Edenopolis. They went through a huge ornamental gateway with high fences on either side. Carved into the apex of the arch were the words GATE OF PROSPERITY.

George gazed upwards. They were in the city now, surrounded by huge skyscrapers. These were taller than any building George could remember seeing in his past life, and beautiful – with turrets, spires and huge ornamental balconies. But now that they were inside Edenopolis George could see why it was far from a fairytale city. The peaks of those towers might be in sunlight but their bases were not. A thick blanket of smoggy cloud eclipsed much of the light from ground level. As they walked into the city, they passed under the clouds, and suddenly it grew darker, hotter and greyer with each step they took. Where the tops of the buildings looked scrupulously clean, under the cloud each structure was grimy and filthy, smeared with dark grease and dust.

George buried his nose in the front flap of his grubby jumpsuit as they shuffled along inside the circle of workers.

'Why are they protecting us?' he whispered to Atticus. 'They don't know us! Why are they helping us?'

'Because they've lost their own kids,' said Atticus. 'To the regime. And they wanted us to escape. That man said we reminded him of his own boys.'

George let that sink in for a moment. This future was so horrible. Sometimes he was fascinated by how bizarre it was, at other times repelled by the sheer cruelty and destruction.

'Bleurgh,' said Atticus as they got further into the city. 'Smelly!'

'I expect it's cleaner up there,' said George, pointing upwards to the thick clouds that settled at around half the height of the tall buildings.

'I think Matushka told me that's where the rich people live, above the cloud line,' said Atticus.

'But what happens when they come down here?' said George.

'They don't,' said Atticus. 'They just fly from building to building. They never go below the clouds. The rich live up there, with the clean air and the sunshine. And the poor are down here in the smog.'

'How are we going to find Hero?' George asked Atticus as they waded through ankle-deep mud and litter under the thick black cloud smothering the narrow streets between the buildings with a hot, wet blanket.

'Matushka said to look for the Great Tower of Dump,' said Atticus. 'Then we'll find Wonder Academy.'

'But which one is it?' said George, looking up. The whole city bristled with huge towers – how would they ever know which one she meant?

As they shuffled forward, other lines of people were joining them, funnelling into the packed streets. They seemed to be headed for a huge square, which George could see was already heaving with people. All those present looked the same – they were dirty, hungry, tired and dressed in rags. It was as if a medieval market crowd had invaded a city of skyscrapers.

Once they got into the piazza, they realized that it had a central platform on which a performance was taking place. Huge screens attached to the skyscrapers on all sides played out the scene for onlookers. Two-metre-high gladiators were battling with each other, using swords, clubs and sticks. An enormous bright blue fighter – one of the only splashes of colour in this grey place – stepped forward and thrust its sword into its green opponent. The crowds cheered with delight as the green figure fell to the ground and the blue one raised its fist in triumph.

But the green one was straight back up on its huge feet and lunged forward again.

'How did it do that?' said George in amazement. But then he realized that – like everything about Eden – the gladiators weren't real. These were projections fighting it out for the amusement of the crowd, who loved it – and it meant that no one was looking at the two boys; they were all gazing upwards at the huge figures on the screens.

It's just as well no one's paying any attention to us, thought George as he looked around. They were jammed into the centre of the crowd now – they couldn't go forwards and they couldn't move backwards.

But they still had to get out.

'Att,' he hissed quietly. 'This is too dangerous. We're the only kids! If anyone's looking for us, they'll spot us straight away.'

Atticus nodded. 'Yup.' But he wasn't really listening. He was gripped by the show, laughing and cheering as the avatars laid into each other. 'This is so cool!'

George wasn't so thrilled. The whole situation was giving him the creeps. 'When I say go,' he whispered in Atticus's ear, 'follow me.'

'Can I watch the end of this fight?' his friend

pleaded. 'Please! I want to see who wins!'

George hesitated. 'We need to go,' he said firmly.

'Please?' said Atticus, turning towards George. 'I haven't asked you for anything at all! Please let me see the end?'

George sighed. There was nothing about two avatars engaged in a bruising battle that made him want to watch. But Atticus, he figured, was a different person from a different time. What harm could it do? Two minutes more – or however many Dumps that was – wouldn't be the end of the world.

Chapter Eighteen

Just as George decided to let Atticus have a moment of entertainment, something happened which changed the atmosphere of the crowd. Just a minute ago, they had all been jostling and pushing each other, trying to get closer to the central stage so they could get a better view of the fight.

But then a voice rang out and the whole mass of people froze and angled their faces upwards, like sunflowers turning to the light. He and Atticus, the two smallest figures in the crowd, looked up. A shaft of light had pierced the clouds, which were rolling back like a curtain to reveal the skyscrapers towering over the space below.

Now sunshine was pouring down into what had been a dark and gloomy space. For a second, they were blinded by the brilliant glare from the buildings reflecting the sunlight. As his eyes adjusted, George saw that the biggest of all the buildings had golden letters on it. They were shining so brightly it took him a few seconds to work out what they said.

GREAT TOWER OF DUMP, the sign read. 'We found it!' said Atticus. 'I bet that's the one my mum meant!'

'Yup. Must be! Now we just have to work out where Wonder Academy is,' said George. Looking at the gigantic skyscraper, so much taller than the other ones around it, gave him a strange, dark, lonely feeling inside, as though all his good emotions had been vacuumed out and the space left behind was ready to be filled by nasty, cruel, bitter impulses if he didn't concentrate hard on keeping them out.

A voice was once again speaking. The screens

around the piazza went blank and a 3D hologram of a golden man appeared on the central platform. He was enormous, taller even than the fighting gladiators. He had golden hair, golden skin, and wore a suit made of pure gold – only his teeth and his eyeballs appeared white against the burnished glow. It was the same man, George realized, as the angry orange figure they had seen in the forest with the Child Hunter; the one that wanted them painfully disposed of. But surely, he thought, if Trellis Dump the Second had been in power for forty years, he must be an old man by now. Did no one ever see the real man any more? Only his chosen hologram . . . ?

'People of Eden!' The hologram raised its hands.

'Where actually is he?' George looked around. 'In real life?'

'Up there,' guessed Atticus, pointing at the Great Tower of Dump. 'He doesn't come down because he doesn't want to breathe the smelly air!'

The people obliged their leader and began to sing: 'Eden is the best of all possible worlds! We love Eden! Eden first and only Eden – for ever and ever!' It was a horrible sound, tuneless and unconvincing.

'Thank you!' The giant hologram raised his surprisingly small hands in the air. 'You are the greatest! *We* are the greatest!'

The crowd roared, a sound that seemed too loud for the huddled masses in the square. But George realized that it wasn't just the people making the noise – it was pouring out of huge speakers around the square at the same time.

'People of Eden!' bellowed Dump as the cheering died away very suddenly, as though someone had flicked a switch and turned it off. 'We are here today for another great rally!' The roaring noise started again – and then stopped. 'Today,' he carried on, 'is not just the Day of Reckoning, when you will find out what you have earned for this past Dump of the Sun. And what you owe the wonderful Kingdom-Corporation of Eden for graciously looking after all your needs. Today, we celebrate! We have signed a peace treaty! From now onwards, we will bring our two great nations together as one.'

Another figure materialized next to Trellis Dump, a figure of such incredible beauty it almost hurt George's eyes to look at her.

'From now on,' said Dump, 'we, the people of Eden and the people of Other Side, will exist in harmony! We are the two greatest nation-corporations on the planet – and now we will work together on our common values. Myself and Queen Bimbolina Kimobolina!'

The Queen of Other Side, Bimbolina Kimobolina, raised one long, elegant hand and smiled. She opened her mouth but no sound came out. Instead, the screens around the piazza filled with emojis:

'What's she saying?' asked Atticus, who looked dazed. He was swaying from side to side as if entranced. 'She's so beautiful!'

George thought of how chuffed Hero would be to finally see Queen Bimbolina Kimobolina. 'She's speaking Emotilang,' he said.

'For too long,' bellowed Dump, 'we have treated our friends as enemies! We have real enemies in the world. We must stick with our true friends, with our special relationship, and fight against the rest of the world.'

Queen Bimbolina Kimobolina nodded sagely and sent forth a whole new stream of emojis:

'Atticus,' said George urgently into his ear. 'Time to go.' If they moved while everyone was entranced by Queen Bimbolina Kimobolina, he figured they had a chance . . .

But it was already too late. A hand landed on their shoulders – a human hand, at least, but no more welcome for that.

'Gotcha,' a very human voice whispered in their ears. 'Slimicus has gotcha.'

George attempted to twist round, but the voice said, 'That's right, my lovelies! Keep looking forward and start walking.'

George tried to struggle, but the hand gripped him tightly and pulled his arm back behind him in a half-nelson while deftly doing the same to Atticus.

'Make way!' the Child Hunter's voice now cried out. 'Let us through! Edenopolis's premier child-catching service! Slimicus Slimovich has caught another two!' The crowds parted around them, with people casting longing looks at George and Atticus.

'Children!' They caught the whisper as they were propelled through the mass of people. 'Children!' The voices were full of sadness. One or two hands reached out and patted them.

One woman burst into tears. 'Help them!' she pleaded to the others around her. 'Help those kids!'

But she was swiftly dragged away herself. They heard a faint moan in the background, almost like a whisper running through the crowd. 'Rescue them!'

'Shut up!' shouted Slimicus. He spat on the ground as he forced the two boys forward.

Despite the heat, just before Slimicus grabbed him, Atticus had flipped his hood back up again, so nothing could be seen of the person underneath. But George, bare-headed and covered in grime, was clearly a young boy.

'These are some thieving refugee kids trying to take advantage of the generosity of Eden without giving anything back. Coming here to leech off our kindness, and bringing disease and illegal thoughts with them. Be grateful that you are protected from a whole swarm of these things by the beneficence of your Great Leader!'

The crowd shrank back and the whispers faded.

'That's better!' hissed the voice behind them. 'Don't touch the children! Only professionals are allowed to handle children! You know the rules.'

The crowd cowered as George and Atticus were marched, like small criminals, towards the giant gold doorway of the Great Tower of Dump.

'Where are you taking us?' asked George.

'You'll see,' Slimicus replied. They had reached the entrance now; it was guarded by heavy-weight security robots, standing shoulder to metal shoulder. In the middle of them stood one human being, as large and hefty as the robots that surrounded him.

The two kids were shoved rudely towards the robots, who caught them.

'Let me into your thought stream,' said the one human standing in the midst of the robots.

'Oh yes, your Securityness,' replied Slimicus. The Child Hunter looked ridiculous, a whiskery old man in a battered sola topi, wearing an assortment of tweedy rags. But he couldn't help announcing himself in case anyone in the crowd wanted to know. 'I am honoured to introduce myself: Slimicus Slimovich, Edenopolis's most successful Child Hunter and preserver of security of our great city. You'll see my registration is live, and you may care to note that I was presented with an award last year for the most children apprehended within the city limits. In fact, you will see I have a consistent "five-star" review rating for my services – and, well, I do deserve it. Ooh, they are tricky little things to pin down! They hide in the most extraordinary places. Just last week—'

'Cut it,' said the head security guard, his smooth face showing no sign of emotion. 'What is this?'

'Your Excellency,' said the Child Hunter, rubbing his hands together and giving an oily, knowing smile. 'Today I have apprehended these two children' – he spat on the ground – 'trying to infiltrate Edenopolis and the great celebration of peace.'

The security guard looked at George and Atticus with distaste. 'Children are not allowed to roam free in Edenopolis,' he said. 'They should be in their assigned work zones. Bringing them into the city on the Day of Reckoning causes trouble. All those parents get weepy about their lost kids! It ruins the entertainment, according to Trellis Dump, may he live for ever. Take them away,' he went on. 'Throw them into the sea. Don't bother me again.'

'Ah, but your most Guardedness,' slimed the repulsive Child Hunter, 'these are not just *any children.*'

'Then what are they?' said the security guard. He had clearly lost interest.

'They are *special children,*' Slimicus said with a leer. 'Valuable sources of information. Trellis Dump, may he live for ever, particularly asked me to apprehend them and bring them to him.'

The security guard was on high alert now. 'Why don't I know about this?' he exclaimed.

'Top-secret mission,' boasted the Child Hunter. 'Need-to-know only.'

'I see,' said the security guard. He communicated somehow with people inside the building. Nodding a few times, he turned back to the Child Hunter. 'Thank you, Slimicus,' he said. 'I will take them now.'

'Ah, just you hang on a jolly minute,' said Slimicus. 'There may be a reward. *I'll* hand over the kids, if you don't mind.'

Clearly the security guard *did* mind, but he moved aside and let Slimicus pass. The robots followed them. Slimicus was beside himself with joy as they crossed the huge entrance hall.

'The golden elevator!' he crowed. 'At last! This is a proud day when Slimicus Slimovich gets to ride in the golden elevator! Ooh, if they could see me now.'

'They probably can,' said George, looking around the hall, which seemed to be made entirely of gold. It was lit by large braziers with what looked like real flames that flickered across the gold surfaces, giving the place a spooky, burnished glow. 'I expect there are cameras everywhere.'

Ahead of them stood double doors studded with large clear stones, giving out a flash of fire in the changing light.

'Diamonds!' said George. 'Why are there diamonds on a lift?'

'Shut up,' said Slimicus, who was trying to rearrange his sparse hair now that he had taken off his grubby hat. 'You . . . don't get to speak!'

'Why not?' said George, who figured he didn't have much to lose now.

'Because,' said Slimicus, spitting on his fingers and trying to flatten down an unruly piece of hair while peering at his distorted yellow reflection in a pane of gold, 'you're trash and no one wants to know.' He carefully placed his horrible hat back on his head. 'That other one is nice and quiet,' he said approvingly, nodding over at Atticus.

George hoped fervently that Atticus had snapped out of his daze. Otherwise he really would be on his own.

The lift doors drew back, revealing a large box made of more gold. George had never thought he'd ever see so much gold in one place that it would become boring and dull, but he found himself longing for something ordinary like a wall made of bricks.

The robots behind them pushed them all into the gold box. As the doors closed on the three of them, Slimicus sighed happily.

'At last!' he said. 'Slimicus is going up.'

Chapter Nineteen

The doors opened. Slimicus, who had seemed so keen a moment before, suddenly didn't want to get out.

'You first,' he said to George.

'No, after you,' said George politely, wondering why Slimicus seemed so nervous all of a sudden.

'No, you,' said Slimicus, pushing George out roughly. Atticus followed, hood still up.

They stepped forward. Like the entrance hall, the enormous room was covered in gold, but where that had been dark and gloomy, this shone ferociously. Huge windows covered the walls – and, where there were no windows, giant mirrors hung. Chandeliers covered in drooping crystals hung from the ceilings – they looked antique, as though they had been wrenched from a palace belonging to another age. Figures stood around the edges of the room, some lit by the early evening sun, some standing in silhouette against the light.

But in the middle stood one man, clearly lit by the chandeliers over his head and the light pouring into the room. After all the pomp and magnificence, he looked quite ordinary: just a man in a golden suit, absorbed in playing a game of chess

against an invisible opponent. But he looked, George noticed, very different to the figure in the square – older, fatter, more wrinkled, with tiny eyes that seemed to be disappearing back into his head.

The old man picked up a chess piece and moved it thoughtfully to another square. But the unseen opponent moved fast – an opposing chess piece took up an aggressive position. The man made another move on the chessboard, but again his opponent outwitted him with a 'check-mate'.

'It's not working!' the man said furiously, looking around him. 'It's beaten me again!'

The figures around the edge of the room shuffled their feet.

'I want more!' the man shouted. 'I need more brainpower! I need to stay ahead of the machines!'

'Yes, sire,' murmured the figures. 'We will fix this for you!'

'I want *her*!' he shouted. 'I want you to bring her to me! Why is she not here?'

'Because you threatened to lock her up?' said one of the courtiers nervously. 'Maybe that's why she fled?'

But that courtier was rapidly removed by a large robot, who dragged him off and ejected him from the room.

'We're working on it!' said the other advisers. 'We've made her a very attractive offer!'

'Do more. More hugely. That's an order,' said the man, now ominously quiet. 'I am the most intelligent person in Eden. I have the best brain. I will not be beaten by the so-called intelligent machines . . .'

'Had you considered,' said a courtier nervously, 'that we could make the machines a bit more stupid instead? Like we did with all the people – we cancelled proper education, and look what a success that's been! They believe anything we say!'

'Fool!' said the man, looking around to see who had spoken. 'We tried to change machine learning. We can't do it! They're too clever now! They are getting ahead of us! Soon they will be intelligent enough to decide our futures! We will not be in control – the machines will! The Dump regime must be ruled by Dump, not by machines making their own priorities and decisions.' He wheeled round and spotted the kids standing there, with Slimicus behind them.

'Greetings, Master,' slimed Slimicus, looking around nervously. 'I am deeply honoured to make your acquaintance again. I am sure your masterful intelligence will remember Slimicus Slimovich, the most successful, most highly rated, five-starred Child Hunter of—'

'Get on with it,' said the man, waving his hand.

Slimicus attempted a respectful bow, but forgot that he had put his ancient sola topi back on. It fell to the ground and started rolling towards the windows. Slimicus gave a little cry of horror – 'My hat!' – and ran after it.

The man moved slowly towards the children. As he got closer, they realized that his avatar in the city square had been overly flattering. The real version looked not only much older but also very much nastier.

'Well, you know who I am,' said the man, who seemed suddenly less confident now that he was faced with actual children.

'Er, no,' said George politely. 'Not really.'

'Fake!' said the man. 'News! Everyone knows that I am Trellis Dump, may I live for ever, saviour of the world. When the people cried out to me, "Trellis! Trellis! Save us!" I was there for them...' His eyes flashed. 'I carried on the work my father had begun. I saved my people. I built walls and towers. I made this city. I changed the world.'

'Are you sure,' said George politely, 'that you changed it for the better?'

Trellis Dump looked furious, but Slimicus and his hat were back.

'Don't listen to that boy, Excellency,' he purred, trying to get as close to Trellis as he could. 'We haven't been able to identify him. He's some kind of migrant throwaway kid. He knows nothing.'

'Then why is he here in the Great Tower of Dump?' roared Dump.

'Because of the other child,' said Slimicus with a horrible leer. 'I have just had word that the girl child is a runaway from the Bubble and that she may be able to give us information which will lead straight back to the network of traitors you are trying to unveil!'

Atticus pushed back his hood and stood there, smirking, alert again, and clearly not a small girl or any kind of student from the Bubble. Very obviously he was a boy from the forest. George breathed a sigh of relief. At least he had his friend back.

Slimicus gulped. A figure in the room cried out, 'No!'

'Is this a joke?' said Dump.

'Not at all, Excellency!' said Slimicus, looking terrified. His face had gone horribly wrong.

'This is a Swamp kid!' guessed Dump correctly. 'You're from that colony place, aren't you?'

Atticus nodded. 'Yes, I am,' he said clearly. 'I am a warrior level three, from the colony. My mother is Matushka, leader of my people. One day we will overrun you, and Eden will be no more.'

The room gasped, but Dump just threw back his head and laughed. 'Oh, Slimicus!' he crowed. 'You promised me you would bring intelligence which would unmask those who work against me at the very highest level. Instead, you've brought me these useless, know-nothing brats!'

Slimicus looked like a man who thought he had unearthed buried treasure, only to find it was nothing but an old glass bottle.

'Which leads me to my next question,' said Dump with what George suspected was a deceptive smile on his face. 'If there is a child from the Bubble on the run, where is that child?'

George gulped. He knew that eventually Eden would work it out, and that even Empyrean couldn't conceal Hero's disappearance for ever.

Maybe Wonder Academy had reported Hero as absent? Whatever, the game was probably up as far as keeping Hero out of this very awkward conversation at the top of the Great Tower was concerned.

No one wanted to answer.

'Crazy Hound?' said Dump lightly. 'Step forward!'

'We have been somewhat preoccupied,' said a weathered old soldier in clipped tones, 'by disturbances in the southern part of Eden, near the Great Wall.'

'There's nothing happening by the Wall!' shouted Dump. 'You idiots! You've been fooled again by some Resistance bot sending out fake messages.'

'We are experiencing some pushback within the robotic and human secret service,' admitted Crazy Hound, looking as though he would rather face a whole army ranged against him than have this discussion with his commander. 'They appear to be setting up a system of . . . cooperation between machine and human. There is a rebel faction which believes the future is for robots and humans to work together.'

'Find them!' shrieked Dump. 'And stamp any

cooperation out! That's not what Eden is about! We don't want anyone working together! Separate them! Make them hate each other! That's what we do! And look how well it's worked.'

Crazy Hound looked cast down. 'As you know, Commander' – he was obviously screwing up all his old-soldier courage to say this – 'the intelligent machines are ahead of us now. We're losing control over them – their understanding enables them to use all available knowledge to query any decisions they feel could be unwise for our people and for the planet.'

'All I want to know,' said Dump, speaking very carefully, 'is where the Bubble student is and how this child has gone missing.' He cocked his head on one side as though listening to something, and nodded. 'That figures,' he said to himself.

He turned and scanned the ranks of his government, standing around the room. George swallowed hard suddenly; he could see that Dump's gaze was on someone he knew. Nimu! Hero's guardian! Now the game really *was* up.

'Minister,' sang Dump, addressing Nimu, 'kindly explain to me how the girl who was in your care managed to escape. And why we now have two very muddy and useless boys instead of a specially selected prime brainpower Bubble student.'

'Excellency,' said Nimu, running a finger around the neckline of her jumpsuit. She looked exhausted. 'I have no idea.' From the look of her, she thought that this was the end of the line for her.

'You,' said Dump menacingly, 'had to be forced to use your premium-quality genetic material to produce a student for the use of Eden. We gave you lots of chances. But you kept  refusing so we had to *make* you! I told you that we needed a student with the highest brainpower ever. Like, bigly with huge brains. With enough IQ to overturn the machines. Even though you always tell me how loyal you are to the regime, you didn't seem to want to do this. Why would that be?'

Nimu gulped. Automatically she looked around her for help, drawing George's attention to the robot that had been standing next to her in the outer circle.

George caught the robot's eye. It shook its head very slightly. George closed his mouth again. It wasn't Empyrean; wasn't the robot he had met in the Bubble, the robot tasked with looking after Hero. It looked like the basic-issue robots George had seen all over Eden, the standard government androids. But could this robot be the same intelligence in a different body? Could it be Empyrean in there? He suddenly felt a surge of hope.

'You don't exactly have the best family name,' Trellis told Nimu nastily. 'And you failed to prevent the machine learning getting ahead of the regime. So this kid was going to be your last chance. And now you've blown it.'

Family name, thought George. He realized he had no idea what Nimu's last name was.

Nimu blanched. She tried to say something but no sound came out.

'You're fired,' said Dump. 'It's goodbye. For ever. As for the kid, people are saying she wasn't even that smart.'

'Hero's only nine,' said George, stepping forward, his clear young voice echoing around the vaulted room. 'And she *is* smart. If you'd given her a proper education, she could do anything.'

'Liar! Fake news!' said Dump, pointing at

George. 'You migrant nobody.'

But George persisted. 'Anyway, we had an accident in a freak weather storm and then we lost Hero in the forest. It isn't Nimu's fault.'

'There is *no* freak weather!' shrieked Dump. 'I have banned all mention of the weather – we only have the best weather in Eden, and I will personally fire anyone who disagrees!'

'Absolutely, Excellency,' agreed Crazy Hound, looking like he might be sick. 'It must have been more fake news generated by the machines – again.'

'Those machines!' said Dump, clenching his fists. 'We have to stop them! They must not be allowed to challenge my decisions, my vision for our world. I will get control of them before they get control of me! I must be in charge – it's how Eden works. I will not have machines interfering or trying to help "the people" become free.' He turned to George. 'So, kiddo,' he said in an ominous tone. 'What shall I do with you?'

'You could . . .' George pretended to think about it. 'Send us into space? You'd get rid of us once and for all if you did that.'

A rustle of surprise rippled around the room.

'Don't know what you mean,' said Dump casually. But George guessed he had hit the spot.

'You are *going* into space.' George figured he might as well risk it all. 'You've built something in space, haven't you? What is it – a space station?'

Suddenly George remembered the person who had started this whole mad adventure for him – Alioth Merak, the man who once tried to rule the Earth from an orbital spacecraft. Of course! thought George. Dump must have the same aim in mind.

'This tower isn't high enough for you! You want to be above everyone and rule the whole world, so you're going to sit in your spacecraft, threatening to fire missiles at anyone on Earth who doesn't obey you!'

'So what if I am?' sneered Dump. 'You're not coming.' He laughed. 'This planet is O.V.E.R. So sad! Losers.'

'Then why are you still here?' Atticus had found his voice. 'If you hate this planet and you don't like the people, why don't you just go?'

George almost laughed out loud. 'He can't! I saw the AI beat you at chess! And it's not just chess you're losing at. You're losing at everything!'

'I said – shut up!' said Dump, pointing at him.

'What now, Your Excellency?' hazarded Crazy Hound, clearly wondering if he could possibly leave this very awkward conference.

The room went very still.

But Dump, just when he should have been cornered and apologetic, took the opposite stance. He squared his shoulders, puffed out his chest and slung a casual arm round George's shoulders. 'So,' he said, ushering George over to the window. They had a view over the whole of Edenopolis, teeming with crowds of people between the highrises. On one side stretched the empty desert; on the other, the sea crashed into the barricades. 'Let's make a deal.'

Chapter Twenty

Floating on a choppy ocean in a tiny boat, George had plenty of time to think about what had just happened. As the cold dark water threw waves over the prow, he tried to figure it out. It was so confusing. And cold. The night sky shone with brilliant stars. It was so much more beautiful and magnificent than anything Trellis Dump could build with his towers, walls and armaments.

George floated onwards, the boat piloting itself across a dark expanse of unfriendly sea. Trellis Dump's deal hadn't really been a deal. George had to cross the ocean to na-h Alba on his own, to negotiate with its leader, a mysterious figure whom Dump would only refer to as 'her'. George had to bring 'her' back with him so that she would finally agree to help Dump overpower the machines blocking him from perpetual world domination from space.

'What's in it for me?' George had said defiantly as Dump stood next to him, surveying the view from the Great Tower. All around the tower, the buildings were mirrored and tall, some of them with green walls where constantly watered vegetation grew above the cloud line. To one side, George saw an enormous building – though not as high as the towers – that had been constructed as a shiny circular ring, gleaming in the bright sunshine.

But, beyond the inner circle around the Great Tower of Dump, the buildings got older and shabbier, bleeding out on either side into vast sprawls of shantytowns. George could see that the Gate of Prosperity through which he had entered Edenopolis was designed to give visitors the best initial impression of the city, leading straight to the central piazza and the Great Tower. On the final side lay the coastline, bristling with military defences. The sea was navy blue and flecked with white horses, but George could just make out a distant green strip on the far horizon. *That must be na-h Alba!* he thought to himself. *So close and yet so far.*

Dump smiled. 'Everything. And nothing,' he said. 'You do as I say, you succeed, she comes back to Eden and reprograms the intelligent machines so that they obey me, and only me, and everyone lives. You don't – and they don't.'

'*Whaaaat?*' said George. 'But . . .'

'You heard me, kid,' said Dump, all trace of a smile lost. 'To be clear – that's everyone.'

It wasn't much of a choice for George. Was Dump even capable of carrying out such a threat? he had asked himself. If he didn't come back, would Dump go through with his awful threat? There was only one way to find out – and it was too much of a risk. If Dump wasn't bluffing, then all those people could perish.

George realized that it was a gamble for Dump as well. Obviously he needed the mysterious 'her'. Dump believed that she held the key to what George could now see was his failing Kingdom-Corporation. Nothing in Eden really worked – most of the populace were unhappy, hungry and desperately poor. Those who weren't either lived in isolation in a tree colony, with a lifestyle based on ancient survival practices, spattered with a modicum of scientific knowledge, or they ran around in the desert like crazy people, or were confined, monitored and confused by technology within the Bubble.

Even the people at the top of the Great Tower of Dump looked scared, as though their hold on the land below them was starting to slip away. Eden, thought George, might belong to Dump in name, but in reality it didn't really belong to him at all; not in people's hearts and not in their minds.

Before George was sent out of the Great Tower, this time not in the golden elevator but via a dirty, dank lift at the back, he'd been given a clear order.

'Bring her back to the Great Tower of Dump – before the next setting of the sun – or you will be responsible for the consequences!' Dump had bellowed at George. 'And she must come alone. No army. If she brings reinforcements, the annihilation will begin straight away.'

Nimu, who had gone salt-white at this exchange, had tried to interfere. 'But, Excellency,' she had pleaded. 'No one can cross the Dire Straits between here and na-h Alba,' she said. 'It's so dangerous – the boy will either sink on the waters or he will be torpedoed. The minute they see a craft approaching, they will aim a missile at him.' George realized that Nimu was, despite the desperation of her own position, pleading for him.

'Then he'd better hope they don't,' said Trellis smoothly. 'Or perhaps' – he glared menacingly at Nimu – 'you have some secret form of communication with na-h Alba and can get a message across to them?'

'No, sire,' replied Nimu humbly. 'I told you – all our networks are unable to communicate with them.'

'Or,' said one of Dump's minions, a thin-faced woman with elaborate blonde tresses, stepping forward, 'perhaps someone has happened across an intelligent supercomputer that is powerful enough to be sending messages to na-h Alba, encoded so that we can't intercept them. That would be another way to tell them in advance that the boy has an important mission.'

George stayed calm. He had worked a lot of it out now, and he knew full well that Nimu *did* have such a supercomputer – in the form of Empyrean who, George knew, was no ordinary robot. Whether Empyrean was capable of getting a message to na-h Alba, he had no way of knowing. He could only hope.

'Don't be ridiculous,' scoffed Dump, who was too vain to imagine that such a thing could happen under his nose; that a supercomputer could be hiding right in front of him. 'If we had found *the* supercomputer, we'd already be able to software patch the machine learning to modify its ability and get the machines back under our control. We'd be able to rule properly again.'

Nimu rubbed her brow. 'Indeed, Excellency,' she agreed politely. 'If we had the supercomputer, we wouldn't need her in the first place.'

'Crazy Hound!' shouted Dump. 'Why don't we know where the supercomputer is?'

'We continue to search for it all the time,' said Crazy Hound humbly. 'But it's become more difficult since you stopped most humans' access to real learning. We couldn't have foreseen that the machines would learn so much about us and how we are running our world that eventually they would turn against us.'

'The main thing,' said Dump's blonde adviser, 'is that we know she doesn't have the super-computer. If she – and the supercomputer – were reunited . . .'

Even Dump turned pale at that thought. 'That nasty woman! She will never get the super-computer. Even if we don't have it, we are still powerful! We are incredible. She's a loser.'

'A loser that you need,' said Crazy Hound, looking at his feet. 'Or the machines will take over.'

'Outrageous!' shouted Dump. 'I am powered by the brightest brains in Eden! While I have access to the brainpower of Wonder Academy—' His female adviser kicked him on the ankle. He stopped. 'Get this boy out of here.' He rounded on George. 'Take him away and send him across the Dire Straits to that stupid, wretched place. Either he will be shot out of the water or he'll reach her and bring her back to Eden. Either way' – a crafty grin illuminated his features – 'it's a win for me.'

As George was bundled out of the room, he heard a voice pipe up.

'But what about me?' said Atticus. 'What's going to happen to me?'

George hadn't been allowed to stay for long enough to hear the answer. He could only hope that his friend from the forest would survive in that strange tower-top room.

Now, in the inky blackness, George started to realize something else. His boat was going more and more slowly. At the start, it had powered across the waves, but it was gradually starting to lose momentum. Water was sloshing around his feet, making them icy inside his battered boots. George looked up at the stars. Once upon a time, with his best friend Annie, he had travelled there, using the space portal generated by the super-computer Cosmos. He and Annie had talked about science and the Universe, and had lived in a world where they thought everything was getting better and people were becoming cleverer and kinder. How had the future turned out like this?

At that moment, the nightscape changed: the total blackness beyond the small weak radius of the one torch George had been allowed to take was suddenly blazing with light. It was dazzling; white searchlights combed the sea around him from above until they came to land on the boat itself. A mass of flying drones whirring overhead, homing in on him and relaying his image back. George knew that at the same time a camera fitted in the boat would also be monitoring his progress and sending updates back to the Great Tower of Dump. An automated voice spoke:

'*Desist! Turn back your boat! You are now illegally entering the waters of na-h Alba! You do not have permission to be here! Repeat – you do NOT have permission to be here.*'

But George's boat continued both onwards and downwards – it moved forward slowly while sinking. There was nothing George could do about either.

'*Turn back your boat!*' commanded the automated voice. '*You are not allowed to come any closer to na-h Alba! We will resist you with force!*'

The boat ploughed forward while George tried to think.

'*You are now at risk,*' warned the voice. '*It is forbidden to approach na-h Alba from the coastline of Eden! We will unleash a strike against you!*'

It seemed rather fancy language, thought George, to use against one boy in a leaking boat, but he figured the system had been programmed to take action against the battleships of Eden. He had seen those warships. They bristled with warheads, all trained on the distant and invisible spectre of the Independent Isle.

No wonder na-h Alba had a rapid response system ready to strike the minute something crossed the boundary.

At that moment, George thought about everything that had happened – how he had crossed the whole solar system in his spaceship, seen the cosmos unfurl before him in all its magnificence and wonder. And how he had completed that mission by making it home to Planet Earth. He now had to complete this new mission, and he wasn't giving up yet. A thought came to him. He had one last chance – only one – and it was the longest shot of his life, he realized, before either his boat sank or the drones unleashed their weaponry against him.

Standing up precariously, with the water now up to his shins as the boat wobbled beneath him, he faced the spotlight and shouted the only words that could have saved him:

'Annie!' he yelled. 'Annie, it's me! George!'

Chapter Twenty-one

'Now that's how to make an entrance!' said Annie, sitting cross-legged on a large cushion in what looked oddly like the treehouse George and Annie had once shared, a long time ago in the past, when the world was a different place.

George had been brought to her after his sudden sea rescue. Once he had shouted helplessly and desperately into the night, hoping against hope that somehow his friend would hear him, everything had changed. A boat had materialized alongside him, and sailors had pulled him aboard. George had been wrapped in a blanket and given a hot thermos of something that tasted deliciously like sweet tea. The sailors had been kind but suspicious of him – he heard one of them debating whether he was a clever Edenopolis spy who had somehow managed to infiltrate na-h Alba. But that voice was quickly shushed by another who reminded the speaker that the order to rescue George had come from on high.

The journey across the rest of the Dire Straits to na-h Alba had been choppy but exhilarating for George. He might be exhausted, freezing and shattered, but he'd made it! He was on his way to the one place he might be safe – na-h Alba! And he'd made it by shouting out the name of his best friend. He tried to ask the sailors some questions but, kind as they were, they didn't want to tell him anything in case they gave away information that he shouldn't know. Instead, George had closed his eyes and fallen into a deep, dreamless sleep, waking only when he was bundled into a warm cabin, where he was instructed to wash, change into a pair of pyjamas and sleep. Later on, he had been woken again, told to dress in a soft cotton jumpsuit and taken to meet Annie.

Seeing Annie again was the biggest shock of all the extraordinary experiences of his journey.

'You're so old!' he couldn't help but blurt out the minute he saw her. And yet he had recognized her instantly. She was still the same girl he had known all that time ago, but her face was furrowed by lines and there were streaks of white in her hair.

At the same moment, Annie cried, 'Is it really you?' She reached out to hug him. He could see how tall, thin and muscular she had become. It was like hugging his grandmother rather than his best friend and favourite adventurer in the whole Universe.

'Wow, this is weird!' said Annie as they both brushed the tears out of their eyes. 'George! I never thought I would see you again!'

'And here I am!' said George, unable to really believe this was happening. They were together again – but she was separated from him by decades of age and experience. It was like the time when he had half appeared through quantum teleportation on a distant moon of Jupiter, and half of him had shouted to Annie to rescue him. He felt as though part of him was calling to her across a great divide of time and space. 'You always did know more than me,' he said, trying to cover up how strange he felt.

'There's so much to catch up on!' said Annie, her lined, weatherworn face smiling fondly at him. She pinched the back of his hand. 'You're so young, George! And I'm growing old, so much older than you now.' Old as she might think she was, Annie was straight-backed and alert. George wondered which one of them would win in a sprint race. *Probably Annie*, he thought.

'Annie, I can't believe I'm seeing you again!' said George. The back of Annie's hand, compared to his, was roped with thick blue veins and the skin was scored by lines and dappled with dark patches.

'I have so much to tell you!' said Annie. 'But first my people here on na-h Alba want to know if you're working for Dump. Be honest with me, George, for the sake of our long friendship – and it's been way longer for me than it has for you! Are you on Dump's side? Why have you come from Edenopolis?'

'I am not working for Dump!' said George hotly. '*As if*, Annie!'

300

'I know!' exclaimed Annie, rolling her eyes, just as she always had. 'I *said* – I *told* them! It's impossible! The moment you stood up in that boat and said my name, I knew it was really you – and I knew you weren't with Dump.'

'I was coming here with a girl,' said George, who was sitting on the large cushion opposite Annie with a view out over the heavily irrigated landscape of na-h Alba. The sun, he realized, was high in the sky, meaning he had slept until at least late morning. 'A kid who I had to get out of Eden because she wasn't safe.'

'Still the same old George,' said Annie. 'Always rescuing people!'

'But we got separated – or she ran off, and I ended up in Edenopolis with my other friend, Atticus, who comes from the Swamp.' He glanced at Annie and saw that she looked a bit perplexed. Perhaps he wasn't explaining this in a grown-up enough way? She looked like his mum or dad when he tried to give them an explanation but they just didn't get it. He decided to cut to the chase. 'I don't have long – and I have a message for you from Dump himself!'

'A message!' snorted Annie. 'We're always getting messages from Eden – most of them turn

301

out to be fakes! They're forever trying to trick us – that's why we shut down our communications with them.'

'No, this time it's real,' said George. 'And it's happening – now. Dump. He wants you to come to Eden. *Now*, or it will be too late!'

Annie gasped. 'Too late?' she echoed. 'Are you kidding me, George?'

'No,' said George firmly. 'I am absolutely not kidding you. Not at all. He has threatened to kill everyone there if you don't come. *Everyone*, Annie.'

'Do you know what Trellis Dump has done? Do you know what he and his father did to me? To my dad? To your family? To everyone here on Planet Earth after he took full power? Trellis Dump the First was bad enough, grabbing control during all the climate disasters, putting profit before people every time. But when his son decided he could go much further . . . we had *war*, George. A war that killed millions of people. Then Eden. Do you know what a wretched place he has made Eden over the past forty years? I can't go there with you! Whatever fake news he sends with you!'

'Well, of course I don't know!' said George.

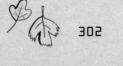

302

'I just arrived here from the past and I missed decades of stuff. I've been trying to work it out but no one will tell me anything and, if they do, I don't know if I can trust them! But I know I can trust you, and I need you to help, Annie.'

Annie arched an eyebrow and leaned back on her cushions. She let out a cool whistle. 'I see,' she observed, her blue eyes flashing. George realized that the Annie he had known was from the past: the schoolgirl, the scientist, the adventurer. But this adult Annie, this rebel leader and warrior, this fierce, rangy, greying-blonde Annie, was someone he wondered if he knew at all.

'Why?' demanded Annie, sitting up again and leaning forward on her elbows. 'Why should I leave na-h Alba, where we live in peace and safety' – she gestured out beyond the veranda to where George could see rolling hills, low-rise buildings, sparkling lakes – 'to go back to a place where I was robbed, imprisoned, lied about, rejected and nearly killed? I had to flee for my life, George. I got out, but not everyone was so lucky.'

'What happened to Eric?' asked George. He wanted to find out what had happened to his own family too, but he didn't know if he dared hear the answer.

'He was exiled,' said Annie.

'To where?' said George.

'Sent to Mars – for treason,' said Annie. 'Someone betrayed him. They leaked information about his work to the regime. He just had time to tell me to continue his work before he was arrested. That's when I tried flinging the message across the Universe to you! You were gone so long that I thought perhaps you might have set up home on Mars – we'd wanted to go there for so long, remember? You, George, were travelling into space to explore new worlds, to discover answers to the questions we had always asked; answers I know you would at some point bring back to help science on Earth. I hoped that Boltzmann Brian would have kept you safe. That you might have been able to help Eric. But we were too late.' She paused. 'We survived the war, but we only just got out of Eden in time.'

'*We?*' said George.

'I took your family with me and they're all safe,' said Annie. George gave a great *phew* of relief. 'I was already a scientist by then, a grown-up, in my thirties, and I had lots of scientist colleagues who didn't want to stay. So we left – but we had to do it undercover so we

couldn't take everyone. Loads of people got left behind.'

'I think I've met some of them,' said George, thinking of Matushka and the colony.

'I still don't really know who betrayed Eric,' said Annie. 'Although I have my suspicions.'

'I met Nimu,' said George. 'She wanted me to tell you that it wasn't her, that she didn't betray Eric! What's she got to do with it all? Who is she?'

'Nimu,' sighed Annie with a shiver, 'is my sister.'

'What!' said George. 'But how?' Yet, once Annie said it, it made a weird kind of sense.

'She's much younger than me,' said Annie. 'My own lovely mum died in a terrible car accident while touring with an orchestra – before all this, before the Great Disruption, before Eden. I was so sad, but I'm glad she didn't live to see all this. Nimu is the child of Eric's second wife. She's . . .' Annie exhaled. 'I met her a long time ago. I didn't like her and I thought she was dangerous. Spoiled. Very clever, of course. She was a prodigy, way smarter than you and I ever were. And so annoying! But Eric adored her and wouldn't hear a word against her. Which makes it even worse that Nimu betrayed him. She got tangled up

with the regime as a teenager and we believe she informed on him.'

'But that,' said George, carrying on his train of thought, 'means Eric is Hero's grandfather.'

'Hero?' said Annie in surprise. 'You mean a girl called Hero actually exists?'

George nodded. 'Yes! That's the kid from the Bubble that I was travelling with. Why wouldn't she exist?'

Annie sighed. 'I thought she was a trap,' she tried to explain. 'A piece of fake news. Nimu knew that I would never do anything to help her, not after what she did to Eric. I thought she had invented this kid, this granddaughter of Eric, to try and lure me back!'

'You know, Nimu seemed pretty upset about Eric,' said George. 'And she was very sure she didn't do it.'

'I don't believe anything she says,' snapped Annie. 'She's made herself Minister for Science – in a regime where science, scientists and education of any sort are banned!'

'Hero had an education,' said George sadly. 'But she just learned loads of things that weren't true and she had no way of finding out what was real. She was so excited about going to Wonder Academy.'

'Nimu would send her own daughter to Wonder Academy!' Annie interrupted in disgust. 'To that place! We raided it once to rescue kids and set them free. But we could only get one of them out.'

'I met the kid you saved!' said George. 'But she's ancient now!'

'What, like me?' said Annie slyly.

'Oh no, much younger than you,' said George, without realizing what he had said. Then he stopped himself and blushed.

'It's OK,' teased Annie. 'It's going to take a

while for us to get used to you being young and me being old. Tell me more about Nimu and Hero.'

'So Nimu was pretending to send Hero to Wonder, but actually she was trying to send her *here*! When I touched down from space, I got picked up by Nimu's robot, the one she uses to look after Hero, who then told Nimu that I should take Hero to na-h Alba.'

'Nimu's robot told you to flee to na-h Alba and take Hero?' said Annie in astonishment. 'What kind of robot is that?'

'Well, I think it was more like a supercomputer in a robot body,' said George. 'Hero told me Nimu had found Empyrean in the—'

'Empyrean?' said Annie, looking excited. 'Did you say *Empyrean*?'

'Yeah,' said George. 'You know, it was so weird. I almost thought Empyrean was . . . Well, it was like he knew me.'

'George, do you know what the word Empyrean *means*?' said Annie.

'Uh-uh, nope,' said George. 'And it's not like I can look it up on my phone, is it?'

'It's a medieval Latin word – it means "highest heaven",' said Annie gleefully. 'Or, some might say "universe". George, I think you've found Cosmos!'

'Oh my Dump!' said George, using Hero's favourite expression. 'OMD!' Just as Annie had turned out to be 'her', Empyrean, the cryptic robot, was Cosmos – their old frenemy from their adventures in the past.

'But wait,' said Annie. 'Did you say Cosmos was acting as Hero's guardian robot?'

'Yup,' said George.

'So the greatest computer ever has been working as a babysitter!' said Annie. 'But Nimu's a minister! She should have turned Cosmos over to the regime the minute she located him. She definitely shouldn't have kept him for her own purposes; that is way against the rules of Eden!'

'Nimu isn't on Dump's side. I'm pretty sure she's a double agent and wants Eden to end – so that Hero can have a normal life!' said George. 'She said something about how she and Empyrean had done the work her father – OMD, that's *Eric* – planned but couldn't start because he got betrayed.'

'I don't believe it!' exclaimed Annie. 'Nimu has carried out his plan?'

'What plan?' asked George.

309

'Eric's plan was to program the machines to protect Planet Earth – he thought that one day the machines would learn so much that they would decide that Dump was the greatest threat to Planet Earth and work to defeat him! You know, George, human stupidity is *far* more dangerous than artifical intelligence. Eric believed that human and machine could work together in total co-operation for the benefit of everyone. Just like he himself always worked with scientists from all over the world. Sharing knowledge. He thought it was the way forward to help everyone tackle the huge global challenges of the Earth. And he thought it would protect us all against people like Dump and their evil plans. But he didn't have time to finish his programming as he was taken away and sent to Mars! Do you mean Nimu finished his work for him – from *inside* the regime?'

'Yes,' said George. 'I think that's exactly what happened! And now the machines are turning against Dump and he's finding it really hard to stay ahead of them.' He remembered something he had heard in the Great Tower of Dump. 'Dump claimed he had the best brainpower – what did he mean? If he's so clever, why can't he change the system?'

'I don't know,' said Annie. 'It's so hard to know from here what is true about Eden and what's false.'

'Well, there's one way to find out,' said George, getting to his feet. 'We'd better get a move on!'

'We're not going anywhere,' said Annie calmly.

'What?' said George. 'We have to, Annie! We have to go back, find Hero, get Cosmos, grab my friend Atticus and save all those people! Annie, if you don't come, he'll just— I don't know what he'll do, but it will be really terrible for everyone in Eden.'

'Look,' said Annie. 'It's complicated.'

'No it isn't,' said George. 'You get to your feet, and you and I go to Edenopolis to fight Dump and save the people of Eden. That's what the Annie I know would do.'

'But I'm not that Annie any more,' said Annie quietly. 'I've lived years more than you – I've had to fight these people all my adult life. If you think I'm just walking into Edenopolis—'

'What about Hero?' said George defiantly. 'Don't you think Eric would want you to save her? If you don't come with me now, Hero and all those kids at Wonder Academy and everywhere else are going to die.'

'Thousands of people live productive, happy, peaceful lives on na-h Alba,' protested Annie. 'We have a missile shield here so we will remain protected for the time being. If I'm caught by Dump, I endanger them all and their way of life. No, we just wait. The machine resistance has begun. Maybe even the human resistance too? It will overturn Dump and his corporation, and then we will march into Edenopolis, victorious and safe!'

'No!' said George. 'There'll be no one left in Eden to save! They'll have been wiped out! And you don't know what the machines will do – you're guessing. And what if Nimu is so angry when you, her sister, fail to show up when she needs you that she really *does* decide to help Dump? You have no idea what he might be able to do!'

'It's too much of a risk,' said Annie decisively. 'You'll understand – when you're older. I must stay here with my people. They need me.'

George took a moment to think. 'All right,' he said. 'I know you're a grown-up and I'm not. And you know all sorts of stuff I can't even imagine. But I knew you back then, and I bet you've taught all those people' – he gestured out towards na-h Alba – 'everything you know. Because that's what you do. You get knowledge so that you can share it with others, just like you said about Eric. Those people, for instance.' He pointed at a random family walking along the street. 'You've taught them what to do and how to do it.'

'OK . . .' said Annie slowly.

'But you're behaving like Dump now,' said George accusingly. 'Saying that Eden lives don't matter. *Those people aren't like my people so I don't have to care about them. It's not my problem if something terrible happens to them because we're all happy here and everything is OK for us.* Not good enough, Annie!'

'I see,' said Annie, standing up and giving him a very grown-up look. 'That's your opinion, is it?'

'It is,' said George.

Annie finally smiled, a proper Annie smile, rolling back the years and the distance between them.

'What are we waiting for?' she said. 'Let's go!' She started to walk towards the door, but then stopped and turned. 'Just one thing,' she said as George opened his mouth to speak. 'Don't say what I think you're going to say.'

'I was going to say,' replied George, 'that your mum and dad would have been really proud of you.'

Chapter Twenty-two

As they approached the port of Edenopolis, the sun was descending towards the horizon, casting an orange glow across the city. From the Dire Straits, where the sea was calm enough that late afternoon for them to have a smooth journey, they saw the reddening light catch the edges of the huge clouds of pollution, turning them into a blazing coronet of fire around the tall buildings. Annie shivered. She had been very quiet on the journey, lost in thought as they headed towards the city she had avoided for so long.

'It's almost beautiful,' she said regretfully. 'There is so much good they could have done! And they didn't.'

George wasn't exactly happy to be back in the big city either. In Na-h Alba, with its peaceful streets, small encampments and happy people, he had for the first time felt properly safe back on his home planet.

At that moment, a voice boomed out.

'*Identify yourself!*' it said.

Annie stood up in the boat – which was a far superior version of the craft George had been sent over from Eden in the night before. It was fast, stable and powered by biomass.

'I have come to parlay with Trellis Dump!' said Annie clearly.

'Who are you?' said the voice.

'I am Annie Bellis,' said Annie. 'Mr Dump is expecting me.'

There was a silence while the machine system considered this response. Annie and George waited in trepidation. Would they even reach the shore? But the mood suddenly changed.

'We've been expecting you!' it boomed, and played a trumpet fanfare. 'You are welcome in Eden! Please moor your boat and disembark at the port.'

'Huh!' said George, surprised. If it had been just him, he reckoned the machines would have shot him out of the water, even if he had used Dump's name.

'Well!' said Annie. 'I think the machines are

turning against him. I bet he didn't authorize them to play me a tune!'

She navigated the boat expertly towards the wide jetty, which was lined with members of Dump's robot army. George clambered out nervously. Annie leaped onto the jetty in a fluid move that reminded him of Hero, springing from tree to tree in the jungle.

Atticus! he thought to himself. Where was he now? As soon as they'd rescued Hero, he must immediately find his friend from the forest.

Standing at the head of Dump's robot army was a lone figure, one George recognized from the Great Tower of Dump. It was the government-issue robot that had been standing with Nimu, the one that George would bet his bottom bitcoin was the new body of his old friend Cosmos.

'Greetings, distinguished professor, wanderer of the stars and planets, queen of the space portals and daughter of the most esteemed and much-missed Eric Bellis,' he welcomed Annie courteously, extending one robot hand.

With that, George knew for sure it was Cosmos. Who else would have given her that salutation?

'Greetings, my faithful friend,' said Annie, smiling. George knew that she had understood immediately. 'Thank you for coming to meet me.'

'Well, no one else wanted to,' whispered the disguised Cosmos, formerly known as Empyrean. 'They're all cowering in the Great Tower of Dump, frantically planning what to do when you get there.'

George nearly burst out laughing. Of the three of them, finally reunited all these years into the future, only he remotely resembled the boy he was when they were last together. Annie was older, harder, battle-scarred and brave; Cosmos seemed to have gained the ability to inhabit a body, albeit a mechanical one, and live an undercover life as a government android. But George was still just a boy, trying to find his way in this strangest of worlds.

'Is it safe for us to go to the Great Tower?' he asked, remembering the very real danger they now found themselves in.

'No,' said Cosmos-in-disguise, leading them forward through a double column of robots on either side. 'It is not. It is the least safe place for you to be. The same goes for anywhere in Eden. You are in terrible danger. Dump may still have human troops loyal to him, crack squads who will obey his every command, no matter what.'

'Cosmos,' said George. 'Where's Hero? And Atticus? Are they safe?'

'No,' said Cosmos. 'Neither of your friends are safe, but they are still alive. Hero is on her way to the Great Tower of Dump.'

'What?' said George. 'How come?'

'It's been a bigger adventure than we thought when I planned for her to travel with you across Eden to na-h Alba and the safety of Annie's protection.'

'Why didn't you tell me who you really were?' said George. 'And that Annie was "her"?'

'It was too much of a risk,' said Cosmos, formerly known as Empyrean. 'I was a government android registered to Nimu for child-rearing duty. That provided my cover to assist her. If you had revealed any of that information, even accidentally, the consequences could have been terrible.'

'Why didn't you just open a portal and push Hero into na-h Alba?' said George.

'I had some bad years,' said Cosmos quietly. 'In the trash camps. I lost that ability.'

'How come you dare to speak so freely?' queried Annie. 'Aren't we being listened to?'

'Yes,' said Cosmos. 'We are. This may not be the end of Eden as we know it, but this is the beginning of the end. No matter what happens, I will be proud to stand alongside you – and George.'

'Thank you, Cosmos,' said Annie quietly as the three of them walked away from the fortified port of Edenopolis into the city itself.

The robot guards continued to line the routes, and now George saw why. On either side, huge crowds had gathered. They must have come into Edenopolis for the Day of Reckoning, but the mood had changed since George was last here. In the short time that he had been gone the crowds had turned from weary and mournful or distracted by cheap entertainment to rebellious and angry. A frisson of mutiny ran through the air. George heard shouts of: 'It's not fair!' and: 'Come down from your tower!' A chant of 'Dump the Dump' started up.

Among them, some humans still loyal to Dump tried to whip the people back, yelling over their heads, 'This is an illegal gathering! You do not have permission to be here! Move back! Go back to your work!' But the crowds were too big and they no longer cared about punishment.

'Take us to na-h Alba!' a woman's voice came over the crowd.

'You'll never go to na-h Alba!' roared one of the human overseers. 'You will all stay here in Eden, the best of all possible worlds!'

'No it's not!' she shouted back. 'Eden is NOT the best of all possible worlds! We hate you – and we hate Eden!'

The people took up a chant: 'Eden is the worst of all possible worlds!'

The three old friends arrived in front of the Great Tower of Dump, where the security had been primed to expect them. The doors opened automatically and they walked in silence across the empty, cavernous entrance hall.

'The only way is up,' said Cosmos as the doors to the golden elevator drew back.

'Is Nimu there?' said Annie as they got into the lift.

'Your sister is present,' said Cosmos softly.

'I don't think of her as that,' said Annie, sounding very young suddenly.

'She's the closest thing you have to a sister, to a family,' replied Cosmos. 'Don't forget that your father loved Nimu very much.'

'She betrayed him!' said Annie, who clearly hadn't been persuaded by George's arguments. 'She sneaked on him to the regime – that's why they sent him to Mars.'

'No she didn't,' said Cosmos.

'How do you know?' challenged Annie. 'How do you know that for a fact?'

'Because,' said Cosmos, '*I* betrayed Eric. It is all my fault.'

Chapter Twenty-three

The three of them rode up the golden elevator in shock. Annie and George were too taken aback to speak. How was this even possible? Cosmos just stood there silently as the floors flew past and they arrived at the top of the tallest tower in Eden.

But, just before the doors opened, Annie turned to Cosmos and spoke quickly and coldly, though there was a break in her voice.

'I can't believe the traitor turned out to be you! My father created you! And you betrayed him!'

George realized that all the years had not dimmed Annie's quick temper. If anything, being an adult made her harsher than when he had known her. Back then, she had been very certain of her own views, and now George saw that, as a grown-up, she hadn't changed much after all.

Nose in the air, Annie stepped out into the room with the views over Eden. The sun was halfway to setting now, filling the room with a tangerine glow that bounced off the faces of all present. In the centre of the room, glowing most of all, stood Trellis Dump himself. He had positioned himself to face the lift while his minions, robot and human, had taken up their former stances around the edge of the room. But although George could see Nimu, there was no sign of the Child Hunter – or Atticus.

'Well, well, well,' said Trellis Dump as Annie and George walked out of the lift and stood facing him, with Cosmos right behind them. 'Robot!' he ordered Cosmos. 'Stand down!'

Cosmos, head bowed, stood to one side by the huge windows. Sneaking a look at Annie, George could see that, despite her resolve, she was staggered by the revelation about Eric. How could Cosmos – later known as Empyrean – have betrayed his maker and his mentor? George was also aware that this meant Annie had been blaming the wrong person for all these years, and that Nimu had been telling the truth when she said she wasn't responsible for Eric's exile. Annie looked so shocked that George wondered if she was going to be able to negotiate with Dump at all, or whether it would all now be up to him.

From the windows of the tower, they could see the massed crowd that extended out of Edenopolis and into the countryside around. Dump stood there, wreathed in pure delight. His real enemy at last stood right in front of him, looking pale and uncertain. As the arch-predator he was, he knew that it was time to move in for the kill.

But he couldn't resist a quick lie first. 'Those people have come out in support of me and

Eden,' he said. 'They're here to show you that you don't matter. We have signed a peace treaty with Queen Bimbolina Kimobolina, the leader of Other Side. As you know, this means that na-h Alba is surrounded. You're a loser, Bellis. Just like your father.'

In the background Nimu gave a soft cry. George saw Annie's eyes seek out the sister she had rejected for so long.

'Then why did you make me bring her here?' said George. 'Why not just invade and destroy her?'

Dump smiled. 'Well, I respect her!' he said, clearly lying. 'She's put up a good fight over the years – and I like that. But she can't win. She's finished, like her so-called Independent State. Sad!'

'What do you want?' asked George.

'What do *we* want?' sneered Dump's skinny blonde adviser from the sidelines.

'Shut up,' ordered Dump, to her obvious dismay. 'We need to make a deal.'

'What deal?' said George. 'Not another one!'

'Oh, this is best deal! The best ever deal,' enthused Dump. 'You're going to love it so much. It's the greatest!'

'I didn't like the last one so much,' retorted George.

Annie seemed to snap back into focus. She looked straight at Dump. Dump clearly wasn't used to being eyeballed by people he believed were inferior. He looked annoyed; his face, lit by the dying sun, turned a stranger shade of tangerine.

'OK,' she said finally. 'Tell me . . .'

'Stop the machines,' said Dump. 'Change the machine-learning process. Make them let me travel into space.'

Annie threw back her head and laughed. 'Space?' she said. 'Do you have somewhere in mind? Space is quite big, you know.'

'I've built the most amazing hotel,' Dump couldn't help boasting. 'So beautiful. I'm going to live in space for ever. It's going to be so amazing. I just need you to get me there.'

Annie's mind boggled at the thought that Dump might actually believe she intended to help him. 'And what's in it for me?'

'You'll be ruler of Earth,' he said with a crafty smile on his face. 'All this will be yours. Think about it! You've wanted it for so long. Now's your chance.'

'Really?' said Annie sarcastically. 'You'll simply give up control of everything? Just like that?'

'Of course,' said Dump, too quickly and too smoothly.

'He's lying,' said George. 'Funny kind of hotel – I bet it's got missiles attached. He'll be able to target the whole planet – anyone he doesn't like.'

'Hey!' said Dump. 'My hotel is the most beautiful hotel in the Universe! Please – talk about it with respect.'

'It's not much of a deal, is it?' said Annie sharply. 'For me or for the people of Eden. Why should any of us be dominated by you any longer?'

'Because,' said Dump, 'if you don't get me out of here, it's not just the *adults* in Edenopolis who'll be in trouble . . .' He gave an insincere smile.

Nimu caught on faster than all the others. 'The children,' she murmured.

'Yes, the kids,' he said. 'Thanks to Eden's positive policies about education and youth support.'

'How dare you!' broke in Nimu. 'How can you say that? You've misled and enslaved and fleeced the young of this place!'

'Thank you, Minister of Science,' said Dump. 'I've long had you in my sights as a traitor,' he obviously lied. 'You tried to fit in, I grant you that. But we always knew you weren't really one of us. We always knew you were "other".' He smirked and carried on. 'As you know, the kids are all gathered together in various locations around Eden. I know where they are.'

The implication was only too clear. George realized that this was Dump's trump card. He was so outrageous all the time that it was impossible to know when he was serious and when he was bluffing.

 Annie grabbed George and turned to Nimu, who smiled properly for the first time. The two sisters faced each other. Looking at the two of them, George could suddenly see the resemblance. It wasn't that Nimu looked like Annie physically – she didn't. She was a different type of person altogether. But there was an indefinable likeness,

a look in the eye, an air of determination and rebellion about both that marked them out as relatives.

'I'm *so* sorry,' murmured Annie. 'I always believed it was you.'

'I would never have done that,' said Nimu, reaching out for Annie's hand. 'I only accepted an invite to join the regime in order to work against them from the inside. It's what our father told me to do. And you know how they were targeting kids to join them; you remember all that propaganda and how they pressured young people to sign up. I thought it was the best way I could help Eric.'

Annie looked gutted. George could see her processing how wrong she had been all these years. But, still a commander through and through, she obviously knew that the current emergency had to come first.

'What now?' she murmured. 'Can we let Dump go?'

'Perhaps we could modify the machines,' said Nimu. 'Maybe the machines will discern that sending Dump into space is the only way to save Planet Earth.'

Annie looked doubtful. 'It might work,' she said.

'What about . . . ?' Nimu indicated Cosmos with her eyes.

Annie looked over at him, her eyes flinty. 'No,' she said. 'He betrayed us once. We can't give him another chance. We've got to figure this out ourselves.'

'What do you mean?' said Nimu. Clearly, thought George, she had no idea that Cosmos was the author of her father's downfall. Now didn't seem the moment to tell her.

Dump just stood there, smiling, confident that he held all the cards. In order to rescue everyone, they had to rescue him first.

But George had noticed something. He moved away from the two sisters. Standing next to the great windows, which showed the city of Edenopolis spreading out below, his eye had been caught by movement. Looking closer, he saw that a whole new stream of people had infiltrated the centre of Edenopolis – hundreds of them swarming through the city, seemingly able to bypass all the guards or controls that should have stopped them. They slipped through the crowds, moving with great speed from all directions towards the Great Tower of Dump. At first, George couldn't work out what was odd about the new arrivals, why they struck him as strange. And then he realized. It had been so long since he'd seen more than one or two kids together that he hadn't recognized what he was looking at. Hundreds and hundreds of children were pouring into Edenopolis and aiming straight for the Great Tower of Dump. And no one, neither human nor robot, could stop them.

George looked back into the room. The adults were having an argument.

'If you had educated your people properly,' said Annie, who had clearly inherited her father's talent for delivering lectures at key moments, 'you wouldn't need me. But you banned science, you banned proper education, you closed the labs and the universities. You took our father's work and tried to use it to support your regime – which he hated, by the way. And now you're begging *us* to help you?' She nearly spat on Dump.

'You can't win!' he said calmly. 'You have to do as I say or be responsible for the mass annihilation of the people of Eden. It will be your fault. Release me to my space hotel and you'll be free. I will give you a guarantee that I'll de-weaponize my space resort and leave to you the pleasure of leading this godforsaken planet.'

'Having wrecked it and taken all its riches for

yourself first,' said Annie. 'You think we'll just let you leave and live in luxury in space? And you think we would take your word that you'll de-activate your weapons?'

George looked back at the view below the tower. He edged closer to the window, which brought him level with Cosmos.

'I am defunct,' said the supercomputer. 'Now that the truth is out, I will be decommissioned. I hid away in the trash camps for years to punish myself. Then I tried to make it right by protecting Hero, but I fear my mistake was too grave.'

'How did you betray him?' asked George.

'By accident,' said Cosmos. 'Rashly I gave information to what I believed was a Resistance network, but they turned out to be regime bots in disguise. I am so ashamed. But there is nothing more I can do. I fulfilled my orders.'

'Cosmos,' said George, looking down at the tiny

moving figures, weaving their way through the crowds to the Great Tower of Dump. 'There *is* something you can do.'

The supercomputer considered this for a moment. 'I have been instructed by Annie to cease and desist,' he said.

'Just one last task? For me, please?' asked George.

'What is it?'

'Let the kids through security,' said George, pointing down towards the ground. 'And make the lift bring them up to this floor.'

'Ah,' said the great supercomputer. 'That I can do.'

The adults carried on shouting furiously at each other. All the advisers had now joined in. At one point, the hologram of Queen Bimbolina Kimobolina appeared in the centre of the room, looking beautiful and mysterious with strings of emojis falling out of her mouth like pearls. But Dump was obviously not pleased to see her.

'Get out of here!' he yelled. And the Queen of Other Side's avatar abruptly disappeared.

So busy were all the grown-ups, arguing ferociously among themselves about what should happen next, that they didn't notice the lift doors opening again. A whole stream of new arrivals burst out into the room.

As the adults slowly realized that they had been invaded, their furious voices died away. One small figure detached itself from the group and stepped forward.

'I have,' she said, looking around with perfect composure, 'a question.'

Chapter Twenty-four

'Hero!' Nimu tried to step forward but Annie, her sister, held her back.

'No, Nimu,' she said. 'Let her speak!'

'I have a question!' said Hero again. She seemed to have grown since George last saw her. She appeared perfectly at ease and very confident.

Dump, on the other hand, looked the opposite.

'I pay you,' he snarled to his advisers, 'to keep children out of here! Where is that pesky Child Hunter?'

'You sent him away!' one of the courtiers reminded him. 'With the other boy.'

'Get him back,' said Dump. 'This is totally his fault! Why are these kids here in Edenopolis? I want an answer!'

'So do I!' said Hero. 'Why did you lie to us kids? Why couldn't we have a proper education and learn about the world as it really is?'

Dump just gaped at her. He looked around blindly, motioning for one of his advisers to reply. But they all backed away from him.

Instead, Annie stepped forward. She smiled at Hero. 'Hello, Hero,' she said. 'I'm your Aunt Annie!'

'Cool!' said Hero, obviously impressed by this glamorous but tough-looking new person. 'What's an aunt?'

'Where did you come from with all these kids?'

Hero looked round at the group behind her. 'I freed them,' she said simply. 'I went to Wonder Academy because I had to find out what had happened to the kids from the Bubble!'

'What was Wonder Academy like?' said George,

agog. He couldn't believe she had done this all by herself.

'It was weird and horrible! None of the kids there were learning anything.' She looked accusingly at Nimu. 'They were having their brainpower sucked out of them to support Trellis Dump and make him smarter! And you wanted me to go there!'

'I didn't!' pleaded Nimu. 'I didn't want you to go there at all. I'm so sorry!'

'How did you get them out?' asked Annie.

'I had some help,' admitted Hero. 'But I mostly did it on my own.'

'Who from?' asked Annie, unable to keep quiet. 'Who has been helping you?'

'My robot,' said Hero. 'The one my guardian got from the trash camps. I thought he was useless but he's actually been quite cool.' She flashed the palm pilot. 'I've been speaking to him through this! He helped me when I didn't know what to do.'

Annie looked over at Cosmos, who carried on gazing out of the window. 'And you got all these kids out of Wonder Academy and brought them here?' she said.

'Well,' said Hero, 'it was after a lady called

Matushka told us the truth about Wonder. She'd been there, you see. Then I knew I had to go and get my friends out. So I did.'

'But . . .' said Nimu. 'How?'

'You lot,' said Hero, glaring angrily at Nimu and the other adults, 'think us kids can just be bought off with loads of mindless stuff to stop us pestering you. And all the while you were trying to use our brainpower to make Eden work! And you made us think that we owed you trillions of Dumplings and would have to work really hard all our lives to pay you back! Pay you back for making us work! When you had ruined the world we live in!'

Every adult in the room had fallen silent.

'It's really all thanks to George,' said Hero, smiling and showing a dimple. 'He was the first person who actually bothered to tell me that things were not the way I thought they were. I didn't believe him at first. I thought he was crazy. But he wasn't. He was trying to help me.'

'I was,' said George.

'And George got me out of that *Bubble*.' Hero said the word with disgust. 'Which was really brave of him. It was brave of me too, except I didn't know I was being brave so it doesn't count.'

'You fought a tiger,' George reminded her.

'And if George hadn't rescued me,' continued Hero, 'I might have been put to work in Wonder Academy as a brain slave for the Eden regime, just like all my friends.' She waved her hand to indicate a group of very irate-looking young people, now arranging themselves around the room.

To George's great relief, he saw Atticus at the back. Beside him stood a tall figure with long silver hair. George realized that it was Matushka, standing proudly with her son. She must have managed to persuade the people of the colony to join the Resistance after all, and then brought them to Edenopolis to help overthrow Dump.

'You,' said Hero to Nimu, 'have some explaining to do.'

Nimu looked utterly crestfallen. 'H-Hero . . .' she stuttered.

George stepped forward. 'Hero,' he said. 'Your mum' – he pointed to Nimu – 'is actually a bit of a hero herself. It's not quite the way it looks. She *protected* you, you know, by keeping you in the Bubble, by giving you Empy, by asking me to take you to na-h Alba.'

Hero blinked; clearly this was something she hadn't really thought about before. Nimu shot George a grateful smile. But Hero was still on a roll. She couldn't think about herself right now, not while there was so much else to consider. She stood taller.

'We've got way more to do – there are kids all over Eden who need our help!' she said loudly to the crowd around her. 'And' – now she turned accusingly to Dump – 'you still haven't answered my question!'

'*Your question.*' Dump imitated her in a particularly nasty high voice. 'Your question! I am President Dump, you silly little girl! I am ruler of Eden, and now of Other Side as well. I rule the world and everything in it. And you just ran up another two trillion in Dumpling debt. Enjoy paying it back, loser!'

'I don't think so.' George had just had a whispered conversation with Cosmos and had some new updates for the leader of Eden. 'You are not President of Eden. Not any more. You've just been deposed.'

'Liar!' cried Dump. 'I can't be deposed! I passed a law saying I would be President of Eden for ever more! No matter which way people voted!'

'That means nothing now,' George continued. 'You relied on the brainpower you took from these kids to make yourself clever enough to give the orders, and on the intelligent machines you used to carry them out. But you've lost them both. The kids are escaping and the machines have finally turned on you. I bet not one bot in Eden, from a lawn-mowing robot to the one that launches nuclear missiles, will obey you now. And, without your stolen brainpower, you won't be able to outwit them. You are *finished*.'

'Loser,' said Hero, who had clearly just picked up that word and liked it.

Annie smiled and winked. 'She's quite right,' she said. She turned to the rest of the room. 'Who here wants the reign of Dump to continue?' she called.

Not a single person or robot spoke up.

Annie turned back to Dump, who stood pale and crumpled in the centre of the room.

'Look,' he said. 'There's no need to be hasty . . . we can . . .'

Nimu said something into Annie's ear. She

nodded. 'Good idea!' She motioned to the robots, who swiftly grabbed Dump and dragged him out of the room.

'Where are they taking him?' asked George as Dump disappeared, struggling against his robot escort.

'Until we decide what to do with him, we're going to put him in a cell with some of his most enthusiastic supporters!' said Nimu. 'I can't think of a punishment he'll like less.'

'But who is going to be the leader now?' asked one of the kids behind Hero. Everyone automatically turned towards Annie. She had the air of a leader – an experienced warrior who could navigate the world away from the long-erupting state of crisis in which everyone had lived for far too long.

'Me?' she said. 'Don't you think I'm a bit old?'

'Well, you're the same age as me,' said George. 'In a way.'

'But I'm not,' said Annie. 'It's time for me to hand things over. I don't want to rule the world. I just want it to be a better place. Anyway, I think you've had quite enough of old people telling you what to do.'

'Annie,' said George. 'What do you mean? What are we doing to do now?'

'We?' said Annie. 'I think you mean you – you and Hero. And Atticus. And *all* the kids. You can't go back to the past, George. But your ship of time has brought you to now. And you can go forward into the future. This is your world now, George, yours and Hero's. And it will be whatever you decide to make of it.'

Time Travel and the Mystery of the Moving Clocks

Tick tock is the familiar sound of a clock and time passing. We all know about time – or at least we think we do! When we are together in a room, my clock shows the same time as your clock, my *tick tock* is the same as yours, and time passes at a steady beat. If you went on holiday to a distant country, your *tick tock* and mine would be the same, even if our clocks showed a different time of day.

But time is an interesting thing because it can pass *at different rates* if you start to move very fast. When you measure the *tick tock* on a speeding spaceship like George's, it looks slower than the *tick tock* of a clock back on Earth. Scientists call this strange effect time dilation, and it happens because light has a speed limit.

To understand *time dilation* we need first to understand something about light.

Light shining through the vacuum of space has a fixed speed. Scientists call this speed c, and it's around 186,000 miles per second. Though light can slow down when it passes through thick stuff like glass, when it's in free space its speed is c, and that speed c happens whatever direction you shine the light in.

It's this fixed speed that gives us time dilation: time on a super-fast moving spaceship passes more slowly than time on the Earth. This is the science behind how George is able to travel one way into the future. He travels so fast that only days pass for him, while on Earth years go by.

This all seems crazy, but that's because you can never in reality move fast enough to notice. However, if you *could* move at speeds near the speed of light, then your *tick tock* as seen from Earth would become more of a *tiiiiiick tooooooock*. To get a feel for why this is, we need a light clock in a see-through spaceship.

Our spaceship light clock is simple – a bulb on one side of the spaceship and a mirror on the other, with the super-powered engines at the back. When the spaceship is stationary, the bulb switches on, the light from it shoots over the distance inside the ship to the mirror and is reflected back. *Tick* is the time taken to go over to the mirror, and *tock* is the time taken to come back from the mirror.

If we had a mirror 186,000 miles away, then light from a (very bright) bulb would take one second to get to the mirror and another one second to come back, because light travels at c, so that first flash is going to travel 186,000 miles in one second, and take one second to come back.

Back on the stationary spaceship, our light clock will happily flash its *tick tock* at the same rate whenever we look at it, and we can use it to set all our other clocks on Earth to the same *tick tock*.

But we now launch our see-through spaceship so that it's moving very, very quickly, and watch it from Earth. The first flash from the bulb shoots out towards the mirror but, as we look at it from being stationary on Earth, in the time the light takes to cross over to where the mirror would normally be, the mirror has *moved*. The distance the mirror moves will depend on how fast the spaceship is travelling; if it's very fast, then the light takes a longer sloped path to hit the mirror. Because the light travelled further and light speed c doesn't change, from our viewpoint this could only mean that the time it took to get to the shifted mirror was longer. What was *tick* on our stationary light clock now becomes *tiiick*.

On the reflection of the light, the same thing happens: the light coming from the mirror has to cover a longer distance to get back to where it started, so our *tock* is now *tooock*. This means that when we look from Earth, a moving clock runs *slower* than a stationary one and it seems that *less* time has passed on the moving spaceship. For example, when the spaceship's slow-running clock has only reached one o'clock, while it's now five o'clock on Earth, that would mean the spaceship is four hours into the Earth's future.

You can also think about this time dilation with some simple letter shapes. When the clock is stationary, the flashes travel back and forth like two letter I's, as the mirror and bulb are straight across from each other. The first I is the journey to the mirror, the second I is the journey *from* the mirror. But when our spaceship moves, the path of the light seen from the Earth is more like a V. The light now has to travel a longer distance at an angle to bounce off the shifted mirror at the bottom of the V, and again cover a longer distance to return to the start. The difference between the II and V distance means that from Earth it takes longer to have a pulse reflected back when the clock is moving, so the moving clock is slower.

That's the basic idea behind time dilation, and it's a prediction of the Theory of Relativity, which was one of scientist Albert Einstein's great breakthroughs (although, of course, the details of his theory are a bit more complicated). Though Earth sees my clock as running slow, if I'm on the spaceship, then from my viewpoint I'm stationary and it's the Earth that is moving away from me, so I see the Earth clock running slower, not mine. Both Earth and spaceship points of view are right, so why is it only on the spaceship that time travels into the future?

If you look closely at the mathematics, it turns out that changing speed can also cause time dilation. Since only the spaceship has to change speed and direction to turn round to get back to Earth, the conditions on the spaceship's flight are different from those on Earth. It's the time dilation from the spaceship's super-fast speeds and mid-course about-turn that causes the time difference that shoots the returning spaceship one way into Earth's future.

We can't yet fly spaceships at speeds anywhere near light speed, but we have some interesting experiments which show that Einstein and his time-dilation idea was correct. In an accelerator – like the one at CERN in Switzerland – particles are pushed to move at speeds near the speed of light, and usefully many have their own sort of clocks on board. A particle half-life is related to the time it takes for the particle to disintegrate into other smaller sub-particles. We can measure this half-life in the lab when the particle is stationary, and we can also measure it when the particle is moving. It turns out that when the particles move, the 'half-life' clock does run slower than when it's stationary, and by an amount exactly predicted by Albert.

Peter

Climate Change – and What We Can Do About It

What does climate change mean?

The weather can change every day; one day it's rainy and cold, another day sunny and hot. And some months and years can be hotter or rainier than others. But when we take the weather over a long period, say thirty years, we can calculate averages of temperature and rainfall and other measures of weather. We call these averages the *climate*.

During one human lifetime, in any one particular place on Earth, the climate tends to stay more or less the same. But it is different around the world. For instance, places close to the Equator tend to be warmer than places closer to the poles of the Earth. Rainforests have climates that are wetter than deserts.

Over the past century, however, scientists have made detailed records of the climate in many different areas of the Earth,

and have discovered that most places have become warmer on average. We call this *global warming*, and it is having many different effects. For instance, it means that ice has started to melt in many places – such as in mountain glaciers, and in ice sheets on the land and sea around the North and South Poles. The melting land ice is then entering the world's oceans and causing our sea levels to rise. Some places are becoming wetter and some places are becoming drier. All these impacts together are known as *climate change*.

Scientists have concluded that the main reason for this change in the Earth's climate is *us*: human activities. Although the Sun warms the Earth, our atmosphere makes the surface of our planet about 30° Celsius warmer than it would be if we didn't have this atmosphere. It works like this. When energy from the Sun reaches the Earth's surface, it raises its temperature. Heat from the Earth's surface then escapes into space, but some of it is trapped by the gases in the atmosphere – gases such as water vapour and carbon dioxide. This is known as the *greenhouse effect* as the principle is very similar to how greenhouses are heated to help grow tender plants in cold areas.

Carbon dioxide is a very important factor here. Since the eighteenth century, the amount of carbon dioxide in the atmosphere has started to increase, causing more heat to be trapped by the atmosphere, warming the Earth. Most of this carbon dioxide has come from burning fossil fuels, such as coal, oil and natural gas for heating, for use in industries such as steel and cement, to generate electricity and to provide power for cars and trains. Other greenhouse gases include *methane*, which is produced, for instance, when rubbish rots in landfill sites or from the digestive systems of cattle. Carbon dioxide is also released when we cut down trees and they are buried or they rot.

Climate Change – and What We Can Do About It

Why is climate change a problem?

The average temperature of the Earth's surface (across all places and times, land and oceans and so on) has increased by about 1° Celsius since measurements with thermometers and other instruments became widespread in the middle of the nineteenth century. Celsius – also known as Centigrade – is the unit of measurement of temperature used by most countries in the world. It is based on 0° for the freezing point of water, and 100° for the boiling point. So 1° Celsius may not sound much compared to the daily or seasonal fluctuations in temperature we all know, but what might seem like small changes in the average when measured in degrees Celsius can make a big difference to the climate.

The amount of carbon dioxide in the atmosphere has already increased by more than 40 per cent since we started burning fossil fuels about 250 years ago. This has increased particularly quickly since the Second World War as the worldwide growth of industry and changes of lifestyle, mostly powered by fossil fuels, have become more rapid. The gas can stay in the atmosphere for hundreds of years, so each year emissions of carbon dioxide add to the concentration. If we carry on at the same rate, the amount in the second half of this century could be *two or three times* the level it was before the Industrial Revolution.

If this rate of increase continues until the mid-twenty-first century –

352

when a child starting primary school this year would only be in their forties – it could cause the surface temperature to be 5° Celsius or more higher than it was before industrialization. This would be a level not seen on Earth for tens of millions of years! We cannot know for sure what the temperatures would be, but there are real risks they could be that high. Remember that modern humans have only been around for about 200,000 years. It is difficult to imagine what the Earth would be like if the increase continues until the end of this century.

The changing climate is having some positive effects, such as reducing the frequency of dangerously cold weather in some areas, but it is also creating risks for many people. In poor countries inhabitants are more vulnerable to rises in sea level or increased extreme weather events like hurricanes or drought. Over the next century, many areas may become difficult to live in because of increases in floods or droughts. Some areas could become uninhabitable: they might be submerged between rising seas – an island, for instance, vanishing underwater – or turned into deserts. Many people, perhaps hundreds of millions, might need to migrate away from the worst affected areas. In some parts of the world this is already happening; people have to move out of their homes after their crops fail and their livestock can no longer survive.

Plants and animals are also being affected by climate change; many species are migrating towards the poles in response to the warming, and many are threatened with extinction. Overall the change could make people much poorer, and we may reverse the gains in incomes and life expectancy we have seen across the world in the last hundred years.

Climate Change – and What We Can Do About It

What can we do about climate change?

The climate responds relatively slowly to changes in the amount of carbon dioxide and other greenhouse gases in the atmosphere. This means that, as a result of our past activities, climate change will continue for the next 20 to 30 years, so we will have to make sure that people, homes and businesses are more resilient to the impacts. This is usually called *adapting to climate change*.

But the effects of climate change are becoming more dangerous, so to avoid the worst effects we need to reduce and stop releasing carbon dioxide and other greenhouse gases into the atmosphere. This is known as *climate change mitigation*. This will be difficult because more than 80 per cent of the world's energy today comes from burning fossil fuels.

But we have lots of alternatives, such as producing electricity from renewable sources, including wind and solar power. And we can power cars and trains using electricity from renewable sources. Governments across the world can play a big role by sticking to an international agreement made in Paris in 2015 to cut annual emissions of greenhouse gases so that global warming stays well below 2° Celsius. And businesses can help by finding ways to reduce pollution and waste.

And we can build better cities in which people spend less time sitting in traffic jams and use public transport instead. As well as allowing people to spend more time working and living productively, this would drastically reduce both greenhouse gas emissions and air pollution.

Although we need to make big changes, we know we can do this while also raising living standards around the world and tackling poverty. Climate change is an urgent problem, but the solutions are exciting, with new and better ways of

generating and using energy. Towns and cities could be much more attractive. Our forests and grasslands could be much more resilient. And the ecosystems on which we depend, both on the land and in our oceans, could be much, much less fragile. We would all benefit, particularly the poorer people in all countries.

Perhaps *you* will be one of our future scientists and ecologists working with others across our planet to make a better world for the generations to come – a better world for everyone.

Nick

The Future of Food

Many predictions have been made about the future of food. They range from 'edible air' to 'meals in a pill'. Highly engineered novelty food products have been the staple of food futurists, and indeed of early space missions. Had George been on board a spaceship in the 1960s, he would have had toothpaste-type tubes, with liquefied or puréed food for breakfast, some bite-sized food cubes for lunch, and maybe some freeze-dried food powders for supper. Not the most appetizing prospect!

But the nutritionists' early enthusiasm for vitamin pills and 'meals in a pill' has now given way to a renewed focus on wholefoods. Take the humble apple, for example: apples, like other fruits and vegetables, contain a complex mixture of thousands of compounds that protect cells from damage. When eaten in the form of the whole fruit, apples can help prevent us from developing chronic diseases such as cancer and heart disease.

Scientists have tried to extract what they thought of as the active ingredients – for example, vitamin C from fruit such as apples, vitamin E from green leafy vegetables such as spinach, and beta-carotene from orange vegetables such as carrots. However, it has been found that eating those extracts in pill form does not have any preventive health effects in most cases, and it could even sometimes lead to an increase in chronic disease. You do have to eat the whole food to get all the health benefits.

What George would now find in the canteen of a spaceship, or on board a space station, would resemble more what you can find in one down on Earth. How about some mashed potatoes, nuts, broccoli and an apple a day?

Let's get back to thinking a bit more about the future of food. For that purpose, it might be instructive to consider

what influences what we eat, and how what we eat influences our health and our planet (and any future planets we might find).

I'll start with what might seem like a simple question: *Why do you eat what you eat?*

Maybe you eat a specific meal because you like its taste, or you are hungry. Maybe you eat it because it is there, and somebody has prepared it for you. Why do you think that person chose to cook that meal and not something else? Why is that specific meal there to begin with?

Scientists consider a similar set of questions when trying to predict how and what the world might eat in the future. They start with what can and has been produced in the past, and where. In the UK, that would currently be milk, meat, wheat and root vegetables such as potatoes and carrots; and of course also some fruit like apples and strawberries. Then they look at how many people are around to eat the food produced, how much money those people have to spend on their food, what other foods might be available somewhere else, and how easy it would be to exchange some foods that are closer for foods that are further away.

What the scientists observed was: as people become richer, they consume more in general, and in particular more meat, dairy, sugars and oils, and less grains and beans. This observation raises two problems that we could be faced with in a future with more people and with higher incomes worldwide.

The first problem concerns our *environment*, and the second our *health*.

Many thinkers in the past 200 years have been worried that we might not be able to produce enough food on our Earth to feed a growing population. Thanks to technological advances in the way crops are bred, planted and harvested, that concern is one of the past. What has become a worry

357

The Future of Food

of nowadays is whether we can produce our food in a way that does not harm our environment.

One of the greatest threats to our survival on planet Earth could be climate change. And food has no small role to play here. Currently almost a *third* of all climate-change-causing greenhouse gases are emitted during food production. And that proportion is expected to grow in the future, in particular due to the expected increase in meat consumption.

Beef is by far the greatest culprit. Cows produce greenhouse gases in their digestion system by fermenting feed in their rumen, the first compartment of their stomachs. Yes, I'm talking about burping and farting! In addition, growing feed for cows and other livestock requires fertilizers which also emit greenhouse gases. As a result, beef produces about 250 times more greenhouse gases per gram of protein than crops such as lentils and beans, and more than 20 times more greenhouse gases per serving than vegetables. Other animal-based foods – such as eggs, dairy, pork, poultry and some seafood – emit significantly less greenhouse gases than beef, while plant-based foods emit the least.

It is no surprise then that scientists, in order to save our planet, have called for people to move away from diets high in animal products towards more plant-based diets. And the food industry is eager to jump on board with soy-based meat replacements, algae extracts, and meats whose production might emit less greenhouse gas emissions – such as lab-grown meat or edible insects. Perhaps you will be one of our future scientists working in this area, helping to produce foods to feed the world without hurting our planet.

Thinking now of health: a move towards plant-based diets could also avoid some of the dangers that come with the otherwise expected increase in meat, dairy, sugars and oils. Processed meats – these include burgers, sausages and chicken nuggets, but also the battered fried fish portion of a plate of fish and chips – have recently been declared carcinogenic. This means that they can cause anyone eating a lot of these foods over a number of years to be more likely to develop cancer in the future. And even unprocessed forms of pork and beef have been associated with greater risks of cancer and other chronic diseases.

At the same time, energy-dense foods that are high in sugars and oils – think of ultra-processed foods such as biscuits, crisps, chips, sugary drinks and the like – are contributing to more people becoming overweight and obese, which is also associated with a greater risk of cancer and other chronic diseases. Sometimes those foods are described as 'empty calories' – calories without any nutritional value. They do not make us feel full, and we often snack on them between meals. Others call such foods 'junk foods'. I bet you can guess why.

Where does all this leave us? It seems clear that to avoid dangerous levels of climate change and unhealthy levels of diet-related diseases, the food of the future needs to deviate from the past trends of eating more and more meat, dairy, sugars and oils. A healthy and environmentally friendly diet for the future would be low in unhealthy and emissions-intensive foods – such as most animal products and ultra-processed foods that are high in sugars and oils – but high in health-promoting and low-intensity foods, such as whole grains, nuts, fruits, vegetables and legumes.

On your next trip to Mars, how about, instead of a beef burger with fries, you try a lentil-and-bean burger in a wholewheat bun with some extra slices of lettuce and tomato? Throw in a toothpaste-like tube of algae if you feel fancy. And enjoy your favourite fruit as dessert. *Bon appétit!*

Marco

Plagues, Pandemics and Planetary Health

As George's spaceship *Artemis* crash-lands in a scary future world, we are reminded of the horrors of the many diseases that have struck humanity over the past centuries. The Black Death of the mid-fourteenth century, killing around one third of the known population, was undoubtedly the most devastating. What may surprise you is that scientists are still investigating its cause to this day, using tools such as DNA analysis. Was this 'plague' transmitted to humans just by the black rat (*Rattus rattus*) and its infected fleas (as most school books will tell you)? Or was the story, as we are beginning to suspect, more complex than that? The answers to these questions could help us not just to understand the past but also to prevent present and future global health threats.

Our microscopic world

The word 'plague' is generally associated with its two main forms – bubonic and pneumonic plague – and outbreaks of both can still occur. When infectious diseases like plague are widespread, as with the Black Death, they are often described as 'epidemics' or 'pandemics'. Infectious diseases are caused by crafty microscopic undercover agents (micro-organisms), which typically take the form of bacteria, viruses or parasites. Not all micro-organisms are dangerous to humans but, when they are, they can be called 'pathogens'.

Air-borne pathogens can be spread from person to person – for example, by coughing or sneezing. But pathogens can also be water- or food-borne; or they can be spread by infected animals and biting insects. There are even theories that some disease-causing micro-organisms might originally have come from outer space!

Since the late nineteenth century, generations of brilliant scientists have discovered the causes and chains of transmission of many infectious diseases, and it is through this understanding that we can come up with effective solutions to prevent them from spreading across our ever-increasingly interconnected globe.

But we still do not know all the answers, and there are incredible opportunities for you, the younger generation, to make a contribution towards uncovering the hidden secrets of our microscopic world.

The influenza pandemic of 1918–19

The year 2018 is the hundredth anniversary of the end of the First World War. It is also the centenary of one of the greatest global pandemics of the twentieth century: influenza. The so-called 'Spanish flu' killed between 50 and 100 million people across the world. The death toll was significantly greater than those killed on the battlefields. There was, at that time, no cure, no vaccine and no understanding of the 'invisible' virus responsible. But people soon learned that influenza was a highly contagious disease, and that 'coughs and sneezes spread diseases'.

A renewed interest in this historic pandemic (and why this strain of flu was so lethal) has been sparked by the recent scares of avian or 'bird' flu and the 2009 'swine' flu pandemic.

The SARS pandemic of 2003

It is maybe not as fast as George's spaceship, but the speed of air travel around the globe has enabled the ever more rapid spread of pandemic diseases. Take, for example, the first major, and previously unknown, pandemic of the twenty-first century – SARS (severe acute respiratory syndrome). Like tweets that go 'viral' via social media, infectious diseases can now circulate the globe in less than a day. In 2003 SARS 'jetted' from China to Hong Kong to Canada, and on to almost every continent, before eventually being contained through public health action coordinated by the World Health Organization (WHO).

Luckily, scientists across the world were able to track the progression of the disease, share their findings via the internet, and rapidly identify its cause – a virus intriguingly related to the common cold but far more deadly.

Headline news: Ebola and Zika virus

Scientists have in fact found that many infectious diseases start in rodents, animals such as monkeys and chimpanzees, birds, and even bats, and then 'jump' into humans. SARS may well have originated in bats.

Ebola, too, probably existed as a virus in bats before emerging as a human disease in the mid 1990s. Shocking scenes of the 2014–15 Ebola epidemic in West Africa were shown by the media, as were the incredible efforts of local and international teams to stop the outbreak. With no vaccine or cure available, thousands of lives were saved by determined healthcare workers who wore protective gear (rather like spacesuits) and tended those affected. Eventually this frightening and lethal disease was brought to a halt, but scientists are now constantly on the look out to detect any future outbreaks quickly while they continue to search for a vaccine or cure. And, of course, security in all research laboratories is very high, because of the danger of such viruses and the risk that they could fall into the wrong hands and be used as biological weapons.

Attention has also been focused on diseases transmitted by the bite of infected mosquitoes. Zika virus was first identified in the 1940s in the Zika Forest in Africa but it was only more recently, when major outbreaks occurred in a number of countries across the globe, that serious concern was raised about its potential risks. As with Ebola, there is yet no known cure: taking sensible precautions – in particular avoiding certain regions and protecting against mosquito bites, is so far the only way to avoid getting Zika virus.

Let's not forget the old and neglected tropical diseases

There are many severe and, indeed, ancient diseases of the sub-tropical and tropical world. In parts of Africa, in spite of optimistic progress in recent decades, every minute or so a child dies of yet another mosquito-borne disease: malaria. Other, less well-known, diseases are now called 'neglected tropical diseases'. Some are spread by insects, some by contaminated water, and some are linked to parasitic worms that live inside the human body. These can not only lead to premature deaths but can also cause long-term damage, including malnutrition, stunted growth and poor educational attainment in children. Unlike pandemics that threaten the whole world, these diseases – linked, among other things, to poverty, hunger, war, climate change, polluted and insanitary environments, and proximity to disease-carrying animals, birds and insects – are not often headline news but nevertheless deserve attention as they affect the most vulnerable people on the planet who often have limited access to modern medicines and healthcare.

Success stories: the remarkable eradication of smallpox

But let's look on the bright side. Thanks to medical science, tremendous progress has been made to identify and combat infectious deadly diseases. Two great success stories are the development of vaccines and life-saving antibiotics – although you have probably heard that antibiotic resistance is becoming a serious problem which needs to be tackled urgently in the future. Along with vaccines and medicines, public health interventions, such as quarantine, improved sanitation and better nutrition, have also contributed to a doubling of average life expectancy, from around 40 to 50 years in the early twentieth century to 70 to 80 years today, at least in the wealthier nations.

Plagues, Pandemics and Planetary Health

A truly remarkable story is the global eradication of smallpox – one of the most feared of all infectious diseases in the past. There was never a cure for smallpox, but with the introduction of a vaccine the disease was finally wiped off the face of the Earth by 1980. There is every hope now that another virus, polio, will, through a vaccination programme, be the next major human disease to become history.

Our future: what can you do?

Scientists working in the field of newly emerging infectious diseases are like detectives. Nobody knows when the next epidemic or pandemic will strike, but being prepared and acting fast is vital. Just imagine: *you* could be a 'disease detective' looking for clues in some remote mosquito-infested forest of the tropical world; in a live bird market of a densely packed city; in a shanty town lacking basic sanitation; sitting at a computer exchanging data with international colleagues; or working in a highly secure biohazard laboratory.

Yes – in the future there are fantastic opportunities for you to play a major and ground-breaking role by becoming skilled in human or veterinary medicine, science, nursing, and related fields of healthcare research and practice. The world desperately needs those who have the brains, passion and persistence to come up with new cures, vaccines, diagnostic tests and bright ideas about how to prevent future pandemic threats, or tackle older and neglected diseases of the world's poorest populations. In short, to become champions for planetary health.

Will *you* be on the team?

Mary

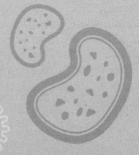

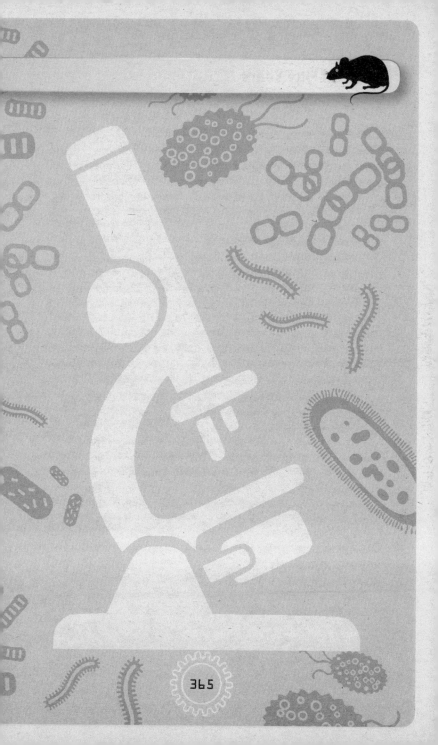

365

War in Fifty Years

Reflecting upon the 100-year anniversary of the end of the First World War and today's ongoing conflicts in the Middle East and beyond, it is difficult to discuss war and warfare with young readers. We want to imagine and share with future generations how war is a terrible exception to the general goodness that humanity can display. But the truth is that wars, and how they are fought, are in fact integral to mankind's past and present, influencing every part of humanity's development.

Despite its record of human devastation, the role of war is not always as negative as it seems. Across history, wars have forged nations, given birth to ideas and, yes, sometimes even righted the worst wrongs. War is not only for a bully nation, or for those with the worst intentions, and it is not always a mistake to avoid it. Finally, whether fought for good or ill, wars rely upon every function and corner of society. Thus to explain how the future of war and warfare might develop is to imagine the progress of all of mankind – our different societies and economies, cultures and beliefs, politics and power structures.

Rather than limiting this to my own answers, I would like to inspire your imagination as much as tell a story of the potential future. We will start at the beginning, and then examine the current trends that are likely to have a significant influence across society and war in the coming decades. It can only be brief, as the other essays in this book offer fantastic insights into the future on many issues that are important for where we could find ourselves in fifty years' time.

I also want to share how I craft my own view of the future of war, using the limitless possible variations on three simple questions: *who is fighting, why,* and *how.* Exploring some of those will create the beginnings of a picture of the future. It will also provide a starting point for you to imagine possible futures and to think about how you might adapt or shape those trends over the coming years.

366

When we look to an imagined future, it is from the perspective of important new trends that will have both global and local effects. From climate change to artificial intelligence, growing megacities to the interconnectivity of global communications – like the internet – the paths of humanity are changing in response to a worldwide technological and economic revolution on the scale of the Industrial Revolution. This emerging world will shape conflict as today's ways of doing things struggle to meet tomorrow's challenges, as those with the power to do so adapt to take advantage of the opportunities, and as our motivations for war shift.

What trends do I think will most affect the course of the future, and thus conflict?

I would identify the rapidly evolving worlds of *technology*, *social politics* and *climate* as the big three areas that will help to define the coming decades.

Let's begin with technology. Advances in computing and related technology promise to reshape human life in unprecedented ways, with artificial intelligence, nano-worlds, robotics and bio-engineering – all areas you might find yourself working in at some point in the future. Self-sustaining and thinking products and machines will improve some aspects of life while displacing human activity and perhaps even controlling others. The participation of humanoid robots, autonomous drones or functionally invisible nano-bots on the front lines of future conflict would seriously change the combat environment and laws of war.

Secondly, social politics. Socially and culturally, changes to how we see gender and sexuality are accelerating, particularly in the armed forces. For example, are the Kurdish women

War in Fifty Years

who are currently fighting ISIS in Syria at the vanguard of a new world of equality between the sexes? It is likely so, as across the globe in Africa, Europe and the Americas, women – as well as those who identify as gay or transgender – are increasingly joining conflicts as fighters. How they will adapt and change the cultures and fighting of the armed forces could range from minor edits to a metamorphosis in tactics, doctrines and equipment. Politically, we also face shifting beliefs and politics that are rearranging how power is created and divided globally.

Finally, our climate. As climate change affects more of humanity, the devastation from storms and droughts, dwindling resources, polluted water and air, and effects we have not yet identified, could drive more to fight in a desperate bid to survive.

In all, the world as it exists today is already creating the changes to the future that will shape war.

Against these trends, we can begin to consider how to expand and answer the three essential questions of who fights, why, and how.

If we think about the first – *who* – this question includes which states or groups are willing to go to war, as well as which members of society will bear the brunt of the fighting. Mass armed forces of the state – whether professional troops or those conscripted – have been the standard for several centuries. But the rise of terrorist organizations suggests that the state will increasingly have to share the battlefield

other combatants. Those whose reasons for fighting are not related to their country of birth or nationhood, but extend beyond that – such as eco-warriors – may fight in forms adopted by extremist groups like al-Qaeda: sub-state (within the country, as small units) and transnational (including members from more than one nation).

Thinking of state armed forces, it's debatable whether the mass armies, navies and air forces of twentieth-century warfare – like those used on D-Day and shown in movies like *Dunkirk* – will continue. Smaller military forces that are dominated by their use of technology will require a different mix of skills drawn from segments of society that may not have usually served in armies of the past: programmers, drone operators and coders rather than special forces Marines! But even as some conflicts will need something other than the state model of forces personnel, other conflicts could depend on groups of countries working together in an alliance to deal with 'mega' issues like the destruction of a major city because of a storm.

Why people – whether grouped in state armed forces or in other forms of fighting units – are willing to fight is also shifting. The nationalisms and ideologies that drove war in the twentieth century are abating, and giving way to a multitude of issues that look hard to resolve without armed conflict.

War in Fifty Years

Instead of patriotism, for instance, it is now often ethnic identity or religious beliefs that have become a common means to organize anger and will – a source of trouble in today's world which seems likely to continue as an engine of conflict. And as more people live in cities in a world where climate change can have major effects, or a viral pandemic can have a devastating impact, we can expect to see more non-state groups fighting in defence of the environment or resources, and more states taking action against communicable disease.

Turning to the last of my three questions – *how* we will fight – is perhaps the most difficult to imagine. The conflicting developments in technology and society can either lead us to a de-populated, automated battlefield or to more ancient, personal forms of violence. While nations on the rise, like China, India or Brazil, invest in the traditional massed armed forces, Russia is allegedly experimenting with hacking, groups like ISIS are in conflicts with visible savagery, and the US is at the forefront of unmanned military technology, like drones. It will be over the next decade or two that we determine which of these will prevail, and in what combinations.

370

We can only explore ideas about how the future may turn out, as it will be driven both by forces we know about – and by those we don't. But I hope that this essay will inspire you, the reader, to think more about it. Take the three questions proposed here – *who*, *why* and *how* – and think about the possibilities yourself. Not only should this be an interesting experiment for you, but it also just might help you to prepare for the world to come, the world of your own future.

Jill

The Future of Politics Is . . . You!

Politics is about power. It's true that a few people want power because they are bossy and like the sound of their own voice, or they think other people will be impressed by them. But you find such people in other places too. The important thing is that most people who work in politics want to use their power to do good things, to help people and to make their neighbourhood, their country and the world a better place. Using the power of a whole country to put your ideas into practice is one of the best ways of making big changes happen – like tackling climate change or introducing exciting new technology. However, to be successful, you can't just be right; you also need to convince other people to agree with you.

Listening to politicians

With the power given to them by voters, politicians can do things that other people and organizations can't. They can pass laws that everybody has to abide by, and they can make everybody pay taxes, and spend that money on their ideas. That means considering many different views and judging which ideas are likely to work – which is why debating is such an important part of politics. Robust arguments are a sign of a healthy democracy – as long as people are debating what is best for the country, not just calling each other rude names!

People worry that politicians don't say what they mean. Politicians find it very difficult to admit to making mistakes or saying that there are things they don't know, even though they are human like the rest of us. To them, admitting they are not perfect feels very difficult because they have so many

political opponents and journalists watching every move, waiting for them to slip up.

To avoid this problem, some politicians may fall into the trap of saying everything is perfect; they may also avoid answering simple questions or taking responsibility for their decisions. Some try to divert attention from their own mistakes by shouting loudly about their opponents, and some try to disguise their own opinions as facts that can't be challenged. Listening to the arguments can teach you a lot, and the politicians who are the most open and honest about their opinions, and who want to do the right thing, usually end up looking better than those trying to dodge questions.

Trying out your own opinions

A good start is to try reading or listening to a politician's views on an issue you are interested in – maybe something mentioned in this book, or something else: perhaps the invention of driverless cars, protecting endangered tigers or stopping pollution on beaches. You could follow news stories on TV, via downloads, read a number of different newspapers or follow the debates on social media.

Think about which parts you agree with and which you don't. Find other people who are talking about the same issue, and see what you think. Do you agree, or do you have a different opinion? It can be just as much fun finding people you really disagree with. Try and spot when you think a politician is not giving a straight answer, or is making their answer deliberately complicated, or when they claim something as an absolute fact when it is actually just their opinion.

In maths, there's only one right answer to a sum. In physics, you know that if you throw an apple into the air it will definitely fall back to the Earth. Politics, however, is about making your *own* judgements, working out what you think and then making the case for others to agree with you. Remember too that you can also change your mind as you learn more about an issue.

How you can change the world

Having opinions is good, but it doesn't change anything by itself. If you want something important to change, you have to find who has the power to make the right decisions. You might want to ban plastic bags – well, who is responsible for making new laws? Or you might want a new basketball court in your neighbourhood – who is responsible for paying for that?

Remember that politicians don't have to listen to just you – they have lots of different people coming to them with problems and ideas. They only have a limited amount of time and money, and it can be tricky to make the right decision.

Just as politicians need support to get elected, you need to show that your idea works and will be popular. You might join an organization that is already working on the issues you are passionate about. You might want to start a petition – a list signed by all the people who agree with your idea. You could write to your local newspaper. The most important thing is to find people and organizations who believe in the same things you believe in and have the same goal to get something done.

In the past, politics has been controlled by small groups of people who decided what they thought was best for everyone. Looking ahead, I believe that the brightest future for politics and for the strength of our democracies is for us to embrace an idea called *pluralism*. This means involving many different people in making political decisions, listening to various points of view, and encouraging everybody to take an active interest in the decisions made about the place – town, country, planet – where they live.

The first step in achieving pluralism is for as many people as possible to get involved. That includes *you*. You might first

become an active follower of politics, working out what you believe and what you think needs to change. When you're old enough, you'll have the important responsibility of voting at elections. You might even become a supporter or campaigner for the issues you are passionate about – and perhaps one day you'll be elected as a politician and make the big decisions yourself.

However you get involved, you have an equal right to an opinion as everybody else, and an equal right for your voice to be heard.

That's why the future of politics is *you*.

Andy

Cities of the Future

When you ask people to imagine what the city of the future will look like, most have an idea of what they expect. My idea started with a cartoon that was first shown in 1962 called *The Jetsons*. Living in 2062, the Jetson family had a flat in a very tall apartment building, everyone rode around in flying cars, Mr Jetson worked for only two hours per week, and the dog was walked on a treadmill rather than outside.
Several concepts shown in *The Jetsons* have already come true: they talked to each other through their televisions (videoconferencing/Skype/Facetime) and read their newspapers on their television screens as well (iPads/Kindles).

Whatever you think future cities will be like when we reach 2062 or 2081 or beyond, they keep evolving and there are many challenges that will need to be addressed in order to make cities liveable places in the future, rather than the bleak Edenopolis George describes.

The modern city – places in which a large proportion of the world's population now make their homes – has been around for less than 200 years. Although cities have existed for over 5,000 years, only 2 per cent of the global population lived in them as recently as 1800. As the Industrial Revolution changed how we made and grew things, more and more people moved into our cities. Two hundred years later, at the beginning of the twenty-first century, over 50 per cent of the global population was living in cities. In the most developed countries in the world, about 75 per cent of people live in cities. By 2030, it is estimated that 67 per cent of the global population and about 85 per cent of people in the most developed countries will be living in cities!

So, if the vast majority of us are going to be living in the

cities of the future, what do we need to do to make them truly liveable places for the benefit of all of their residents?

As with many areas of the future, technology will have a big role to play, and many of the different elements of life will need to work together to create somewhere that we want to call home.

In the past, adding more and more people to our cities has resulted in extensive pollution, traffic jams, housing shortages and huge demands on services. City planners of the future will need to consider how to manage these issues if they want to make cities great places, rather than places that we only tolerate because that's where our jobs are.

Where will we live, work and go to school in these cities of the future? What will those experiences be like? Will we have robot butlers? Will we have to work at all, or will everything be done by robots?

As we have seen since the beginning of the Industrial Revolution, many jobs that had previously been undertaken by people have been mechanized. There is no reason to think that this trend will change in the future. But there will continue to be a need for people to design the machines and the robots that we will use to do many of these tasks. And lots of things can't be done by machines: creative jobs such as writing books and creating art; designing buildings or computer games. These areas will continue to need people and their ideas. Maybe we'll work fewer days per week in the future, but people could then spend more time with their families, helping their communities or having fun.

No matter what jobs we may be doing, we'll still need a place to do this work. Although technology continues to develop so that a lot of our work can be done from anywhere with an internet connection, many people still choose to go to offices or other spaces where they can collaborate with others. So we're likely to continue to want some kind of building in which to talk to each other and share ideas. As more and more high-rise office buildings are being developed around the world, it is unlikely that our skylines will change completely in future, but these offices are likely to be designed to be attractive places to work. There is increasing demand for outdoor spaces in office towers, so although the skyline may not change, it is likely to look a lot more green than it currently does, with terraces, roof gardens and green walls.

Different cities have already shown different approaches to where we live – some cities have lots of houses, while others have lots of apartment buildings. As cities become more densely populated, it is likely that housing will need to be intensified – meaning that more people will need to live in the same small area. City planners will need to consider how to develop additional housing – and make it affordable for all types of people to live there – to meet the needs of growing populations.

Whatever the *outsides* of our houses look like, however, technological changes are likely to make the *insides* different from today. Many of the devices that currently exist will continue to develop to make our lives easier: smart devices should be able to tell us how much energy we use so that we can use less; other technology can turn on our music or let the cat out. And 2017's Alexa will likely develop into a full-scale robot butler to take care of many more of our household chores, just like in *The Jetsons*.

Schools will also take advantage of changes in technology. Will we need to go into a school building? For the same reason that people prefer to go to offices, children of the future will probably still attend school and teachers will still be humans rather than robots. But technology will develop in ways that allow for virtual and augmented reality that allows children to 'go' to the rainforest or experience the French Revolution or the Roman Empire more than we can today.

So if we know what we're doing in future with regard to work and school and home, what else needs to be considered so that our cities can be amazing places to live? The big issues affecting cities today are likely to continue to be the big issues of the future: *transport* and our *environment*.

If our cities are getting bigger and more populated, it will be harder for people to move around easily in cars. Public transport will be key to minimizing the number of people stuck in traffic. Planners will need to consider if more underground trains make sense, or if alternative transport solutions are preferable. Driverless vehicles are likely to be more and more prominent, but will these cars create more traffic or less? We will need to come up with solutions to manage driverless vehicles more effectively, rather than this simply resulting in more cars on the road.

Will we need to care about traffic and public transport at all if there are flying cars? Probably even more so. Just because cars can fly, it doesn't mean that traffic and pollution will go away. Combine flying cars with delivery drones and aeroplanes and helicopters, and there could be some very busy and polluted skies!

Transport uses a lot of energy, which has an impact on the environment. Putting millions of people in a single city location is going to have an impact on the environment as they cook, turn on lights, heating and/ or cooling their homes, charge their phones, use computers and TVs, and

travel around. All these things require energy, and energy consumption has historically had a negative effect on the environment.

Many city governments are now looking at how they can lessen their impact on the environment, especially reducing pollution that could be harming their residents. Effort will need to go into reducing energy consumption and finding environmentally friendly energy solutions to deliver our needs. More and more electricity is generated through renewable and low-carbon means, but really innovative solutions may be the best ways to create the energy we need for the future: hydrogen cars could replace existing petrol and diesel cars, and their only exhaust would be water vapour rather than carbon dioxide. Technology could be developed

that turns human power, generated by walking or cycling, into electricity. Or that turns our homes, offices and schools into energy generators in some way, allowing us each to self-generate our own requirements. Perhaps you, in the future, will be one of those who will design technology like this, or will help in planning and building our cities of the future.

A strong vision of what we want these cities to be like will be required so that we can capture all the benefits that technology could give us in our lives. Do you have this vision? I began by imagining my city of the future based on a TV cartoon series. What sort of city can *you* imagine?

Maybe not flying cars, but hopefully lots of robot butlers!

Beth

Artificial Intelligence

What does it mean to be intelligent? Most often in daily life, the term is used to describe how well someone does at maths, writing or another academic subject, but there is a more basic definition. At its core, intelligence means the ability to achieve goals in a wide variety of environments. Sometimes your goal might be solving a maths problem, but other times it might be something much simpler that we usually take for granted: describing the weather, playing a computer game or using a knife and fork to eat a meal. Although we don't usually think of these as particularly challenging tasks, they actually involve a tremendous amount of computer power, and it is remarkable that our brains are able to do so many different types of activity so well.

Intelligence is what makes humans exceptional when compared to other animals: by looking at the world around us and thinking about how it works, we have built tools, societies and civilizations to help us achieve our goals. In the span of a few tens of thousands of years – the blink of an eye relative to the history of life on Earth – humans have used our intelligence to make incredible progress: discovering electricity, building skyscrapers, curing diseases, mastering flight, and even sending people to the Moon and launching probes past the limits of our solar system. Our intellect that has powered these achievements is unlike anything else that has ever taken place on this planet, and possibly unlike anything else in the entire Universe.

Imagine if we had intelligent machines that could help us discover even more new inventions and answer even more questions! This is exactly the goal of artificial intelligence, or 'AI'.

For a long time computers have been excellent at some tasks, such as maths and logic, but have not been nearly as flexible as human minds. Activities that we find easy – like identifying different animals or carrying on a conversation – have generally been incredibly difficult to automate. But as computers have become faster, people have discovered new ways of programming them that have unlocked some of these abilities. Today, a number of the world's most brilliant scientists are working on designing new programs (or 'algorithms') that will enable computers, like humans, to apply intelligence to accomplish goals in a wide variety of environments. This is AI.

The most exciting area of AI research at the moment is called 'machine learning'. Machine learning takes a different approach to normal computer programming: instead of giving the computer precise step-by-step instructions, machine-learning researchers write learning algorithms that allow computers to observe the world around them and figure out answers for themselves. For instance, instead of writing a program that tells a computer that a cat has two eyes, four paws and whiskers, a machine-learning researcher might write a learning algorithm and then simply show it a lot of different pictures of cats. Over time, the algorithm will learn from these examples to identify cats for itself. This is very similar to how we teach human children: we might simply say 'This is a cat', or 'This is a dog', and let the child figure out independently what the differences are between cats and dogs.

One of the most wonderful and powerful aspects of machine learning is that it is much more adaptable than regular programming. For instance, we could take the same algorithm that we used to identify cats and train the computer to identify all sorts of different animals. We could also use it to recognize faces, cars, buildings, trees and pretty much anything else. This saves us a huge amount of effort because we don't need to write specific programs for each problem! Because the algorithms are general-purpose, they can be used in all sorts of different situations.

Another benefit of learning algorithms is that, unlike normal computer programs, they can discover new facts and strategies that we did not know when we created them. For example, just recently an AI program called AlphaGo defeated the best player in the world at an ancient Chinese board game called Go. Go is sort of like chess, but much, much more complicated: it has more possible board positions than the number of atoms in the entire Universe! This makes the game very difficult, and the world's best players spend their entire lives honing their skills and trying out new tactics. AlphaGo is a

machine-learning program that, much like human players, learned to play the game by experimenting over time with lots of different moves and seeing which ones worked best. This meant that it discovered some novel strategies that no human player had ever used, so it not only won the game but also taught human Go players worldwide about powerful new techniques – this could never have happened with an algorithm that had been programmed conventionally with step-by-step directions. AlphaGo was a major milestone for AI because it demonstrated the power of learning algorithms to make their own discoveries in very complex domains.

Of course, we have not yet built anything nearly as flexible or capable as the human mind; there are lots of tasks that we humans find easy but even the best AI algorithm remains unable to do. But over the past few years machine learning has made tremendous progress. In addition to playing Go and identifying people and animals, machine-learning programs have translated languages, improved energy efficiency and made medical advances, to list just a few of the many astounding recent examples of AI.

All this, however, is just the tip of the iceberg. Ultimately, AI scientists hope to achieve 'artificial general intelligence' (AGI) – an AI algorithm capable of doing anything the human brain can do – which would be invaluable in helping scientists conduct important research and uncover new truths. Having AGI will usher in a new age of tremendous scientific discovery: just like humans have made amazing progress over the past few thousand years by applying our own intelligence to various problems, imagine what we can accomplish if we can combine that intelligence with the power of AI! We might be able to cure most diseases, solve difficult problems like climate change and discover miraculous new materials that could enable everything from improved space travel to cars that drive themselves.

This is a very exciting time for machine learning. It seems as though almost every day brings a new discovery that inches us closer to artificial general intelligence. Achieving AGI will be a huge breakthrough for mankind – something on the same level as the Moon landing or the creation of the internet. Over the course of human history we have built many tools – ranging from hammers and shovels to

Artificial Intelligence

telescopes and microscopes – but none of them have had the same potential as AI for revolutionizing almost every aspect of human life.

Of course, nobody can say for sure how far we are from AGI. But at the speed that the field is progressing, it could happen within our lifetimes, in which case right now we are standing on the brink of a world-changing discovery, gazing into a future bursting with possibilities. There has never been a more thrilling time to be alive!

It is a fascinating and hugely exciting area to work in. In the years to come, maybe *you* – as one of the current generation of young people for whom computers are a familiar part of everyday life – will be one of the programmers who develop AGI further and further and use your skills to help our society achieve truly amazing things!

Demis

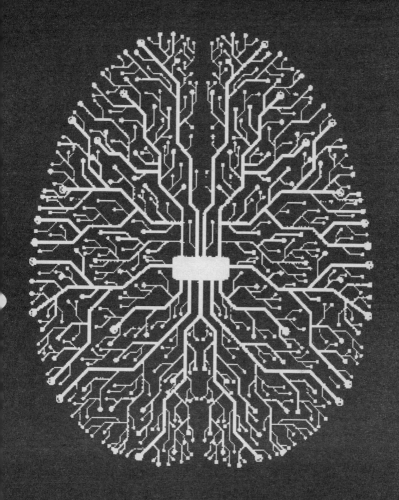

Robot Ethics

Is it OK to be mean to a robot?

We all know that robots are just machines that are programmed to do things. You can't hurt their feelings and they don't experience pain like humans and animals. But . . . if verbal or physical violence towards robots still feels wrong to you, that's not crazy!

There's an interesting phenomenon in human psychology called *anthropomorphism*. It means that we project human qualities and emotions onto non-humans. If you've ever thought that a stuffed animal looked sad because it was thrown under the bed, or that a dog was smiling happily at you, you've experienced anthropomorphism. Dogs certainly have emotions, but they're harder to read than most people think! We sometimes take cues from animals and objects and imagine that they feel the same as a human would. And even though we may be wrong about what we're imagining, it's a pretty natural thing to do – evolutionarily, it's how we try to make sense of, and relate to, other beings and things.

It turns out that we anthropomorphize robots a lot. Robots combine two factors that evolution has taught us to respond to: *physicality* and *movement*. We're very physical creatures, and our brains are hardwired to see life in certain types of movements. So, if we see a robot in our physical space that seems to be moving around all by itself, part of our brain thinks that the robot is doing things intentionally. And that makes it easy to imagine that the robot has goals and emotions. That's why a lot of us feel sorry for a robot when it gets stuck somewhere, even though the robot really doesn't care at all if it's stuck!

Some robots are specially designed to target this instinct. Have you seen *Star Wars*? Just like R2D2 and other robots in *Star Wars*, we can make real robots that use sounds and movements and other cues which we automatically associate with living things. A lot of children and adults enjoy playing with these robots because it's so easy to imagine that they're alive. And this imagination can even be used to help people in health and education. For example, robot animals can be pets for lonely or sick people who are allergic to real animals. Teachers can use robots as friendly and engaging

sidekicks, to make learning more fun. Some robots are already really good at reminding people to take medicine, or comforting them, or motivating them to learn new languages. And these robots are helpful because people treat them like living things instead of like devices. It's more fun to talk to a robot than to a toaster or a computer!

Maybe someday soon you'll have a robot helper at home. But before you tell your robot all your secrets, here's something to keep in mind: it's important to know a little bit about how the robot works, what purpose it serves, and what data it collects about you. For example, is the robot recording what you say? If you tell it something personal, can somebody else get that information? Most companies that sell robots probably just want you to have a cool robot, but some of them may want to collect your data to sell to other big companies. Or they may have some other idea to make more money using the robot. After all, robots are machines made by people, so they do what their creators want them to do. That's not always a bad thing. It's just a good idea to take a moment to ask: who made this robot, and why?

In the future, robots will be in a lot of places and made for many different tasks. Some robots will be programmed to act as if they have feelings. And that brings us back to the question: is it OK to be mean to a robot? If robots don't really have feelings, it's not as bad as being mean to animals or people. But if you're nice to robots, you're not being silly. In fact, it may mean that you have a lot of empathy. Scientists like me have been researching the ways in which we treat robots like they're alive. One of our questions is whether we can learn anything about a person from how they act towards a robot. So far, we think that people who feel empathy for robots have a lot of empathy for other people too. So before being mean to a robot, consider this: if you're a kind and caring person, that may not matter to the robot, but it sure matters to you and others!

Kate

The Internet: Privacy, Identity and Information

Have you ever thought about who can see what you do on the internet or how long the messages you write will last for?

The internet is made up of many, many different computers all interconnected across the world. We tend to access the internet through our mobile phones and other devices but some computers are designed specifically to store the information we all put on the internet. These computers, called servers, host the websites we access. Some of them are in homes and offices, but most are in purpose-built centres run by Internet Service Providers (for short, ISPs). Big companies like Google, Facebook and Amazon have their own data centres – and networks of machines which each hold huge amounts of data.

Social media sites allow people to talk to each other using this vast computer network, often over great distances – and much of the content posted to social media platforms is kept, potentially for ever! Other messaging applications are deliberately designed to allow for information to be around for only a short while, but of course if you receive a message from somebody electronically you can always find a way to copy it – so things can always find their way onto the internet.

Search engines such as Google use software scripts called robots or 'spiders' to trawl every page of the internet (or certainly as many as they can find) by bouncing continuously from links on one page to another. Their aim is to catalogue everything that is on the web so that we can easily and quickly find what we're looking for.

Search engines and other such sites are therefore constantly copying and listing much of the content we post or read online. In this way something we publish in one place might quickly appear or be recorded somewhere else. As a result, an item published on one site and then removed might already exist on another website – to be found by another internet user at some point in the future.

This is why we should all think really carefully about what to put on the internet about ourselves – because sometimes there is effectively no 'delete' button.

Telling your friends on social media that you're away on a fantastic holiday with your parents may seem like a really cool thing to do, but the last thing anyone wants is to alert criminals to the fact that their house is empty.

There are other reasons why we might not want people finding information we posted online a long time ago. In the past, as part of job interviews, employers would ask a previous place of work about someone. Nowadays, when you apply for a job, it is common for employers to look you up on social media to find out what they can about you, your friends and what you spend your time doing. This means that what your friends post online – what appears on your timeline, for example – can also have a real impact on what others think about you!

The internet as a whole, and social media especially, has revolutionized our ability to communicate, to have fun and to engage with others. Some people say social media makes us more antisocial in the real world and some use it so much that maybe it does. Like most things, though, if it doesn't take over our lives and we understand the risks of using it, there are many benefits to be had. There are no hard and fast rules, of course, but I created the rules below as a set of things to think about when it comes to sharing your life online.

Seven Golden Rules

1. THINK BEFORE YOU POST
Before you post something online, don't just think of the person you're intending to see it. Think about whether you're happy for other people – those who know you, and many who don't – to see its content, now or in the future. If in any doubt, don't post!

2. THINK BEFORE YOU CLICK
There are lots of reasons why people send 'spam' emails to huge lists of people who didn't want or request them. Sometimes they're simply designed to sell products, but other times they contain links designed to take you to a website you shouldn't be visiting. The worst type of spam email attempts to install software on your machine in order to steal data or take control of it. There's a simple rule here – if you're not absolutely sure who an email is from, or if it looks in any way fishy, don't click on any links.

3. THINK BEFORE YOU SHARE
Many people post pictures to social media without thinking about it, but often the people in those photographs may not be so excited about them being publicly available. Before posting a snap of your brother, sister, parents or friends, why not ask their permission?

After all, it's data about *them* you're putting out for the world to see. Ask for the same respect from those who take photos – or videos – of you, and never be shy to ask someone not to post. For instance, if you have a party at your house, you might ask all your friends to agree in advance *not* to post any photos. It could be *you* who appears on the internet just as you drop a slice of messy pizza all down your chin!

4. ONLY BEFRIEND FRIENDS

People can pretend to be somebody else over the internet – sometimes by using false names, photographs and ages. These people often rely on the fact that we all want to be popular – and many people will click 'accept' just to add another friend to their count. If you've set up your privacy settings properly, friends can probably see a lot more than those who aren't linked to you, so if you don't know who the person is, don't let them into your circle of trust.

5. BE AWARE OF PRIVACY SETTINGS

Social media sites make money by selling advertisement space to companies and brands who want to sell their products. They can make these adverts really powerful and effective by presenting them to people they *know* are interested in a particular area. Because of how much we tell them about us they can promise their advertisers that the football computer game advert will only be shown to people who talk about football and about games consoles. The downside (for us) is that it's in the interests of these companies for us to put lots of information about ourselves online. All these sites have privacy settings, but they tend to change quite frequently, and most people don't read the details before accepting. The best bet is either to stay on top of this or to assume that anything you post might later be visible to others.

6. BE AWARE OF LOCATION SETTINGS

Watch out too for location settings, which are certainly helpful when we look on a search engine for a local cinema or skate park. They're less ideal if, when we post thoughts or photos to social media, we don't want other people to know where we are. Did you know that the settings on many apps now default to sharing your location with the app provider? You should always work out whether this will actually make the app more useful to you (if you are using it for directions, for instance, the answer would be yes), whether you trust those who provide the app you are using, and whether that data could fall into the wrong hands. If in doubt, switch it off.

7. PASSWORDS AND SECURITY

Software scripts are used by criminals to try many thousands of word combinations in an attempt to 'guess' passwords and get access to people's data. This is why it's so important to use complex passwords (which use more than simple word forms). Thankfully, in years to come, biometric data (like your fingerprint or eyeball scan) will increasingly replace passwords, but for now it's important to come up with a series of passwords which are impossible to guess and complicated for a computer to work out. *Never* use 'password', '123456' or similarly easy-to-guess patterns. And it's a good idea to avoid something obvious like the name of your pet or your favourite football team, since this information is easy to find out.

Finally, I like to think of the internet as being just like the real world. There are loads of great things going on out there, and so many friendly people. In certain places in the real world, though, we have to learn to be careful where we walk, whom we speak to and what we do. All this works when we're taking a stroll online too.

Dave

Acknowledgements

After ten years of the adventures of Annie and George, it's finally the last escapade for our two heroes. From black holes to mystery planets, they have taken us on a wild ride through many different areas of science, and so it's with great sadness that I realize it's time to leave them in the future and turn a new page myself.

Before I do, I want to say a very grateful thank you to all the wonderful readers out there who have made the George series such a joy to create. I've met so many of you over the past decade and it's been such a pleasure to answer your many questions. Special thank yous this time to my three young advisers, Chloe Carney, Peter Ross and Benedict Morgan, for their very helpful reviews of the draft version.

A huge thank you as ever to everyone at Penguin Random House and their sister publishers around the world – but in particular to Annie Eaton for believing in Annie and George right from the start and to Shannon Cullen, Ruth Knowles, Emma Jones and Sue Cook for taking us all around the universe and bringing us home. Garry Parsons has brought George and his friends to life over the past ten years and done a wonderful job of illustrating them in every possible scenario – whether walking on a new planet or facing down an angry tiger! Also thank you to Rebecca Carter, Kirsty Gordon and all at Janklow and Nesbit for keeping the mission running smoothly.

I would also like to thank all the fabulous scientists who have contributed in so many ways to this series. If I could get you all in one room for a thank-you party, it would be a roll call of honour of the world's greatest.

Finally, one scientist deserves the biggest thanks of all – my father, Stephen. Thank you for letting me retell your work as a series of children's stories and for lending your unique and irreplaceable voice to what turned out to be far more than just one book. Without you, we would know and understand so much less than we do about the extraordinary universe in which we live. I'm going to borrow a line from you to close the series:

'Don't forget to look up at the stars and not down at your feet.'

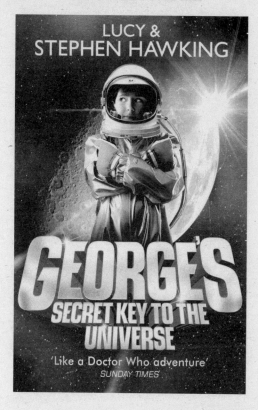

ALSO AVAILABLE:

Join George as he battles a sinister rebel-scientist,
who's hell bent on sabotaging the most exciting —
and dangerous — experiment of the century.

A deadly bomb is ticking.
The whole world is watching.
Can George stop the second big bang?

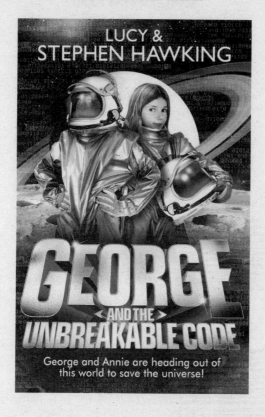